THE
HOLLOW
GIRL

A Moe Prager Mystery

THE
HOLLOW
GIRL

A Moe Prager Mystery

Reed Farrel Coleman

TYRUS
BOOKS

F+W Media, Inc.

Published by
TYRUS BOOKS
an imprint of F+W Media, Inc.
10151 Carver Road, Suite 200
Blue Ash, OH 45242. U.S.A.
www.tyrusbooks.com

Hardcover ISBN 10: 1-4405-6202-4
Hardcover ISBN 13: 978-1-4405-6202-0
Trade Paperback ISBN 10: 1-4405-7301-8
Trade Paperback ISBN 13: 978-1-4405-7301-9
eISBN 10: 1-4405-7274-7
eISBN 13: 978-1-4405-7274-6

Printed in the United States of America.

10 9 8 7 6 5 4 3 2 1

Library of Congress Cataloging-in-Publication Data

Coleman, Reed Farrel,
   The Hollow Girl / Reed Farrel Coleman.
     pages cm
   ISBN 978-1-4405-7301-9 (pb) -- ISBN 1-4405-7301-8 (pb) -- ISBN 978-1-4405-6202-0 (hc) -- ISBN 1-4405-6202-4 (hc) -- ISBN 978-1-4405-7274-6 (ebook) -- ISBN 1-4405-7274-7 (ebook)
   1. Prager, Moe (Fictitious character)--Fiction. 2. Private investigators--New York (State)--New York--Fiction. 3. Missing persons--Fiction. 4. Mystery fiction. I. Title.
   PS3553.O47445H65 2014
   813'.54--dc23
             2013044500

5414 8464 6/14

Cover design by Sylvia McArdle.
Cover images © 123RF/Piotr Marcinski/Alex Stokes.

This book is available at quantity discounts for bulk purchases.
For information, please call 1-800-289-0963.

To Moe's fans. Thanks from us both.

Also by Reed Farrel Coleman

Moe Prager:
Walking the Perfect Square
Redemption Street
The James Deans
Soul Patch
Empty Ever After
Innocent Monster
Hurt Machine
Onion Street

Dylan Klein:
Life Goes Sleeping
Little Easter
They Don't Play Stickball in Milwaukee

Gulliver Dowd:
Dirty Work
Valentino Pier

Joe Serpe:
Hose Monkey
The Fourth Victim

Standalone Novels:
Gun Church
Tower with Ken Bruen
Bronx Requiem with Det. John Roe

Acknowledgments

I would like to thank Paula Schwartz, MD, Suffolk County ADA Ming Liu Parson, and Karen Olson. I want to express my appreciation to Ben LeRoy and David Hale Smith for helping to revive and sustain Moe. To Sara J. Henry, Peter Spiegelman, and Ellen W. Schare. As always, to Judy Bobalik. And a special nod to Dylan T. Coleman for helping with the cover design for this novel.

I need to thank Rosanne, Kaitlin, and Dylan for making all the sacrifices they have made for me. Only my name goes on the cover, but they have stood by me at every turn. Each of them has helped bring Moe to life by bringing love and understanding to mine.

But always where she goes there is rain.
—Kathleen Eull

. . . and the Hollow Girl knits her clothing out of self-loathing.
—anonymous fan

PROLOGUE
1993, Lenox Hill Hospital

Nine years had passed since Israel Roth and I had placed pebbles atop Hannah Roth's headstone. I didn't know it then, but that day in the granite fields, on the crusted snow and icy paths, was goodbye. Husband was never coming back to see wife again. I couldn't have known it then. Mr. Roth never said as much, but I had since learned to recognize goodbye. Goodbye has its own feel, its own flavor, a flavor as distinct as my mother's burnt, over-percolated coffee. Sometimes the taste of it comes back to me, that black, god-awful goop that poured like syrup and had a viscosity and flavor more akin to unchanged motor oil than coffee. Sometimes, that's what goodbye tastes like. Goodbye also has its own aroma, its own scent. Sometimes, like today, it smells like a hospital room.

"So, Mr. Moe, where are you?" Israel Roth asked, his voice weak and strained. "You seem far away."

"Sorry, Izzy, I was time traveling."

He smiled up at me. "I'm the one who's dying, here. You think maybe I'm the one what should be entitled to going back in time?"

"I was thinking about my mother's coffee. Trust me when I tell you you wouldn't want to go back in time for that."

"That bad, huh?"

"Worse. You know the saying about what doesn't kill you only makes you stronger?"

"Sure."

"By that measure, I should be Hercules."

"You're plenty strong, Mr. Moe. You shouldn't fool yourself otherwise." His eyesight almost gone, he blindly reached his hand out for me to take hold of. I noticed that the skin of his forearm was so loose that it folded over on itself, obscuring at last the numbers tattooed there.

I took his hand, squeezing too tightly. "I've never been very good at self-deception," I said.

"It's no gift, lying to yourself. I'm not so blind as you think, Moses." He only ever called me that when he was serious. "You see the skin covers the numbers those bastards put on me like cattle. Not seeing it doesn't fool me that it's not there. Only when I am so many ashes, when I am dust and teeth and bits of bone, will I be free from that number. You know what, sometimes I think even then, when you scatter me to the wind, that I will be only a number."

"Never to me, Mr. Roth. Never to me."

He squeezed my hand back, but didn't say a word. We sat there like that for a few minutes, his hand clutched in mine, both of us time traveling.

Goodbye, as Emily Dickinson might have said, has a certain slant of light. Maybe I was imagining it, but the angle of the afternoon light coming through the vertical slats of the blind seemed to whisper goodbye. I wasn't ready for it, whispered or shouted. In Mr. Roth's company was perhaps the only place I ever truly fit. When he was gone, where would that leave me? Where would I fit? Although I'd loved being on the job, the job never quite loved me back. Shit, most of the guys I worked with wouldn't have known who Emily Dickinson was, or when she lived, or if she wrote, or what she wrote. None of them could have quoted a line of poetry if their lives depended on it. But their lives never depended on it. Has anybody's life ever depended on such a flimsy thing? Only I knew about that slant of light. Only the college boy who had become a cop on a drunken bet.

Not even now, not after sixteen years away from the Six-O, did I feel like I ever quite fit in. I was always stuck somewhere in between, always apart from and a part of at the same time. Mr. Roth's fate was at hand. I wondered if mine was to always be stuck above or beneath. Maybe that's why I'd wanted my gold shield so fucking bad, to show that I fit in, that I was one of the guys. It was nonsense. I didn't fit in any better in the wine business. If anything, it was worse. I never wanted any part of it. No gold shields in the wine business.

"So, Mr. Moe, where are you traveling now?" Izzy broke the silence, his hand clenching tighter still. "Back to Momma's coffee?"

"No. I'm all over the place. I've never been able to live in the moment."

"Such a stupid phrase, 'in the moment'. It's foolishness, no? When is the moment? Now is just the past in waiting. As soon as it's here, it's gone. You can't live in a place that vanishes as soon as it comes. The present, Mr. Moe, is always coming and then always gone. Live for the future, and live in the past. There is only that."

I opened my mouth to argue. No words came out. I wanted to think it was because Mr. Roth seemed to have drifted into sleep, but it wasn't that at all. It was that the truth of what he'd said had knocked me silent. But whatever the nature of the relationship between past, present, and future, there was one inescapable fact: Israel Roth had very little future left. And when he was gone, a piece of me would go with him. Then, when his hand went suddenly slack, I knew that wherever that piece of me was going, it had just arrived. Mr. Roth was right: There is only future and past. Now is fleeting. Now is gone.

CHAPTER ONE
2013

Humpty Dumpty had nothing on me. No egg ever cracked so well, no window shattered into as many ragged pieces. Me, so hardened, so sure there was nothing new the nonexistent God could put on my plate. It galled me that in the end, my mother—think Nostradamus vis-à-vis Chicken Little—had been right. "When things are good," she used to say, "watch out." But I hadn't watched out, because I had a new grandson. Because after surviving stomach cancer, and burying my childhood friend Bobby Friedman, and finally asking Pam to marry my sorry old ass, I'd stood high on a mountain of my own self-assuredness and waved my middle finger at the universe. It waved it right back. *Fuck you, Moe Prager. Fuck you!*

If you need a lesson about the appalling lack of fairness in the universe, let me give it: I was still alive and Pam was not. I'd lost my folks, Katy, Mr. Roth, Rico Tripoli, Bobby, and a hundred other people from my past, but the grief those deaths had caused was a warm-April-sun-on-your-face-all-the-hotdogs-you-could-eat-on-opening-day-at-Citi-Field compared to this. Because with this came guilt, the gnawing guilt of *coulda done* and *shoulda done*. I hadn't known guilt, not really, not until I heard the sirens, not until I looked out the window of my Sheepshead Bay condo and saw half of Pam's body sticking out from beneath the front of a car, the poor girl who'd hit her sitting on the Emmons Avenue curb, arms folded around herself, rocking madly, wishing it would all just go away. I wanted to scream down at her that not all the mad rocking or self-comforting behavior in the world would make anything go away.

Guilt is like that, a permanent infection. Not chronic, permanent. The thing you've done to bruise the universe may fade, but the guilt never goes. Not really. Not ever. Oh sure, there are bad days and worse days, and you come to see the less bad days as good ones. That's a lie. I wanted to scream down to the girl that the guilt was mine, not hers. That it was me who'd sent Pam down to get the *Sunday Times*. That I could have gone myself, should have gone myself. That my car was in its parking spot in back of my building, so that it wouldn't have been a trade-off, my life for Pam's. That I was nearly fully recovered, but that I'd grown old and lazy and used to people doing for me. I did not scream down to her or go down to her, not immediately. I don't think I cried. I was frozen there in front of the window.

I wasn't a forgetter. Even at my drunkest, I'd never blacked out. Like the rest of my life, that all changed the night Pam was crushed beneath the wheels of Holly D'Angelo's new Jeep Wrangler, a high school graduation gift she had received that very June day. Sometimes I find myself thinking about Holly D'Angelo—a pretty neighborhood girl who kept saying "I'm so sorry, mister, I'm sorry"—and the gift of guilt that would keep on giving. I wanted to take her hurt away. I really did. We all fuck up. We all fall down. But we shouldn't have to pay forever. Holly D'Angelo shouldn't have to, anyway. That was for me to do, to pay.

I do remember that I was standing in front of the uniform from the Six-One Precinct, his face not a blur exactly—a blank, his face was more of a blank. I remember speaking to him, but looking back and forth between Pam's motionless body and Holly D'Angelo's endlessly rocking one. More than that, I don't recall or don't want to recall. The guilt, that's another matter. There's been no escape from that.

CHAPTER TWO

I was conscious of someone standing over me. For a brief second, I thought it was Pam. She was like that, getting up early, leaving me to sleep, making us some fancified breakfast that I'd barely touch, then she'd come to wake me. She wouldn't kiss me, but rather lean down close so that I could feel her warm breath on my neck. Then she would brush the back of her hand against my cheek. Is there anything quite as subtly intimate as a lover's touch on your cheek? In the depths of my illness, during the worst of the chemo, I swore it was Pam who willed me to live. I was too sick, too weak, too unhappy to have willed myself to do anything but surrender. And oh, how I wanted to surrender. How I longed to shut my eyes and have it all go away. Pam wasn't having any of that.

She didn't pretend that I was well, didn't ignore my symptoms, but she also refused to treat me like a leper. When she was down visiting from Vermont between cases, she always shared my bed. Even at the lowest points, when I was bald and ashen and skeletal, when I couldn't stand to look at myself in the mirror, when I reeked from coming death, Pam slept with me. Cancer is an isolating experience. You can't imagine just how isolating. Treatment and recovery are worse, in their way. When I needed someone to keep me tethered to life, Pam kept me tethered.

Then that brief second ended and reality flooded back in. It wasn't Pam standing over me. Pam was never going to stand over me again. I would never see her again. Never taste her again. Never feel the brush of her hand against my cheek again. Pam was gone. And gone was gone forever. The truth of that was hard enough to take, but it was the guilt the truth came wrapped in that made me close my eyes to the light, to the figure throwing shadows over my bed.

"Moses. Moses. Get up. Get up!"

"Go away," I heard myself say, voice slurred and sandpapery. I was grabbed by the shoulders, yanked to a seated position, my head snapping forward. "You've got that wrong, bartender: I prefer to be stirred, not shaken." I fell back onto my bed.

"Very funny, little brother. Get up." It was Aaron.

"What time is it?"

"About four hours after you should've gotten up."

"That's my brother, the King of Rights and Wrongs. Leave me alone, Aaron."

"For chrissakes, Moe, you smell like a barroom floor. And when was the last time you shaved?"

"Gimme a drink. And how did you get in here, anyway?"

He jangled keys on a ring. "You gave me these when you were sick."

"Give 'em back. And get me a fucking drink!"

"No more drinking for you. Unless it's water." He shoved a plastic bottle in my hand.

"Leave me alone. My fucking head is pounding. And plastic bottles are bad for the environment."

He placed three ibuprofen tablets in my other palm. "C'mon. Take these. Get up. You've got a client to meet."

Client? More than anything else my big brother had done or said since I became conscious of his presence, that word got to me. I swallowed the tablets and drank the water.

"What client?" I asked, the faint sound of hope in my voice. I wanted no part of that, no part of anything that might interfere with my dark, and as of yet unsuccessful, plunge into numbness. "I thought you didn't want me to come into work until I was ready. And since, according to you, I smell bad and need a shave, I don't think I'm ready to kiss some wine buyer or caterer's ass so that we might—"

"Not that kind of client, you idiot. A client for you."

I knew what he was saying. I understood the words, but they didn't move me, at least not in the way Aaron had wanted them to. I tossed the empty water bottle to the floor and rolled back into bed. "Fuck you and fuck the client."

"You really are a coward."

"Sticks and stones, big brother. Sticks and stones."

"Maybe I should let her see you like this. Then maybe she'd come to her goddamned senses. She's been looking for you for a week, calling all the stores. She left so many messages that it finally got back to me. That's why I'm here."

"Call her back and tell her to go fuck herself, whoever she is. Tell her someone else can go spy on her husband or find her missing cat. The only lost cause I'm interested in is my own. I think I have Carm's number up in Toronto. Let her call Carm or Brian Doyle. Besides, I'm not up for making new friends."

"She's not looking for a lost cat, Moe. She's looking for you."

"Not interested."

"You know her."

"I used to know lotsa people."

That did it. Aaron blew up. He threw the apartment keys at my head, barely missing. "You know what, little brother, fuck you!

For years, for our whole lives, I've carried you. I put money in your pocket and food on your table so you could play cops and robbers. Where would Sarah and Katy have been if I didn't drag you kicking and screaming into the wine business? How would you have put a roof over their heads or sent your daughter to school, by being a PI? And for all our lives I've had to deal with your sneering contempt for my being someone happy to do normal things, responsible things. Well, no more. I don't care anymore. Fuck you!"

"Yeah, you said that."

"Her name and phone number are on the coffee table. You're supposed to meet her at two for coffee at the El Greco Diner. Go, don't go. I don't give a shit."

The door slammed. A few minutes later, I got up to answer nature's call and to pour myself a drink. I toasted the front door with a half-tumbler of Dewar's and took a healthy swig. I snatched the note up from the coffee table, as ready to crumple it up as I had ever been ready to crumple up any piece of paper in my life. But when I saw the name written on it, I stopped. I looked at the man in the Deco mirror Pam had bought for the apartment at a Vermont antique store. The man looked very sad and very old. He put the drink down and went to turn the shower on.

CHAPTER THREE

The too-thin man in the diner vestibule mirror looked like a changed person. He was cleaner, smelling more of soap and fresh-cut-grassy aftershave than of barroom floor. His head still throbbed, but not fiercely. He watched as he ran his fingers over the trim goatee he'd shaped out of the gray chaos that had covered his face only a few hours earlier. His mostly salt with some pepper hair, which had grown back thick and defiant post-chemo, had been combed and brushed into something akin to submission. His casual dress, his light, navy blue sweater over jeans and boots, lent him an air of easy composure. He knew better. He turned away.

I turned away from the mirror because there was nothing composed about my shaking hands or the sick feeling in my belly. But I was too old to play Prince Hamlet. I had already chosen *to be*, although given my behavior over the last few months I would've been hard pressed to prove it. In spite of my drinking, I'd fought too hard to survive and to hold my grandchild in my arms to chuck it all now. The problem was, I hadn't seen or held Ruben since August. Sarah was pretty mad at me for being drunk that day. Then I'd made it worse.

"It's been six weeks, Dad," she'd said, pulling me off to a corner. "Stop it. Please stop punishing yourself. Pam would hate this, you're making yourself sick again."

But I was several sheets to the wind by then and not in the mood for a lecture. "Don't tell me how to grieve, kiddo."

"Grieving. Is that what this is? Seems more like wallowing to me."

"You're just pissed off because I didn't go this far down the rabbit hole when your mother was killed."

The expression of horror on my daughter's face would have cracked glass. She looked up at me, tears streaming down her cheeks like when she was a little girl and she'd scraped the skin off both knees.

"I know you're hurt, Dad," she said, struggling against the sobs, "and you blame yourself for what happened to Pam. I know you're a grown man whose life is his own. I will always love you, but I don't like you this way and I won't have Ruben around you when you're like this."

I didn't blame her. I didn't blame anyone for their anger at me. No one was angrier at or more disappointed in me than I was. No one. I had called to apologize, but it was no good. I hadn't stopped drinking or beating myself to a pulp. After our last call, I'd given the self-immolation a rest for a few days because Sarah invoked the Prager family holiest of holies.

"What would Mr. Roth think of what you're doing, Dad?" she'd asked.

I hadn't answered. The truth was that Israel Roth would have understood. As someone who'd avoided the showers and ovens at Auschwitz, while the rest of his family had not, no one understood survivor's guilt like he did. What he wouldn't have approved of was my pretense of trying to get numb, of playing at making the pain go away.

"There is no magic trick, Mr. Moe. No presto change-o, no abracadabra," he would have said. "There is no making it go away, only living with it. So stop already with pretending and make a friend of your guilt. What choice have you got? What choice do any of us have?"

So as a nod to his memory, I'd stopped drinking for a week. But then I saw something in the paper about a girl killed in a traffic accident, or I heard it on the radio. I can't recall. Whichever it was, it was enough to get me going again.

Now I had another ghost to face. One that had, in her way, haunted me for many more years than either Pam or Mr. Roth. One who had the potential to pry the lid off a piece of my past, a piece I would just as soon forget.

I opened the door that led from the vestibule into the dining area and spotted her sitting at a booth. She sat hunched over a cup of coffee, staring into it as if into a well. I'd first met her in January of 1978, thirty-five years ago, during my early days in purgatory. Fresh from getting put out to pasture by the NYPD, wracked with pain from yet another negligibly successful knee surgery, it was like being a kid at Brooklyn College all over again: aimless, with no career and no prospects. What I had was my brother Aaron pestering me to come up with the last ten thousand dollars we needed to buy into our first wine shop. Talk about mixed feelings.

I loved my big brother, though we were essentially different people. He used to joke that I had been adopted from the space orphanage. There were times I wasn't so sure he was kidding. He was an anchor and I was anchorless. His dream had always been to go into the wine business and have me for a partner. Me, I neither had dreams nor cared much about wine. I had the business sense of a housefly, and the only partners I ever had or ever wanted wore blue uniforms and badges. Still, I wasn't stupid. There wasn't much else out there for me. When you don't have dreams of your own, the next best thing is to hitch your wagon to someone else's, right? Then my best cop buddy from the Six-O Precinct, Rico Tripoli, threw me what I thought was a lifeline.

There was this college kid, Patrick Michael Maloney, the son of some political mover and shaker from upstate New York who'd gone missing in Manhattan that December. The cops had gotten nowhere on the case nor had the PIs hired by the Maloneys or the hundreds of volunteers who came down to the city from the kid's hometown to search for him and hang posters. Rico was related to the Maloneys through his wife and he had convinced the kid's old man that I was magic. That I had a sixth sense about missing persons. That I would find his son. I wasn't magic. I hadn't even made detective before getting retired. What I was was lucky, and then, only once.

"Been a long time," I said, sliding into the booth across from the woman who'd hunted me down.

She nodded in agreement. "It has, a very long time. Thank you for coming."

The Nancy Lustig I'd met thirty-five years before was a poor little rich girl. Lucky, too, in some ways. In others, not so much. Lucky, because . . . well, she was rich. She had lived in Old Brookville on Long Island in a mansion the size of a jumbo jet hangar. Little, because then she was young, an underclassman at Hofstra University. Poor, because she was ugly, not hideous, certainly, but not pretty enough to be called plain either. Unlucky, because she had had the misfortune of getting romantically involved with Patrick Michael Maloney. Before disappearing, he'd gotten her pregnant and nearly strangled her.

I'd liked her back then, liked her a lot. She was brave and brutally honest about her missteps, her desires, her jealousies, her foibles, and, above all, her appearance. I think—no, I know—that I'd fallen a little bit in love with her. After only a few minutes with her, I'd stopped seeing her looks or stopped caring about them. It wasn't a romantic love. I didn't *want* her. It was the love of spirit, the kind of thing the poets I'd wasted my time studying before I became a cop would have understood. *Stone walls do not a prison make, nor iron bars a cage* . . . . That kind of love. But not even the love of spirit endures.

I flagged down the waitress. "Irish coffee. Heavy on the Irish. No whipped cream."

"Irish coffee?" Nancy said, still staring into the well. "You never struck me as a drinker."

"And you never struck me as a woman who would turn into one of those vain, self-obsessed women from Long Island who divide their time between shopping on the Miracle Mile, playing tennis, and studying the next great innovation in plastic surgery."

"Ouch!" she said, smiling. "You've become quite the diplomat in your dotage, Moe."

"Surviving stomach cancer and grief, they kinda give you license to speak your mind."

I'd seen Nancy Lustig only once again in those thirty-five years. By then she had transformed herself into everything the old Nancy wasn't. She'd had a lot of "work" done on her nose, her teeth, her breasts, her body. Her Coke-bottle glasses were gone, as were thirty-plus pounds. When I stopped by her house in 2000, she was impeccably put together: the hair, the nails, the tan, the achingly blue contact lenses. But I didn't resent her wanting to be pretty. Who doesn't want to be pretty? It was that she had seemed to have turned ugly inside in direct proportion to her newly crafted attractiveness.

The woman who sat across from me had aged well and appeared to still be the woman I'd met that second time, although she had traded the blue contact lenses for rich brown ones more suited to her eyes' actual coloring. Her hair, now a darker blonde with perfect highlights, was parted down the middle and fell past her shoulders. Her redone nose and cheekbones and thickened lips were beautifully made up with products that came from Orléans and the Orient. Her skin was taut and tanned. The neckline of her camel-colored cashmere sweater plunged to reveal more than a hint of cleavage between her gravity-defying breasts. There was some age on her hands, though she tried hard—too hard—to keep them young. That was what the French nail job and the five pounds of jewelry were for. The diamonds, emeralds, and gold she wore in the form of rings and bracelets were as much about distraction as attraction.

"So what's this about?"

"My daughter."

"Your daughter?"

"Yes," she said, finally looking up from her coffee cup to meet my gaze. "My daughter, the Hollow Girl."

CHAPTER FOUR

After the waitress served my very Irish coffee and I took half of it in a swallow, Nancy pulled an iPad from her Prada bag. She tapped the screen, her sculpted nails click-clicking as she worked. Then, when she had what she wanted, she made a stand of the iPad's beautifully tooled custom tan leather cover, and placed it in front of me.

There, frozen on the screen, was a girl about the same age Nancy had been the first time we met. She was obviously Nancy Lustig's daughter. Not the Nancy Lustig who sat across from me, not the bionic woman who had reshaped herself with her will and her checkbook, but ugly-beautiful Nancy. Although this girl was thinner, a bit prettier than her mother had been, she had not reached escape velocity from the gravity of her mother's double-helix. This girl had lovely blue eyes—probably from her dad's side of the family—and a less bulbous nose. Still, the dumpiness, the thin lips, the weak chin had all been passed on from mother to daughter. Her bare, pale arms were tattooed, if not ridiculously so, and she wore a diamond nose stud. She was dressed in a plain white men's T-shirt, loose-fitting faded jeans. Her feet were uncovered, and she sat on a barstool in front of a white wall.

"What's her name?" I asked.

Nancy chose to answer a question I hadn't asked. "I can read your mind, Moe. You're thinking it's too bad plastic surgery can't be passed down from mother to daughter."

I didn't deny it, since I *was* thinking something along those lines, if not exactly in those words. "What was it you called your daughter before, a hollow girl? What's that about?"

"The Hollow Girl," Nancy corrected. "I'm surprised you've never heard of her. The Hollow Girl is an Internet legend. Go ahead, press play."

I tapped the screen and the frozen image came to life. The girl spoke in a whisper, her expression sullen.

February 14, 1999, Valentine's Day, the blackest day of my life. A lot of you will be getting roses today, chocolates, gold lockets, diamond rings. I'll get nothing. I was on the phone with Lionel all last night, begging him to take me back. Begging! Do you know what it's like to beg? Do you have any idea what it's like to really beg? I mean, we say it all the time, but we don't know. You don't know. I do. Now I know what it is to make an idiot of myself, to completely demean myself, to plead and plead and plead until there isn't a single ounce of pride left.

And when he said he wouldn't have me back because he was tired of having an ugly white bitch like me at his side and hung up the phone on me the last time, you know what I did? I ran across campus to his dorm room and rang his bell till he came to the door. When he came to the door he wasn't wearing anything at all. "Okay, bitch," he said, "y'all couldn't make this easy and jus' go away. So now you here, c'mon, we gonna do this the hard way."

He pushed me into his bedroom, and there in the bed was Victoria. You know Victoria. I told you about her, beautiful, perfect Victoria who I used to dream about kissing. Beautiful, perfect Victoria who I used to masturbate thinking about until I was sore. Victoria, who got drunk at our end-of-term party our freshman year and made out with me. Beautiful, perfect Victoria, who was so embarrassed she had let me touch her that way that she dropped me as a roommate. That Victoria, she was in Lionel's bed, and when she saw me she laughed. "Make her watch, Li. Make her watch. I want her to watch." He didn't have to make me. I would have stayed no matter what, because, like I said, I had no pride left. I wanted to see how low I was willing to sink. So I sat at the edge of the bed and watched them fuck. I listened to them sigh and grunt.

Then, when they were finished, when the room smelled so much of them I almost fainted, you know what I did? [Sobbing.] *I . . . I stabbed myself. I stabbed myself.* [Lifting T-shirt to expose bandage.] *I stabbed myself. I let the blood . . . I let . . . I let it run onto my hand and I wiped it all over Victoria's perfect, beautiful face.* [Lifting bandage to reveal stitches, raw red skin] *And Victoria started yelling and clutching at her face.*

"You crazy, bitch! You crazy!" Lionel screamed, grabbing me by the hair and throwing me out of his dorm.

Now I know what I have to do. This wound would heal, but I'll never heal. My hurt won't ever go away. [Steps out of frame. Returns carrying a full glass of red wine and a white plastic pharmaceutical bottle. Uncaps bottle.] *I know what I have to do. I was right. I have nothing left inside of me. I'm just the hollow girl.* [Alternates swallowing pills and drinking.] *Goodbye.* [Thirty seconds later, glass falls to floor. Wine splatters. Glass shatters. A few seconds later, she collapses out of chair.] *Help! Help me, please. Help me . . . .*

But when I looked up, Nancy Lustig was smiling with her great white teeth and plush, red lips. To say I was confused was profound understatement.

"When that got posted in '99, there were a record number of 911 calls in several cities across the world. You should hear some of the tapes. People were panicked. 'You have to help her. She's killed herself. You have to help the hollow girl.' But no one knew who she really was, or where to find her. The 911 tapes are available. You should listen to them. It's kind of pathetic, really."

"I'll take your word for it. But I don't get it. Was she okay?"

"What don't you get, Moe? It was theater. Of course she was fine. Clearly the people who watched her didn't know that. They thought she was some poor, homely girl away at college, in way over her head. Until that post you just watched, people called her Lost Girl. Lost Girl had thousands and thousands of online followers. There were chat rooms devoted to Lost Girl. She had fan clubs. Some university psych classes made watching Lost Girl's daily posts required homework. But after the night of the 'suicide'—" Nancy drew quotation marks in the air around the word *suicide* "—everything changed. She became the Hollow Girl. She caused quite a stir. Hollow Girl went viral before the term was in common usage."

"But what was the point?"

Nancy tilted her head at me like a confused puppy. "The point? It was performance art. Would you ask Van Gogh the point of *Starry Night*? She had been going for acting lessons since she was ten. Performing is all she ever wanted to do. She even did stints at Juilliard and Yale Drama, but she was only seventeen and still in high school when she came up with the idea of this video blog about a nameless character she created out of herself. Amazing, isn't it?"

"That isn't the word that comes immediately to mind, no."

"Don't be silly, Moe. My daughter grasped the power of the Internet and became one of its first real stars."

Finishing my drink, I made eye contact with the waitress, and made the universal sign for another round. She nodded. *Message received.* "Okay, Nancy. This was fourteen years ago. She's what, thirty, thirty-one now? You said she was missing."

"She is. She has been . . . for a month. I want you to find her."

"Telling me her name might be a good place to start."

Nancy shrugged her shoulders. "If you insist. Sloane."

"And what did I do to earn the honor of finding Sloane?"

The waitress delivering my coffee prevented Nancy from answering. And before the waitress left, I ordered another round, only this time without the coffee.

"Rude of you not to ask me if I'd like something, Moe." Nancy turned to the waitress. "Any single malt Scotch?"

"We got Glen something or other."

"Glenlivet?" I suggested.

"I think so."

Nancy frowned. "Nothing else?"

I snapped at her. "This ain't the Gold Coast. It's a diner in Sheepshead Bay. You think they're gonna carry Lagavulin and Talisker? Take what they have and run with it."

"A double of that Glen something or other. Neat."

"Forget the Irish," I said. "I'll have what she's having."

The waitress smiled at me but left sneering at the back of Nancy's head.

"So you were about to explain to me why you think I'll be able to find your daughter."

"Because the cops can't be bothered and the other firms I've hired can't seem to make any headway, or don't seem to want to."

"Always heartwarming to be told you're somebody's Plan C."

"Well, you wouldn't have been if I could have reached you."

"Touché. Okay, so you found me. The cops probably think it's none of your business. And maybe the PIs can't find her because she doesn't want to be found. Is she married?"

"For about five minutes, four years ago."

"Boyfriends? Girlfriends?"

"Both, I think, but it's not like we have a Hallmark Channel relationship. We don't do girls' nights. We don't put on our flannel jammies and watch *Steel Magnolias* and have a good cry. We don't meet in the city for lunch and the museum. We never have."

The drinks arrived. I gave the waitress a twenty. "That's for you. Thanks."

Nancy seemed offended by the tip. "What was that for?"

"So she doesn't spit in the food I order after you leave."

"Am I leaving?"

"After your drink, yeah." I raised my glass to her. She touched her glass to mine and we drank.

"You'll take the case?"

"Such as it is."

"What's that supposed to mean?"

I ignored the question. "You still live in Old Brookville in the same house?"

"Same address, very different house. But yes, I live there."

"I'll be there tomorrow morning." I drank some more. She drank the rest of hers. "I'll want the name of the cops you spoke with, the contact information for the PIs you hired. I'll want her address. The keys to her apartment, if you have them. I want a current picture of your daughter. Names and addresses of friends, et cetera. Are you married?"

"Not for many years," she said, staring into her freshly emptied glass.

"Does Sloane use your ex's last name or yours?"

"Neither. After the stir the Hollow Girl affair caused, she had her name legally changed to Siobhan Bracken."

"I'll want all the info on your ex. Any siblings?"

"None. Anything else?" she asked.

"Yeah, it would be nice if you could muster up some genuine feelings, like you used to have when we first met. Your worry's not exactly palpable."

"Worry about whether my money's palpable, Moe. My feelings are my business." She wrinkled up her nose and dropped the corners of her mouth.

"I don't need your money, Nancy. I'll take it, but I don't need it. What I need is the distraction. Till tomorrow morning, then."

"I don't like being dismissed," she said, sliding out of the booth and standing close to me. I had to confess, she smelled awfully good.

"That's not what I'm doing, dismissing you. I have to get some food in me and I have to do some research on my own. I have to get started."

"Okay, then." She reached out her hand as if to touch my cheek. Reflexively, I grabbed her by the wrist before her hand could touch me.

"Please don't do that again." I let go of her wrist, the stones on her bracelets leaving little red marks in the flesh of my palms.

Nancy Lustig shook her head at me and walked away, her heels making sharp clacking sounds on the unforgiving terrazzo floor. I did not look after her. Instead I waved to the waitress and opened the menu that sat before me, untouched until then.

CHAPTER FIVE

What the fuck was that all about? That was the question I kept asking myself as I walked from the diner back to my condo. The weather had turned cool on me. I stopped, about-faced, and used my hand to block the light from the sun that hung fierce and low in the western sky. It had already begun telling its late September lies. My hand could shield me from its light, I thought, but not from its lies. Soon, early darkness would follow. Too bad life wasn't like that, darkness following the lies. It was my experience that a lot of life was built on lies, mostly the ones we tell ourselves. I had reached a kind of Zen about the ones I told myself. Most of my life had been a wrestling match with them. Not anymore. Om. But it wasn't my lies or the sun's that concerned me. I was thinking about the ones Nancy Lustig told herself, and the ones she would tell me.

When I got inside my flat, I poured myself a Dewar's and thumbed through the mail. It was the usual daily mix of bills and begging. That particular day's charity requests claimed that my contribution would cure pancreatic cancer, diabetes, AIDS, and autism. My donation would feed the poor of Africa, continue to reconstruct Long Island in the aftermath of Hurricane Sandy, and rebuild the lives of our wounded veterans. I was a powerful man, apparently.

It wasn't that I was cold to the begging. I wasn't numb. I believe my prodigious drinking in the wake of Pam's death had proven as much. It was just that everything had been turned into a crusade. Not everything is worthy of a crusade. Sometimes it became just so much noise that translated into *Give money, stop death*. It was the biggest lie we shared. That if we only gave a few dollars more, we could all spread lamb's blood above our thresholds and the angel of death would walk on by.

I put the glass of blended Scotch to my lips, then put it quickly down. Instead, I decided to call Sarah. I wanted to test some of what Nancy had told me. If the Hollow Girl was as legendary as she claimed, I wondered if Sarah would know the legend. I also longed to hear my daughter's voice, and hoped she would put the phone in front of Ruben. I held the phone in my hand, punched in ten of the eleven digits, and stopped. What if she was screening her calls and wouldn't pick up? I wasn't sure I could take that. The thought of it, of Sarah staring at my number on the screen, refusing to pick up, made me want to reach for the Dewar's again. Even during the years she had shut me out in the fallout from her mother's murder, Sarah answered my calls. Of course, our conversations in those years were stilted and contrived, more chilling than if we hadn't spoken at all. Still, I never doubted she would answer my calls. Things were different now. She was married, a mother. Her husband, her son, they were her life now. But what is life without risk? I punched in the last digit.

I got her answering machine, but then she picked up: "Hey, Dad, sorry, I was changing Ruben." I couldn't speak for the tears. "Dad, Dad! Are you all right?"

"Fine," I finally said. "Sorry. No, I'm good. I'm good."

"Okay . . ." she said, those two syllables thick with suspicion.

"I've taken a case."

"My dad, the PI. That's great." She sounded like she meant it. "What kind of case?"

"Missing persons. Listen, kiddo, have you ever heard of the Hollow Girl?"

"Oh my God, Sloane Cantor is missing?"

"You know I can't talk about that. So you've heard of—"

"Heard of! Dad, I used to be glued to my computer every night. For a year, the Hollow Girl was all we used to talk about in school. She was like this phenomenon."

"Did you begin watching her when she was the Lost Girl?"

"Yeah, but after that suicide thing . . . it got crazy. She totally blew up after that."

"What was the appeal?"

"She spoke to the ugly girl in all of us."

"But you're beautiful. You were always beau—"

"You're my dad. You're supposed to feel that way, but the world is tough on girls. Even pretty girls never feel pretty enough. We're never thin enough or big-breasted enough, or we're too big-breasted, or we're too this and not enough that. The Hollow Girl spoke to that in all of us because she looked how we felt, and she felt it harder than we did. It's like that show on HBO about the young women living in hipster Brooklyn. It's about women in their early twenties, but it speaks to all women at some level because we either were that age, are that age, or will be that age, so—"

"Thanks. Can you put Ruben on the phone?"

"Sure, he's right here. Hold on a second. Ruben, it's Baba Moe. Say hello to Baba," she said in her high-pitched happy mommy voice. Then I could hear my grandson squealing with joy into the mouthpiece. I wasn't so egocentric to think it was because Baba

Moe was on the other end. It was enough to hear him be happy because Sarah was happy. "How was that, Dad?"

"Great. Thank you for e-mailing me all those photos of him. He's getting big."

"Okay, Dad, I've got to go. He's gonna be hungry soon."

"I love you guys, kiddo."

"We love you too, Dad."

I breathed a giant sigh of relief. Any conversation that didn't include the phrases, "Have you stopped drinking, Dad?" or "Are you still trying to drink yourself into a coma?" was a good one. It was progress of a sort, and it was great to hear Ruben's voice again. Then, as I was enjoying my little reverie, I realized I was sipping the Dewar's.

I put the glass down again and went to my computer. I typed "the Hollow Girl" into a search engine and couldn't quite fathom how many hits I got. If the search engine was actually an engine and if life was a cartoon, sparks and smoke would have shot out of my desktop. Apparently, neither Nancy nor Sarah was exaggerating. The Wikipedia page alone scrolled down the length of a football field. Sloane Cantor, as my daughter had called her, was the cause of a minor revolution at the close of the last millennium. But as is often the case, the Hollow Girl's high point was her low point too. Within two months of her suicide posting in December of '99, it all came undone. First came the outing—"That's Sloane Cantor. She's not even in college."—then the outrage, heartfelt and otherwise, the lawsuits, the investigations; then it was over.

Even after the Hollow Girl was outed as just some aspiring high school actress, she had a huge following, an even bigger one than when she was just lost. It quickly evaporated. When the women and girls who were vicariously living or reliving their own trials and tribulations through the traumas of the Hollow Girl discovered it was an act—inspired though it may have been—they felt cheated and betrayed. There were angry tirades about the Hollow Girl in women's magazines and several op-ed pieces in papers large and small about the "hoax" Sloane Cantor had perpetrated on the world. Her attempted suicide act had transformed her from an "everygirl" hero into a kind of Evel Knievel/Harry Houdini hybrid: What stunt would she pull next? When none was forthcoming, her followers vanished. Age has some benefits. If she had been a bit more experienced, Sloane might have realized that once the suicide bit aired, she would be in the position of playing *Can You Top This?* with herself.

The lawsuits came to nothing. By the time depositions came around, the world had moved on. Besides, Sloane had been underage when the postings aired and there was no indication of malice on her part. In her own small way, Sloane's Hollow Girl suicide had produced a reaction not dissimilar to what had happened in 1938 in the wake of the *War of the Worlds* broadcast. What surprised me was how little mention there was of the Lost Girl, the Hollow Girl, or of Sloane herself after 2002. Oh, there were clippings from the New Haven and Yale papers about some great performances in small roles by Siobhan Bracken, "an actress to watch," but very little else. There was a thing in *Variety* about a pilot for a sitcom that was an updated version of the old show *Hazel*. Siobhan Bracken, née Sloane Cantor, "who first came into the public eye as the Internet's Hollow Girl, is slated to play the lead." That, too, came to nothing. Either the pilot was never made, or, if it was, the show wasn't picked up.

After my brief session of playing catch-up, I decided I'd watch a few old, random postings to get a feel for what the Hollow Girl's more typical diary entries were like. When I finally looked up from my computer screen, it was 1:42 A.M. I had been totally sucked in for hours. I could not stop watching her. Sloane Cantor was a compelling presence onscreen. She had a knack for turning the mundane details that make up all of our lives into joy and heartbreak. It was no wonder to me that she had attracted a huge following. I think if I would have known about her, I would have followed her, too.

I wasn't quite finished. I did a search for Siobhan Bracken. I wanted to see if there was anything remarkable about her under that name, or anything about going missing. If there were any police reports that had leaked into the public domain, or if some enterprising TV reporter or entertainment reporter had picked anything up. Nothing. I shut down my computer, my mind wandering back to earlier in the day to my thoughts on darkness and lies. Though I was well-versed in darkness, I got the feeling I would need help navigating through the minefield of lies that had already been told to me, and the ones laying in wait.

CHAPTER SIX

In spite of the sun's 9:00 A.M. position in the sky ahead of me, I wanted a drink. There wasn't anything particularly novel in that desire. Since Pam's death, thirst for alcohol had been my baseline state of being. But it hadn't just happened. There wasn't any genetic predisposition toward alcoholism in my family. The only things the previous generation of Pragers were predisposed to were abject pessimism and failure. For the most part, Aaron, Miriam, and I had managed to steer a pretty solid course away from those things. Then why could I hear my late mother's voice in my head? She whispered, It's never too late for things to fall apart. It's never too late. Disappointment is always just a breath away. When my downward spiral had begun, there was a determined willfulness in my drinking that had morphed into something else, something disconnected from my will.

I'd made the drive east toward Long Island hundreds, if not thousands, of times. Our third and most profitable store—Red, White, and You—was located in an obnoxiously fancy shopping center on the cusp of the Gold Coast. We opened the store at the end of the 1980s, but little had changed about the store or its setting in nearly two and a half decades. The parking lot was always so full of Porsches, Jags, Beemers, Mercedes, Bentleys, and

Maseratis that it felt more like an ultra high-end auto mall than a parking lot. Around these parts, driving a Cadillac meant you were either an iconoclast or your portfolio was underperforming. The population had churned, but not changed, really. Whereas the old Gold Coast had been populated by the Vanderbilts and Astors, its current incarnation smelled of new money. Our customers at Red, White, and You tended to equate price with quality, so was it any wonder that it was our most profitable store, or why it was my least favorite?

Nancy Lustig lived off Route 107, less than a mile away from the store. And when I pulled down the driveway, I saw that she hadn't lied about everything: The address remained the same, but the house no longer remotely resembled the one that had sat on the property thirty-five years earlier. The old house had been mostly just big, a lovely red brick colonial with a cobblestone driveway, nothing that was going to give Gropius or Gehry the hives. That was no longer the case. The new house was something out of the Hollywood Hills. Three stories high, it was all angles and beautifully sculpted concrete. The concrete was perfectly smooth, painted a flat black, and the interior, obvious through the miles of glass, was almost completely white. Some of the interior seemed to flow directly out into the exterior. The four-car garage, made of the same materials, was set off to one side, but more traditional in shape and function.

I pulled up next to the brushed steel front door, which swung open even before I got out of my car. I wasn't exactly shocked that my presence had been noted. Since 9/11, it felt like the whole world had surveillance cameras. In Manhattan, it was safe to assume that every step you took was being recorded somewhere by someone. And when you had a house in the fancy-schmancy part of Long Island that seemed like it was built mostly of glass and open spaces, you needed security cameras, a lot of them.

Nancy greeted me just inside the door. She was dressed in a silky white robe that accentuated her breasts and curves and revealed a lot of the tanned skin of her still-muscular legs. She was barefoot, I suppose to give me the impression that she had only recently gotten up and was just lounging about. *Yeah, sure.* I wasn't buying it. No one who had sculpted herself out of the unremarkable clay she had begun with would come to the door freshly out of bed.

She was perfectly made up, her hair falling just so: this much in front of her shoulders, that much behind. And her brown legs fairly glowed with the skin cream she had probably rubbed on them not a half-hour before I arrived. At least she had been wise enough not to load on the jewelry. That really would have murdered the illusion. Still, I had to confess that Nancy had turned herself into a very attractive woman. It was difficult to reconcile old Nancy with the new. And as she had the previous day, she smelled awfully good, like a hint of honey mixed with raw, freshly crushed herbs.

She caught me off guard, leaning in and kissing me on the cheek. God damn me if I didn't flutter some. I tried not to show it. I'm not sure how successful I was at that. Now the urge to drink, which I had pretty much battled to a draw on my way here, was reasserting itself.

"You look like you could use a drink," she offered, turning, walking straight ahead.

Maybe she really could read my mind. "Nothing for me. Thank you. I'm fine," I lied, and tried deflection. "This is an amazing house. Awfully white in here."

"Thank you. I helped design it. Come on out to the pool."

I followed her out through one of those interior/exterior spaces. Here, though, the white concrete flooring not only flowed outside, it flowed directly into the heated pool, wispy clouds of steam rising off the water as it blended with the crisp fall air. The pool was one of those multitiered infinity edged designs with a cascade feature. It was constructed of a dark gray slate, or what looked to be slate. It was hard to know what was real and what was make-believe around Nancy. Beyond the pool, the rear yard was a blend of styles, none of them native to Long Island. I could see a Japanese rock garden, koi pond, and a lone bonsai tree. On the opposite side of the pool, where the table, grill, wet bar, and cabana were, the design was vaguely Southwestern. Somehow it all seemed to blend well together.

When we got out by the pool, Nancy stopped. She half-turned to me and said, "There's coffee, tea, and scones on the table and a full bar over by the cabana. Help yourself."

With that, she undid her robe, letting it fall to the floor at her feet. She hesitated a beat before walking slowly into the pool. The beat of hesitation was purposeful. She wanted to make certain I noticed her, noticed that she was wearing only her tanned skin, noticed the six-pack abs, noticed that the only hair on her body was on her head. For a woman in her mid-fifties, she was in incredible shape. Seeing her that way was equal parts exhilaration and sadness, for apparently she had exchanged her soul for beauty. When we'd first met, she was guileless and honest, whereas everything Nancy did now seemed to come with a secret or not-so-secret agenda. The problem for me was trying to sort out if whatever was going on was about Nancy, or her daughter, or me.

I watched Nancy long enough for her to be swallowed up by the water, then I headed over to the table and poured myself a cup of coffee. I buttered up a raspberry scone. The fire pit was going full blast and its heat blew at me in pleasant waves. I chose to watch the flames and not Nancy. I heard her step out of the pool, listened to her wet feet slapping the baby-smooth concrete as she walked. At least she had the good taste not to ask me to dry her off, though I would be lying if I said there wasn't at least a part of me that wanted her to ask. She stopped by me, again only briefly, so that I might get a close-up view of her wet body glistening in the mid-morning sun.

"I'll be out in a minute," she said and moved on to the cabana.

Fifteen minutes or so later, she emerged: hair dry, face made up, a bottle of Irish whiskey in her hand. Now she wore a long, white, terry cloth robe tied at the waist. She didn't say anything, not at first. Instead she busied herself with the whiskey and a cup of coffee.

She waved the bottle at me. "Would you like some?"

I held my cup out to her and she poured. "That's fine. Thanks." I sipped as she sat down close but at an angle to me. "So you wanna tell me what this tango is all about? Is your daughter even missing? And if she is, do you actually give a shit?"

"Is she missing?" she repeated, shrugging her shoulders. "Maybe. She might be. I don't know. She vanishes sometimes, but usually she gets in touch with me after a few weeks. This time it's been about a month and I'm worried . . . a little. Do I give a shit? I do, because I failed her as a mother. Like I said yesterday, we aren't exactly close, but I am her mom."

"That's two outta three answers. What about the big question? What's this dance about?"

"You, obviously . . . and me."

I put my cup down. "What about us?"

"Everything."

"Well, that clears it all up."

"Sarcasm. God, it makes me wet." Nancy placed her hand over her crotch.

"That was the pool water."

"More sarcasm." She pulled a face. "Say something else and I'll come."

I stood to go. "Look, Nancy, I don't have time for this bullshit. I could be spending my time doing some serious drinking or, God forbid, working."

She grabbed my wrist with both hands. "Please, don't go. I'm sorry. I really am worried about Sloane."

"Siobhan," I corrected just to bust her chops.

"I detest that name, but yes, Siobhan." She still had my wrist. "Please sit down. Please."

And for the first time, even behind the contacts, I saw a glimpse of old Nancy. "If you give me my wrist back, I'll think about it."

When I sat back down, she said, "I lied to you that time, the last time we saw one another before yesterday."

"In 2000? When I came about Patrick."

"I pretended not to know who you were. I knew about what had happened to Patrick, and I remembered you. Believe me, I could never forget you."

"What does that mean, you could never forget me?"

"When I was in college and you came here to the old house to talk to me about Patrick, I kind of fell in love with you. You were older, not too old, and so handsome and you treated me like . . . like a person. You told me the truth and didn't try to spare my feelings. I remember every word from that day. I told you things I wouldn't have told anyone, like about the sex club and the abortion. I didn't know you at all. You were just some broken-down ex-cop who came to my house looking for Patrick, yet there was something about you. I trusted you immediately. You made me feel safe. I felt this spark between us. I'd hoped you felt it too, but I was hideous. I knew I was just being a stupid, romantic girl. That someone like you would never feel something for a stupid little troll like me."

I laughed, shook my head, thinking about how incredibly wrong she was. "You weren't pretty, Nancy, no. But you were the most honest person I think I'd ever met. Your honesty almost made me dizzy."

"Do you know what it was like for me to look in the mirror? God, I hated myself. There were times I regretted that Patrick hadn't killed me after the abortion." She was crying now. "All these years later and I'm still that ugly girl. You just don't see her anymore." She stood up and removed her new robe. I turned away. "Don't turn away. Please, don't turn away. Please, look at me. In a very real way, Moe, this was for you. All the surgery and exercise and dieting, all the pain and hard work, it was so I could have a man like you."

"I don't know what to say to that."

Nancy took a step to me, knelt down, and placed her cheek against my thigh. "Don't say anything. Just come upstairs with me. It's so chilly out here and we could be so warm together."

I found I was stroking her hair. "You were wrong, you know. That day I first came to your house, I did fall a little bit in love with you. My brother and I own a wine store not a mile from here. I used to hope you would come in someday, but you never did."

"I know, but you were married then and you had a little girl."

"How do you know—"

"Please, come upstairs with me."

"I can't, Nancy. I'm . . . I just can't."

"Is it Pam?"

I shot out of my seat, the force of it knocking her back and to the ground. "What the fuck, Nancy? Are you stalking me?"

And for the second time that day, I saw the old Nancy in her eyes and expression. "I'm sorry, Moe. I really am. You can't possibly appreciate how much." Red-faced, she scrambled to put the terry cloth robe back on. When she got it tied up, she turned to me. "I do want you to find Sloane or, at least, to find out that she's okay. All the pictures and information you asked for are in a brown envelope next to the front door. There are keys to Sloane's apartment as well. I've also included a retainer check for five thousand dollars. I didn't know what your rates were."

"There's something about me you *don't* know?"

"I guess I deserved that." She looked at the ground. "I realize now isn't the best time to ask and that I've gone about this all wrong, but would you please give me a chance to explain, maybe over dinner? I promise, no more stunts. No more manipulations. Just dinner."

"Swear to me that this thing with your daughter isn't bullshit."

"I swear," old, ugly Nancy said from beneath the million-dollar veneer.

"I take it your phone numbers are in the envelope."

"They are."

"I'll call you in a few days with a progress report. We'll talk about dinner then."

"Thank you."

"Don't thank me yet, Nancy. First let's see what's up with Siobhan."

"Will you do one more thing for me, Moe?"

"Depends."

"Just hug me. Just a little. It would mean a lot to me."

"Just a hug?"

"Just a hug. That's it."

I didn't say a word, but stepped up to her and wrapped my arms around her, my fingers sinking into the thick terry cloth. We stayed like that for a few seconds, her head on my shoulder, our arms around one another, then we pulled apart.

"Thank you," she said.

"I'll call."

I walked back into the house. The envelope was where she said it would be. Funny, it must have been there the entire time.

I picked it up, let myself out, and settled into my car. But I didn't drive away, not immediately. No, I just sat there for a long couple of minutes lost in time, unable to get the smell of her perfume out of my head.

CHAPTER SEVEN

The stuff was all there, including the keys and check. I laughed at myself. Someone had to. It had been so long since I took a paying gig as a PI that I wouldn't have known what to charge Nancy or what to ask as a retainer. I didn't know where my license was, or if it was valid any longer. But it had never really been about the license for me. Looking back, I wasn't sure what any of it had been for. For so many years I thought it was about getting my gold detective's shield. Then it was about being a PI. Then . . . .

In the end, it's true: The older you get, the less you know; at least, the less you know for sure. No matter. Somehow I got the sense that on this case—if it actually was a case and not pure manipulation—there wouldn't be much need for me to display current documentation.

I did still carry my badge on me. I toted the old tin in my pocket, not so much to use it—for chrissakes, I was beyond a relic in cop years. I could maybe flash it at a blind man and get away with it. No, I think I carried it as a kind of talisman. It connected me to a distant past, to a time when I dressed in blue and things were decidedly more black and white than unendingly gray. I had, on the other hand, stopped carrying my .38 since I'd taken up drinking as an Olympic sport. Handguns, clouded judgment, and old man reflexes were a bad mix. The same was true for driving. Once I got back into the city, I was either going to have to lay off the booze or refamiliarize myself with the subway map.

The subway map would have to wait because my first stop was only several miles to the west of Nancy Lustig's Old Brookville manse. Great Neck, the town I was headed for, was a pretty wealthy area in its own right. The northernmost part of Great Neck, Kings Point, was rumored to have been the model for West Egg in F. Scott Fitzgerald's *The Great Gatsby*. I smiled, thinking that Fitzgerald would have soiled himself at the notion of Great Neck having been a predominantly Jewish enclave for the latter half of the twentieth century. Tom Buchanan surely would have. Somewhere, Meyer Wolfsheim was smiling.

The law offices of Cantor, Schreck, Forbus, Jordan, Halle, LLP took up the top two floors of a four-story glass and steel sarcophagus on Northern Boulevard. The Cantor at the head of the partners list was, according to the paper in my hand, Julian L. Cantor, Nancy's ex and Sloane's father. I knew the firm from when my second wife and I ran our own security outfit. Many of our steady accounts had been law firms representing one side or the other in personal injury suits. Though we never worked directly for Cantor, Schreck, et al. we had done jobs for law firms that were allied with them on class action suits. While they weren't a huge firm by New York City standards, they were big players on Long Island and very well respected.

The semicircular reception area was straight out of the suburban law office playbook. There was plush gray carpeting and floor-to-ceiling blond wood paneling with the firm's name in big block letters behind the circular receptionist's kiosk. To the right of the kiosk was a designated waiting area consisting of six severe black leather chairs and a curved coffee table covered in magazines that might interest someone with a seven-figure income. I can't say that *Polo Month* or *Yacht and Jet Weekly* piqued my curiosity.

"Mr. Cantor, please," I said to the receptionist.

Attractive, with short cropped brown hair, she was maybe thirty, but she had older eyes and a professionally cool demeanor. "Do you have an appointment?" she asked, already knowing the answer.

"Sorry, I don't."

"Then I am afraid Mr. Cantor is unavailable. Would you like to make an appointment?"

"Look, I'm not trying to be difficult, but it's important that I speak to Mr. Cantor as soon as possible."

She didn't like it or me. "In reference to . . . ?"

"His daughter."

"You'll have to be more specific," she said, her voice neutral, her expression far less so.

I handed her one of my old company cards from a little leather case. "Please tell Mr. Cantor that I have been retained by Nancy Lustig, his ex-wife."

The receptionist's expression changed from skeptical to suspicious. She hesitated for a moment, but then put her fingers to a screen. "Yes, hi, Jess," she spoke into the tiny mic at the end of the curved tube on her headset. "I have a Mr. Moses Prager in reception to see Mr. Cantor . . . his card says he's the president of Prager & Melendez Investigations . . . no, this isn't a solicitation. Mr. Prager says it's about Mr. Cantor's daughter and that he has been retained by Mr. Cantor's ex . . . okay, Jess, I'll hold on." About thirty seconds later, the receptionist nodded. "Fine, I'll have him wait. Thank you, Jess." She looked back at me. "Please have a seat, Mr. Prager. Miss Lourey will be down to get you in a moment."

"Thank you."

But she had already moved on to something else. I was as good as invisible to her, or dead. I went with invisible. I'd recently been too close to dead to find that option even mildly amusing. Almost before I could sit, a woman seemed to appear before me out of thin air.

"Mr. Prager?" She stretched her hand out to me. "I'm Miss Lourey, Mr. Cantor's administrative assistant."

I shook her hand as I stood. She had a firm handshake, long but tidy black hair, and was dressed in a gray business suit with sensible black pumps. "A pleasure," I said out of habit.

"This way."

After a short, painfully silent elevator ride, Miss Lourey dropped me off at Julian Cantor's corner office. She handed her boss my card, which he gave a cursory glance.

Cantor greeted me with an insincere slap on the back. He was a trim, plain-faced man with a million-dollar smile and the same blue eyes as his daughter. He was dressed in the standard uniform of a senior law partner: dark blue pinstriped suit, powder blue shirt with white cuffs and collar, red tie, red suspenders, gold cuff links, Piaget watch, alligator belt, black wingtips. His gray hair was expertly coifed, his fingernails trimmed and polished, his face clean-shaven. He smelled vaguely of cigar smoke and sickly sweet, locker-room aftershave. That was the new rich man's affectation. They seemed to enjoy smelling like they did when they went for their first haircuts.

"So what's this about?" he asked, glancing at my card again and gesturing to a chair in front of his desk. I sat as he moved around the desk to his chair. "What's my ex upset with Sloane about this time?"

I ignored the question for the moment. "I notice neither you nor Miss Lustig call your daughter Siobhan."

"What, are you a psychologist all of a sudden?" Cantor asked, affecting a Yiddish accent, his face frozen in a plastic smile.

"Just curious is all."

It was his turn to ignore me. "Look, Prager, my ex-wife is a guilt-ridden woman. She feels she did a shitty job as a mother."

"Did she?"

"She was no more a bad mother than any of the other women who moved in our circle. In fact, she was better than most of those rich, worthless whores. Sloane learned early on that she could get to Nancy by pushing her buttons and she has never stopped pushing them."

"How about your buttons?"

"I know your firm, Prager. At least I used to. You know what trial lawyers are like. Not so easy to mess us about," he said, proud as could be. "Sloane was a handful. Precocious, manipulative, talented, high-strung, a screwed-up adult in a little girl's body. Now all that's changed is she's a screwed-up little girl in an adult's body."

"What's your relationship with her like now?"

"Look, Prager, I'm not in the mood. I already have an analyst, okay? What's going on?"

"Your ex says your daughter has been off the radar for almost a month now, and that's a little longer than she's used to."

Given Cantor's previous glibness, I expected more of the same. *What, the kid doesn't check in and my ex sends for the Marines? See, the kid's just pushing Nancy's buttons again like she always has. So what? Maybe my kid's finally making a life for herself apart from Nancy.* But that wasn't what I got, not at all. The lawyer screwed up his lips. Pensively stroking his cheeks with his left hand, his eyes filled with worry.

"A month? That is a long time for Sloane not to bust Nancy's balls. Are you sure it's been that long?"

"That's what your ex says, Mr. Cantor."

"All right, Nancy is pretty accurate about that stuff. If she says it's a month, it's a month. Look, Prager, keep me posted too." He reached into his desk drawer and pulled out one of his cards. "This has all my contact info on it, including my home number, cell, et cetera. Anything you need, just ask."

"Why the concern? I mean, it's pretty apparent that your daughter does this kind of thing on occasion."

"It's complicated. You have to understand Nancy and Sloane to understand the situation, Prager. They've always been bound together in a strange kind of dance. It's almost planetary, the way Sloane revolves around her mom. Two weeks and not a word from Sloane. Then, like clockwork, she calls to hurt her mom. Lord knows it wore me down. I have never seen two people who love and hate and need each other more than those two. Nancy never really needed me anyway. She never needed anyone or anything but a mirror. And Sloane only ever needed her mother. I got tired of being an afterthought," he confessed, now staring intently at my card. "Moses Prager . . . Moses Prager. Do people call you Moe?"

"Everybody calls me Moe."

His mouth readjusted itself into a crooked, knowing smile, and he clapped his hands together. "Moe. Ah, so you're the famous Moe."

"If you say so."

"You're the guy who Nancy met when you were looking for her old boyfriend, Patrick, in the '70s."

"You know about Patrick Maloney?"

"Of course, but only as a means to talk about you. You've always been her white knight, you know that, right?"

"I didn't."

"No offense, Prager, but I don't see it. I mean you must've been pretty good looking as a younger man, but . . . I guess it's always tough, competing with a fantasy."

"I wouldn't know, Mr. Cantor. I just try to get by. When I walk, I put one foot in front of the other."

"Nancy fuck you yet?"

"Thanks for the card." I stood up, refusing to take his bait. I didn't see the point. The surgery, chemo, and radiation had not only gotten rid of my cancer, they had largely gotten rid of my temper as well. Too bad they were woefully ineffective against guilt. "I will call if I need anything."

"She will, you know . . . fuck you, I mean. She's always wanted to, and Nancy's always gotten everything she's ever wanted, except you and Sloane's affection. Now she can cross one of those off her list."

I walked to the office door, then turned back. "It's funny, Mr. Cantor, how hard it is for people to see the stuff right in front of their faces. I don't think Nancy's ever gotten anything she ever wanted, not really."

With that, I left. I wasn't judging Cantor. I had been twice divorced myself, both times because I was blind to the things right in front of my face. But I was getting the sense that maybe there was a case here, and that I'd better start taking things seriously.

CHAPTER EIGHT

When I saw the building that matched Siobhan Bracken's address, I can't say I was surprised. The Kremlin, as it had come to be known, was a fifteen-story-tall red brick apartment building on East Houston—that's HOW-ston, not YOU-ston—Street on the Lower East Side of Manhattan. It wasn't ugly, nor was it much to look at. It got its nickname because of the whimsical art installment on its roof that featured twenty-foot-tall statues of Lenin, Trotsky, Stalin, Khrushchev, and Brezhnev holding hands and doing a circle dance. It was visible from surrounding streets. Behind the dancing comrades was a four-sided metal structure shaped like rows of dark green, red-starred ballistic missiles. The array of fake missiles covered up the building's water tower. So, no, I wasn't surprised at all by Siobhan's choice of address. Like mother, like daughter—things weren't what they seemed.

Across Houston Street from the Kremlin was Katz's, the world's most famous Jewish deli. Opened in the 1880s, Katz's was well known to all New Yorkers. But it became nationally famous during WWII when it adopted—some would say stole—the motto "Send a salami to your boy in the army" from a competing deli and made it its own. Stolen motto or not, Katz's served the best pastrami and corned beef in the world. Besides being sent into a state of bliss by the aroma of cured meats, grilling hot dogs, sweet chicken soup, and the vinegary tang of sour pickles, stepping into Katz's was another journey back in time. They did things the old-fashioned way here. There wasn't a mechanical slicing machine in sight. The meats were all hand carved and piled in small mountains atop soft, fragrant rye bread.

It was also a kind of sacred shrine, the place Israel Roth and I had always visited when he was up from Florida. It was corned beef for him, pastrami for me. Russian dressing for him, mustard for me. Dr. Brown's cream soda for him, Dr. Brown's Cel-Ray for me. A round kasha knish for him, a square potato for me. We both preferred sour pickles to half sour. That last time, he hardly touched his food. He was very old then, and dying. He knew it. I knew it. He refused to discuss it, and I was happy to let him refuse. We'd sat mostly in silence . . . well, as much silence as was possible in Katz's. The place was always busy and noisy with clattering dishes, clanging silverware, shouted orders, hundreds of half-spoken sentences in thirty different languages. But whatever tiny bits of food Mr. Roth ate that night—one bite of his corned beef, a forkful of knish, a few sips of his soda, half a pickle—he seemed to savor. He knew these flavors would have to last him an eternity.

As I walked across Houston, I saw the doorman at the Kremlin unloading groceries from a cab for one of the tenants. I was a bit disappointed not to be able to speak with him. A cooperative doorman is a great resource. No one, except maybe the superintendent, knows the inside skinny like the doorman. It wasn't a total loss, though. It wasn't like the doorman wouldn't be there when I came out. I didn't even have to use the key to get into the lobby. A young Japanese couple with wildly spiked hair, dressed in matching lime green leather jumpsuits and white marshmallowy boots, came bursting through the lobby door without giving me a second thought. *Ya gotta love the Lower East Side.*

Siobhan's apartment was on the fifth floor. When I got out of the elevator, I followed the sign on the wall and turned left. It had been many, many years since I'd lived in a large apartment building, but I'd grown up in one. There was a kind of familiar comfort in the competing odors that filled the hallway. Whether it was a building of luxury flats in Manhattan or a tenement in Coney Island was beside the point. As I made my way to 5E along the zebra-patterned carpeting, my nose told me that someone in 5B was frying onions, garlic, and ginger. That the person in 5C was getting stoned; the earthy, burning-grass aroma of high-grade marijuana was intense. Think Allman Brothers, *At Fillmore East*, circa 1970. And then, as I passed 5D, I got gut punched by the scourge of apartment building life, the stench of overfried fish.

For some bizarre reason, I was smiling. It was like remembering my mom's coffee—horrifying and wonderful all at once. I was young again, a kid in Coney Island; my life just one long summer's day of basketball, stickball, touch football, and friends; a life of the Cyclone, the boardwalk, and the beach; a life of first kisses. My smile vanished as quickly as it had come, because beneath the nostalgic stench of the fried fish my nose detected the dark grace notes of another sickening scent. This brought me back, too, but not to the Cyclone or to first kisses. I was twenty when death introduced itself to me. I recalled that night in more detail than the night I'd lost my virginity. It was February of 1967. That first whiff never leaves you, and as a uniformed cop I had breathed in its rancid glory a hundred other times.

I forced myself to be calm. There was no reason for me to believe that death was calling from Siobhan's apartment, or that it was even human death. Pets die, too. People go on vacation and their refrigerators break down. Meat rots. Flies lay eggs. I lied to myself that it was just as likely a broken fridge as anything else, but as I'd told Mr. Roth only moments before he passed, I wasn't very good at self-deception. I'd smelled human death too many times, and I was too old to pretend. I couldn't even manage to convince myself the odor wasn't coming from beneath the white metal door marked 5E. As I got closer, the smell got stronger. And when I got to the door I knew.

My right hand clenched so tightly that the edges of the keys dug into the skin of my palm. They hadn't drawn blood, not yet, but my skin had been cut. I had decisions to make. There was no turning back, no phoning this in anonymously. Caller ID had kind of put an end to that trick. The doorman might not have seen me, but the Japanese leather twins had—even if they paid me no mind—and I had counted at least three security cameras that had followed my progress. No, the only decision I had to make was whether to call the cops now or wait until I'd had a look around the flat. The former choice would be easier and smarter; the latter, foolish and of questionable legality. I put the key in the lock, turned it, used the pinky side of my right hand to move the door handle, and stepped inside.

Bang! The rank stench of death, of feces and urine, caught me full in the face. So much for the broken refrigerator theory. It was all I could do not to puke. I held my right hand tight against my mouth. It didn't help. I knew there was never any getting used to the odor, but experience had taught me that if I held the nausea off for just a little bit longer, I could stop myself from being overwhelmed by it. So I stood there, taking slow, shallow breaths. As I did, I scanned the place. The apartment smelled nearly as powerfully of money as of death. The place looked like something out of a snooty-assed magazine or designer showcase. Everything was just so, and just so expensive. The one thing missing, from what I could see, was a body.

Now I had another decision to make. Every step I took deeper into the apartment, every surface I touched, meant I was contaminating a possible crime scene. Still, I'd come this far, and if anyone was going to find Siobhan Bracken's body, it felt right somehow that it should be me. Don't ask me why, but I got the sense Nancy would find solace in that. Having buried so many people close to me, I didn't want to rob Nancy of even an ounce of solace. As I stepped toward the bedroom, the odors got stronger, and then I saw long streaks of dried blood on the hardwood flooring in the passageway between bedroom and bathroom. That was enough. I called it in, but hung up on the 911 operator before she could ask me any particulars. The responding uniforms could get those in person.

I knew I had about two minutes to find the body, and stopped tiptoeing about. It didn't take me more than fifteen seconds to locate her. I found her in the bedroom, face-down in the carpet, left arm splayed, right arm outstretched as if reaching for the bed. There was blood here, too, a lot of it. She was nude, her clothes, bra, and panties, strewn along the side of the bed. She'd been dead for a while, bloated and in bad shape, gravity having forced her blood to pool in the parts of her body close to the floor. I didn't step into the bedroom, nor did I step into the bathroom. I only saw what I could see from the hallway. That was plenty. Yet I couldn't shake the feeling that something wasn't right. Yeah, I know. There was a dead woman, probably a murdered one, not ten feet from where I stood, but it wasn't that. I turned and left the apartment to wait for the cops. By the time I closed the door behind me, I could already hear the sirens.

CHAPTER NINE

My old badge came in handy for once. It bought me some respect and a little less bullshit from the two 9th Precinct uniforms who responded to the scene. They didn't treat me like a moron or a civilian even if, by their reckoning, I was as old as dirt. I explained to them who I was and what I was doing there, and they didn't seem to give a crap about my having contaminated the crime scene. They left that part up to the pair of detectives who'd caught the case.

"Fuck," said one uniform to the other when he saw the detectives stepping out of the elevator. "It's Frovarp and Shulze."

"Yeah, you got the shit end of the stick, Prager," the other uniform agreed. "Them two are real ball busters, especially Frovarp. Watch yourself with her."

Frovarp was a willowy woman in her mid-forties with short gray hair and a *don't-fuck-with-me* demeanor. Shulze, tall and thin, had a kind of hangdog smile and an "aw shucks" manner about him. It wasn't hard to figure out who played good cop and bad cop when they interviewed suspects. Neither of them seemed to like me very much. That made three of us, but they were pretty unpleasant about it.

First they made me wait for over a half-hour before they even acknowledged my existence.

"Him, he stays here until we're ready for him, okay?" Shulze told the uniforms without making eye contact with me.

I watched the Crime Scene Unit and the guy from the ME's office go in while I sat in the hallway, waiting my turn with the Inquisition. I'd thought about calling Nancy, but I still couldn't get a finger on the feeling that something wasn't right about this whole situation. No matter. Siobhan wasn't going anywhere. I wanted to make sure that when I called Nancy, I had as much information as possible. The last thing relatives of a victim want to hear is *I don't know*. Relatives want answers, explanations. With murders, especially, they want to know as much as possible.

"What the fuck, Prager? You could smell it out here like the vic was in front of the damned door. Why the fuck did you go in there and mess with the crime scene?" Frovarp barked at me when she came out of the apartment.

"I didn't know the smell was coming from her apartment. I'm not a fucking beagle."

"C'mon, man. That's bullshit and you know it," said Shulze.

"Thing is, I had keys. I went in hoping the smell wasn't from inside the apartment. When I found the body, I called it in. I was careful not to mess up the crime scene."

Frovarp didn't buy it. "You wanna merit badge for that, Boy Scout?"

"No, I'd like you two to tell me what's going on so I can call my client."

"You're not calling anybody about anything until we go over the preliminary statement you gave the responding officers," Shulze said, looking down at his notes. "You say the vic is Siobhan Bracken, aged thirty-one. That she—"

"Sorry, Detective Shulze, but that's wrong," interrupted the ME, a guy named Dougherty, popping his head through the open door. "You've either got the wrong vic or the wrong age. That woman in there is forty-five if she's a day. And to add to your headaches, she's not a vic . . . at least not of a crime."

"What the fuck are you talking about?" Frovarp screamed loud enough to be heard at Katz's. "There's blood all over the fucking place."

"We won't know for sure until we do the autopsy," said the ME, "but my guess is myocardial infarction is the COD."

"A heart attack?" Frovarp liked that less than she liked me. "Bullshit on that."

Dougherty shrugged. "Or possibly an aneurism, but I'd bet on heart attack. Maybe the fall killed her."

Frovarp was skeptical. "The fall?"

"And the blood?" Shulze wanted to know. "Last time I looked, none of that shit you're talking about comes with external bleeding. Unless I'm seeing things, there's a lot of blood in that apartment."

"Almost all of it came from a gash on her forehead and wounds on her face. I'll show you."

The ME turned and walked back into 5E. Frovarp and Shulze were so pissed that they didn't notice I followed them into the apartment. We huddled in the passageway between the bathroom and bedroom.

"Here's what your CSU guy and I think must have happened," Dougherty said when he saw we were there with him. "The victim undresses to take a bath or a shower, or just to get ready for bed. She starts heading into the bathroom, but the MI or the aneurism seizes her before she makes it fully inside, and she falls headfirst onto the tile floor. You can check with CSU. They say there's a cracked tile under that large area of dried blood. If you look carefully, you can see it."

"Okay, keep going," Frovarp said.

"She's stunned or unconscious, which is why there's such a large amount of blood in that one area. She wasn't moving. Head and facial wounds tend to bleed very intensely. She finally rouses. Realizing she's got to call for help, she crawls back into the bedroom to find her cell phone. That accounts for these streaks of blood on the floor here and leading into the bedroom. Unfortunately, she expires before she can find the phone or use it."

"So if that's not Siobhan Bracken, who is it?" I heard myself say.

"Get the fuck outta here, Prager," Frovarp groused. "Go wait in the hall."

"Hey, this is one less case to close," I said. "What's eating you?"

Shulze gave me a less than gentle shove. "Outside, Prager. Wait outside!"

I went outside all right, but I didn't wait. Those two asshole detectives weren't going to give me any information or make my job any easier, so I didn't see why I should make their charming lives any easier. And there was no doubt they were the types to give me a hard time simply because they could. *No, thanks.* I wasn't in the mood. I hadn't committed any crime. Well, I guess, technically I had, but it wasn't the type of thing people got prosecuted for. The uniforms who had first responded were long gone, and the guys who had replaced them didn't know who I was. They just let me walk right onto the elevator and go.

I didn't figure I'd have much time to chat with the doorman after Frovarp and Shulze realized I hadn't stuck around. So as I left the building, I handed the doorman my card and a couple of twenty-dollar bills. "What time you get off your shift?"

He didn't bother looking in his hand. "Six, but you know what I'm thinking? I'm thinking maybe I might be busy tonight, you know?" he said with a familiar Bronx Italian inflection.

"There's more where that came from, so make sure you're not busy, okay? I'll meet you at Grogan's Clover on Avenue C at 6:15. You know it?"

He was a dark, good-looking man with a tough guy attitude. "I'll find it. Is everything okay with Siobhan—I mean, Miss Bracken? She's real nice to me. I would hate it if like somethin' happened to her, you know?" he asked, his hard exterior cracking slightly.

"I'm not sure, but there's a dead woman in her apartment that's not her. You got any ideas?"

"A few, maybe, yeah. Depends, you know?"

"Don't push me, wiseass. Gimme a first name or you can buy your own fucking drinks."

"Millie."

I wasn't going to dig harder just then because I got the sense my time was running out. "Later."

CHAPTER TEN

The call I made to Nancy Lustig was your classic good news, bad news kind of deal: The bad news is there's a dead woman in your daughter's apartment. The good news is that the body isn't your daughter's. I didn't begin the call that way, but I also didn't spend twenty minutes discussing the weather or the spot price of sweet Texas crude oil, either. When I told Nancy about the dead woman, there was a moment of stunned silence.

"Do you know who the dead woman is?" Nancy asked.

"By now I'm sure the cops have searched the place more thoroughly, and they've probably got a preliminary ID."

"What do you mean, by now? Where are you? Why aren't you still at the—" She was screaming into her phone. Panic does that to people.

"Breathe, Nancy. Breathe. I'm not at the apartment because the cops weren't happy I was there in the first place. They weren't gonna tell me anything, and they were likely to arrest me just to break my balls. I can't find Siobhan if—"

"Sloane," she interrupted, still shouting. "Her name is Sloane!"

"Have it your way. I can't find Sloane if I'm having a pissing contest with the cops or if I'm spending the night in a holding cell at the 9th Precinct."

Nancy was calmer now. "I'm sorry, Moe. You're right, of course. But do you have any idea who the dead woman is in the apartment?"

"I was hoping you could help me with that."

"How?"

"I've got a first name: Millie."

"Was she pretty, blue-eyed, forty-ish, light brown hair?"

"She wasn't very pretty to look at when I saw her. She was in really rough shape, but I guess that's a fairly good description. Who was she?"

Nancy ignored that last part. "What do you mean, she was in rough shape? Oh, my God, was she murdered?"

"Relax. The medical examiner doesn't think it's a homicide. He thinks it was probably a heart attack. Then she fell and cracked her head open. So at first glance it looked like murder to the cops. It looked that way to me also. Who was she?" I asked again.

"It sounds like it must be Millicent McCumber."

"Millicent McCumber, the actress?"

Nancy laughed an odd, staccato laugh. "Millie McCumber," she repeated. There was pity in her voice, but it was also full of sharp, angry teeth. "She was a has-been who hadn't been for a long time. She hasn't done more than a bit part in fifteen years. Christ, she couldn't even get hired on *Law & Order* and that franchise has cycled three times through every New York actor still blessed with a pulse."

"Why wasn't she working? She was good. I remember them calling her the next Meryl Streep."

There was that machine gun laugh again. "The next W.C. Fields, more likely. She drank so much, she should have had gills instead of lungs. Millie was also a diva extraordinaire. Even though she hadn't had a meaningful role in a movie since the second Clinton administration, she was harder to tame than Medusa's hair."

"So you knew her."

"I had the displeasure, yes. Some people have pets, others have causes. The Ancient Mariner had an albatross. Sloane had Millie.

She kind of made her a reclamation project because Millie had once been beautiful."

"You sound angry. Maybe even a little jealous."

"I am—I was," she confessed. "Sloane is so talented and could have really been somebody. She still could be somebody, but instead she chose to weigh herself down with that human skirt of rocks."

"Were they lovers?"

"At first, I guess maybe they were, but not for a long time. In fact, for a few years, Sloane had seemed to shed Millie. Then a few months ago, they started hanging around together again. Probably because Sloane knew it would irk me."

The more I listened to Nancy talk about her daughter, the more I gave credence to what Julian Cantor had said about the relationship between mother and daughter. It really did seem as if their lives were bound together in very unhealthy ways, but I hadn't taken this on to do family counseling.

"Did Millie live with Siob—with Sloane?"

"No, but she had keys to the apartment, and Sloane let her use it when she was away."

"So that's good. It means that Sloane's away and not missing."

"You find a dead woman in my daughter's apartment and that should make me feel better?"

"Well, when you put it like that . . . . But if Sloane only let Millie use her apartment when she was away, it might mean—"

"Might," she said. "Might."

"Don't worry, Nancy. I'm not trying to get off the case. I've already got someone lined up to talk to. I just wanted to let you know that there are other scenarios than the worst one."

"I'm sorry. It's just—"

"You don't have to apologize. If it was my daughter, I'd be crazed, too. I'll keep you posted."

CHAPTER ELEVEN

Grogan's Clover was a bullshit joint, a hipsterish papier-mâché version of a New York Irish bar. See, here's what people don't get about New York City: Manhattan isn't like the outer boroughs. Not only is it like a different city, it's like another planet. Only in Manhattan would somebody dream up a scheme to borrow hundreds of thousands of dollars to recreate something that is perfectly fine as is. There must have been a few hundred authentic Irish pubs spread throughout the city, reasonably friendly places that served beer, liquor, and edible food without requiring you to sign over your firstborn for payment. Maybe the TVs weren't flat screens the size of solar panels, but they showed the same games and were equally distracting. And maybe their jukeboxes didn't always play downloads from bands with names like Grizzly Bear or Das Racist, but music came out of them nonetheless.

Sadly, the vampires who feed the appetites of scruffy hipster ghouls were busy turning parts of my beloved Brooklyn into Manhattan. *No, thanks.* The Brooklyn I love likes itself a half-step behind and a few years out of date. It likes its yearning. The yearning where making it means somewhere across the river, not across Bushwick Avenue. My Brooklyn doesn't consider its decay ironic or a statement about something bigger. My Brooklyn is what it is, and says that's enough because it has to be. That's all there is. Brooklyn is necessarily a place that used to be, not a place that's happening. God, please, let it happen somewhere else. Anywhere else.

My breath stuck in my throat with an audible gasp when I caught a flash of the bartender's profile. She looked so much like Holly D'Angelo, the girl who'd hit Pam, that all the pain of late June came flooding back into me. With her practiced Manhattan callousness, she hadn't noticed my reaction or, if she had, she sure hadn't let it show. What she showed me instead was a vague hint of a smile that itself seemed like a Herculean bit of theater. I guess I should have thanked her because if she had shown me even an ounce of genuine humanity at that moment, I would have ordered a double Dewar's and not looked back. But because her chilly tattooed veneer so pissed me off, I refused to go diving into the whiskey abyss.

"Club soda and lime," I said.

It must have sounded like *Go fuck yourself.* She tilted her head at me, as if wondering what she'd done to earn my contempt. She didn't waste much time in contemplation, putting my drink up on a coaster and moving on down the bar.

The doorman from the Kremlin came bouncing into Grogan's at 6:37. Out of his ridiculous gray visored felt cap and matching tunic with shiny brass buttons and wide red piping, he looked young and hungry. He was definitely a workout rat, and his civilian clothes were meant to show off his V-shaped torso. When he strutted into a place, he wanted everyone to notice him, expected them to notice him. But this was Alphabet City, not Arthur Avenue. Around here, his Bronx outer-borough charms were lost on the locals. He didn't like that, not even a little bit.

"Whatta dump," he said, sitting on the stool next to me. "Yo, honey, gimme a Ketel One on the rocks, and put it on grandpa's tab, huh."

"You're late."

"Chill out, gramps. I'm here, ain't I? The freakin' cops kept me around askin' me questions, you know."

"Fair enough."

The bartender put the doorman's drink down in front of him and gave me a refill on the club soda. We didn't bother toasting. The doorman polished it off in a quick swig.

"No offense, pops, but I don't like this place and you ain't exactly my idea of a wing man. Show me some money or I'm gone. You know what I'm sayin'?"

He gave me the opening and I waltzed through it. "Well, if I didn't already know about Millicent McCumber and Siobhan Bracken's arrangement, I might be tempted to show you some more money. But since I do know about them—*all* about them— you're gonna have to sing for your supper and earn your money, junior."

"Fuck you!" is what came out of his mouth, though his face showed disappointment. In his head he'd already spent the money he was now risking with his bluster.

I offered him a second chance. "We'll start easy with a simple question. What's your name?"

"Nah, I ain't playin' this game. Keep your fuckin' money." He got up from the stool, but hesitated, waiting for me to make him an offer to stay.

I played a different card based on a not-so-wild guess. "Suit yourself, junior, but my guess is the management company that runs the Kremlin won't be pleased to find out you were fucking one of their tenants. Not only will they fire your ass, but you won't be able to get a job cleaning toilets in a city housing project. Now sit the fuck back down and talk to me."

He puffed out his chest, leaning into me like he was going to prove me wrong by smacking the shit out of me. Something he no doubt could have done, and would happily have done. The thing is, he knew I was right. Of course, I was only guessing at his relationship with Siobhan, but I wasn't born stupid. Although I was basically a stumbler as a PI, I was good at picking up on the little things. I had known Nancy as a young woman, and I suspected Siobhan, like her mother before her, would have been incredibly susceptible to a handsome, well put-together guy like the doorman.

"C'mon, c'mon." I patted the stool next to mine. "Sit back down and tell me your name." I said it as friendly as I could manage, and ordered him another drink.

He sat. After his second, then third, vodka, he finally told me his name was Anthony Rizzo and that he and Siobhan had a deal of sorts. For two hundred bucks a throw, he'd service her.

"She wasn't bad for her looks, you know. She liked a little kink. Liked me to her call bad things and fuck her really hard. Sometimes it was both Siobhan and the older broad, Millie. That bitch was freakin' wild, man." After two more drinks, Anthony started to confess something else. "Sometimes for a few hundred extra—" He stopped, clearing his throat, his face turning deep red. "Sometimes . . . ."

"So," I said in a neutral voice, "there was another guy involved, too. What was his name, Anthony, the other guy?"

He was cowed, hanging his head. "Giorgio," he whispered. "He was one of Millie's friends."

"Last name?"

"Don't know it, man."

"But you have his number, right?"

He shook his head. "Not on me."

I slid five twenties to him across the bar. "My cell number's on my card. Text it to me. Did you ever go to his place?"

"Once, yeah. I needed the extra scratch, you know? He owns a brownstone in Hell's Kitchen somewheres."

"Text me the address too."

After another drink, Anthony fed me the basics, the more mundane stuff that any doorman who wasn't sleeping with one of his tenants would have known. The last time he'd seen Siobhan in either his capacity as a doorman or paid lover was at the very end of August.

"She was goin' on one of her trips, you know, probably international because the cab I hailed for her was takin' her to JFK, not LaGuardia or Newark."

"Any idea where?"

"Nah, she didn't discuss shit with me. When she saw me outside of the bedroom, she treated me like the hired help . . . worse, maybe. But she used to go on a lotta trips."

"For how long?"

"Most of the time, a week, ten days maybe; two weeks max."

"So she's been gone a long time, then?"

He nodded. "Yeah, I guess so. Yeah, it's been a while, you know?"

"How long has Millie been staying in Siobhan's apartment?"

"A month maybe. She'd been around a lot lately."

"When did Millie first start coming around?"

Anthony thought about that for a minute, rubbing his forehead as he did. "A couple of months. I think Siobhan introduced me to her in May. Told me Millie had keys and that I should let her in and to treat Millie the way I treated her."

"How long have you had your little arrangement with Siobhan?"

"A year, maybe. We'd do it about once a month, like when she needed it bad, but since Millie showed up, I been in 5E a lot, you know. Even after Siobhan split for wherever, I was up with Millie a few times. She was a generous bitch, man, and she could really fuck," Anthony said, pumping his fist. "She was the best I ever had. Too bad about her, huh?"

I wasn't sure if Rizzo was more upset by the loss of future income, or by the thought he was never going to sleep with Millie again.

"So if you'd been servicing her a lot, weren't you curious when she stopped calling?"

"Hey, I ain't a 7-Eleven, man. I don't work there seven days a week, twenty-four hours a day. I figured the bitch split, like Siobhan. People in that building come and go without telling me shit." He looked at his watch. "Can I get outta here now?"

"Soon, Anthony. In a minute. Just one more question."

"Fine."

"Did you have any idea of who Siobhan and Millie were?"

"What the fuck does that mean, who they were? One was a hard-up bitch with a lot of money who liked to get fucked hard, for whatever reason. And the other was a drunken whore who loved cock and pussy more than anybody I ever met, you know?"

I handed him two more twenties, reminded him to text me Giorgio's contact info, and told him I'd be in touch if I needed anything else. He didn't look pleased for someone who'd just drank about eighty dollars' worth of free vodka and who'd made almost two hundred bucks cash in the last hour and a half. I suppose he preferred making his money the old-fashioned way: hustling for it and working for tips. I guess I didn't blame him for resenting me. No one likes having a hammer held over his head, and the hammer I was holding over Anthony's was a heavy one. But leverage is a funny thing and much harder to use than people would expect. I learned that lesson a long time ago at the hands of Brighton Beach's mob boss, a guy we called Tony Pizza. It was a lesson I have never forgotten.

CHAPTER TWELVE

I thought about killing time until I received Anthony Rizzo's texts about the mysterious Giorgio, but chose to play a hunch instead. Giorgio, I figured, could wait until tomorrow. So when I walked out of Grogan's, I turned north, then west. I'd decided to go sniff around Kid Charlemagne's on 2nd Avenue and 7th Street. Kid Charlemagne's, like Grogan's Clover, was one of those Manhattan meta creations—a theme restaurant as Venus Flytrap—a place created by an elitist asshole so that he and his friends could laugh at the great unwashed masses who innocently wandered in for a burger and a beer. My bet was that Kid Charlemagne's owner, a C-list artist and A-list junkie named Nathan Martyr, would be well acquainted with the likes of the Hollow Girl and Millicent McCumber.

I'd walked about a block when I noticed I was being followed, and not very skillfully so. My tail, a nondescript white guy in his mid-thirties wearing a pristine motorcycle jacket, Ralph Lauren jeans, and two hundred buck Nikes, had gotten a little too close when I left Grogan's. Then, instead of just walking on by me, as he should have, he abruptly changed course and rushed to cross the street. I could see him paralleling me up Avenue C, and when I turned left to head west, he did the same, keeping to the other side of the street. He wasn't a threat. His incompetence didn't exactly breed fear in me. Still, I was wary all the same. He wasn't a cop, that was for shit sure. The question was, if he wasn't a cop, who was he and why the hell was he following me around the Lower East Side?

I ducked into a busy restaurant, allowing me to make sure I was in fact being followed and not simply succumbing to a bout of paranoia. My view out the eatery's darkly tinted plate glass window reassured me that I wasn't being paranoid. To say my tail wasn't much of a pro was an understatement. When I entered the restaurant, he should have kept on going, then doubled back and hidden himself out of my line of sight. But no, there he was, directly across the street, pacing a rut in the sidewalk.

I waited for a group of people to leave the restaurant. When a party of five headed out, I tucked in behind them, kneeling below car top level—no easy task for an old man with bad knees—as I went through the front door. Working my way about ten car lengths back east, I popped my head up and looked through a car windshield. *Oy!* I almost felt sorry for this schmuck with the expensive jeans, because he was still across the street from the restaurant, craning his neck, waiting for me to exit. Confident of my tail's inexperience, I crossed to his side of the street, hid in a doorway, and waited him out.

Ten minutes later, it must have clicked that he'd lost me. He went into the eatery to make certain. When he came out, he was so pissed he kicked a parking meter machine. If it hadn't already been easy enough to follow him, his self-inflicted limp made it cake. Eventually, he worked his way back down toward Houston Street. He got into a sleek, metallic maroon BMW coupe with idiotic vanity plates that read P EYE 7. This clown was almost too much to bear. At least I now had a good sense of who he might be. I was confident he must have been Julian Cantor's lead investigator.

The thing is that there are all kinds of PIs for all kinds of jobs. Some require a police background and some don't. Some require a deep level of high-tech skill. Some require a bit of acting craft, while others require nothing more than patience and a strong bladder. When Carmella and I owned our security firm, we tried to have a mix of all kinds of skilled people. But when you were an investigator who worked almost exclusively on personal injury and malpractice suits, you basically had to be good at three things: taking photos of cracked sidewalks, taking statements, and understanding medical terminology. When you did it for a big firm like Cantor, Schreck, it also meant you could afford to be incompetent at street skills and could also afford a fancy BMW with vanity plates. At least now I wouldn't feel conflicted about not calling Julian Cantor. He would find out about the late Millicent McCumber soon enough.

As I waited for P EYE 7 to pull out of his parking spot, my phone buzzed in my pocket. I'd gotten the texts from Anthony Rizzo with Giorgio's info. I thought about forgetting Kid Charlemagne's and heading to Hell's Kitchen to chat with the mysterious Giorgio. I decided to skip both. I was beat, and a little shaky. I hadn't been awash in alcohol for so long as to get the DTs. I didn't black out or see rabbis dancing on pinheads, but I'd been at it long enough to know when I needed a drink and when to sleep. I found my car and aimed it at the Brooklyn Bridge.

CHAPTER THIRTEEN

One drink. That was all I had. Sleep came rather more easily than I expected. I guess working a case made me more tired than I'd expected. It had been a while. When I was sick and getting treated, I was tired all the time. Between the damned drugs and radiation, it was as if the doctors were busy trying to kill me and the cancer at the same time, and it was a toss-up to see which would outlast the other. Even after the cancer was gone, the exhaustion stayed with me as a reminder of my fragility. As if I needed reminding.

I hadn't dreamed, that I could recall. In the immediate wake of Pam's death I'd dreamed all the time, none of it very pleasant. Strangely, those dreams were rarely of Pam. I didn't picture her being crushed beneath the wheels of Holly D'Angelo's Jeep. Nothing like that. Mostly I dreamed of Katy, my first wife, Sarah's mom. She was the only woman I think I'd ever loved to the point of stupidity, but we'd been doomed from the start. I would dream over and over and over again of the baby Katy had miscarried in the early '80s. Imagining I had seen the baby's face, that it had talked to me and wagged a tiny accusatory finger at me, I'd wake up in a sweat. Regardless of how hard I tried, I could never remember its face or what it had said or sounded like. I couldn't even remember if the lost baby had been a boy or a girl. All that stayed with me when I awoke was the translucence of the skin on the baby's tiny finger, how I could see the blood pulsing through it.

Showered, shaved, and coffeed up, I sat down to scan the papers. Millicent McCumber's death wasn't exactly front-page news. She was like a thousand actors before her—pretty, talented, full of promise and potential that came to nothing more than a footnote or afterthought. She had died not as a celebrity remembered, but as someone people *thought* they might've remembered. A chasm exists between those two things. There was a listing of her acting credits: a few Off-Broadway plays, Ophelia in a Shakespeare in the Park production of *Hamlet*—the role that got her noticed—plus two Broadway shows, six movies, and a five-episode run on a star-crossed prime time soap about a wealthy New England family that lost their money during the Depression.

Although there was no explicit mention of the cause of death, an NYPD spokesperson was quoted as saying, "There is no reason to suspect foul play." I knew the ME had a working theory about a heart attack, but given what Nancy and Anthony Rizzo had told me about Millie's wild and addictive nature, I wasn't so sure. I was awfully curious to see what the toxicology report would say. My curiosity would no doubt fade in the six weeks it would probably take to get those reports back. Six weeks, as I had learned during my illness, could be a lifetime.

One thing that grabbed my attention was a statement from Millie's agent, Giorgio Brahms. Poor Giorgio was heartsick at the loss: "We'd been through some very tough times together, but lately Millie was re-energized and we were excited to put her back out there." It wasn't the statement that so much caught my eye as the person who gave it. Old Giorgio didn't know it yet, but he had an appointment with me that afternoon. There was at least one other person I wanted to see first, so I made a few phone calls as I waited for my computer to boot up.

* * *

Michael C. Dillman was happy to see me as long as he believed I had come to his offices at 7 Hanover Square down by Wall Street in order to enlist his assistance in diversifying my portfolio. Dillman was a fit and slender African-American man of thirty-one with a handsome face, close-cropped hair, and a well-trimmed mustache. Everything about Dillman was well trimmed and well appointed, including his clothing and his office. There were photos of his lovely wife holding their twin daughters. His Yale BS and Wharton MBA were proudly displayed on the wall to the left of his desk. It was all peaches and cream between us until I handed him my PI card and mentioned Sloane Cantor by name. Then the cream curdled, the peaches went bad, and his mood went severely sour.

"What kind of nonsense is this?" His voice was cold and he shook his head in anger. "Get out of my office or I'll call security." He picked up his phone to emphasize the point.

"Sloane's missing," I stated, as if it was a fact.

He twisted his mouth into a sneer. "And this should concern me because . . . ." Regardless of the sneer and bravado, he put the phone back in its cradle.

"Maybe it shouldn't, but when it's the cops who come looking for her and not a PI friend of the family, your office is going to be the first stop on their list."

Dillman tried unsuccessfully to act unfazed. "Why would that be, Mr. Prager?"

"Because after five minutes even a blind detective will know all there is to know about the Hollow Girl and Lionel, her cruel, abusive boyfriend who made her watch as he fucked her friend Victoria. And then there was that order of protection thing she took out against you . . . ."

He shot out of his chair. "Fuck! I thought all this idiocy was behind me forever. God dammit! This is bullshit. I did none of those things. Lionel was as phony as the rest of Sloane's Lost Girl routine."

"Not the order of protection. That was real enough."

"Look, Sloane and I were friends in high school. We were both in the Drama Club. For me, it was just something to do to break out of my shyness. For Sloane, Drama Club was her life. We had done all the school productions. It bonds people together in a way that's difficult to explain. I thought I could trust Sloane with my life. How was I supposed to know when she asked if she could use my photograph for this project she was doing that it would turn into a nightmare? I have too many regrets in my life, Mr. Prager. I can't undo any of them, but if I could undo one thing, it would be giving my permission to Sloane to use my picture. You have no idea how bad it got there for a little while."

"I think you'd be surprised at the ideas I have. I take it you got a lot of hate mail."

"And death threats," he said, staring out the window at the harbor, Brooklyn, the Statue of Liberty, Staten Island. "Even though people knew it was a sham, they thought I really was Lionel and that somehow I had done all those horrible things to the Hollow Girl. That I had practically forced her to commit suicide. I had no idea about any of it until it was too late. It was like my family was hit by a tsunami, and without any notion it was headed their way. I could take what happened to me, but what had my parents, my brothers and sisters, done to deserve any of it? I guess I lost it. I was a senior in high school. What did I know about life? I didn't know how to react, so I said some very stupid things that I should never have said. With Sloane's dad being a powerful lawyer, one thing led to another."

"I can see how things could have spiraled out of control. But you seem to have done very well for yourself, Mr. Dillman."

He turned back to face me. "Sloane's dad wasn't the only powerful father on the block, so to speak. My father was a powerful man as well. The order of protection was vacated and we all moved on with our lives, or so I thought."

"Apparently, it was pretty bad for Sloane, too. Did you know that she changed her name?"

"I didn't know that and please . . . ." He held up his hand. "Don't tell me what she's changed it to. I don't want to know."

"Do you hate Sloane?"

"I suppose I did, but if she's missing, it's nothing to do with me. I've moved on from all that."

"I believe you."

"Do you think I should contact my lawyer, Mr. Prager?"

"You probably should, just in case. If there's another tsunami coming, it's good to be prepared."

"Thank you for that. I will get in touch with my attorney as soon as you go."

I stood up to do just that. I shook his hand and thanked him for his candor. As I was almost out his office door, he called after me. "Have you ever met her?"

"No, I haven't. Why?"

"Sloane is—was an odd duck. I suppose all of us were back then, but Sloane was different."

"How so?"

He laughed, a bitter sort of a laugh. "It's kind of ironic that she became known as the Hollow Girl, in spite of her beginning as the Lost Girl."

"I'm not getting you," I said, turning fully to face him.

"To be lost you have to have once been present. Sloane was never really present. She was always kind of empty. I used to think the only times she was ever truly alive were when she was being someone else. It was as if Sloane was only ever Sloane when she was Eliza Doolittle or Lady Macbeth. I know that doesn't make much sense."

"Lots of things don't make sense, Mr. Dillman."

I left it at that. Who Sloane Cantor or Siobhan Bracken was or wasn't didn't concern me. I hoped it never would. I'd been hired to find out if she was missing, whoever she was.

CHAPTER FOURTEEN

Coming out of 7 Hanover Square I noticed a maroon BMW parked nearby. This putz was persistent, if not very subtle. I admired persistence. Just now, however, it was annoying the shit out of me. I didn't mind so much that I'd been tailed here or that P EYE 7 had anticipated my next move. Like I'd explained to Dillman, any yoyo would come sniffing around, given the bad blood between him and Sloane Cantor. I was a generous guy by nature, but I had my limits. I didn't want P EYE 7 anywhere near Giorgio Brahms. Not everyone a PI interviews is apt to be as forthcoming as Dillman. There were times you had to work to develop a level of trust before someone would open up to you. Even then, there are no guarantees. The last thing I needed was for this schmuck to show up at Brahms's door while I was there, or ten minutes after I left.

I thought about using traffic to shed the BMW. Regrettably, using traffic in Manhattan to lose a tail wasn't a sure thing. The streets were too congested, traffic moved too slowly. I opted for another approach. Post-9/11, there was always an army of cops around the financial district. So it was less than challenging for me to find a uniform to help me out. And when I explained that I used to be on the job and that there was this annoying asshole in a

BMW following me around because I was in the midst of a messy divorce . . . I didn't stick around to watch the festivities, but it was easy to picture the look on my new friend's face when he was asked to step out of his car.

It was a straight shot up West Street to get to Giorgio Brahms's address. He didn't live too far from where the *USS Intrepid* was docked along the Hudson River. When I was growing up, this part of the city was a real shithole. The waterfront was falling to pieces. The cargo business was moving to New Jersey, and the cruise business was moving down to Florida. Hell's Kitchen, never the garden spot of the city, was under the control of a violent Irish mob known as the Westies. But there's this New York City phenomenon that exists, because the city has no room to grow: The neighborhoods cycle and churn. It's what transformed Williamsburg, Brooklyn, from a forgotten backwater area populated by Hasidic Jews and Puerto Ricans into hipster heaven, and what turned Long Island City, Queens, from an inert industrial wasteland into a hot part of town. There are inevitable downsides, too, of course. Rents skyrocket. Traditional residents get displaced. Hell's Kitchen, a moniker that persisted in spite of the real estate hyenas' attempt to rename the place Clinton, had undergone a slow churning into respectability and hipness. I mean, who but a Bible-thumping, God-fearing servant of the Lord wouldn't want to say he lived in Hell's Kitchen? As a dyed-in-the-wool Brooklynite, it even appealed to me.

Brahms's brownstone could have used a little churning and urban renewal of its own. The chipped and flaking façade looked as if it had survived a WWII battle, barely. The wrought-iron gate was rusted and unstable. The front steps were cracked and wilted. All the street-facing windows seemed to have been produced before industrial glass became the rage. Only in New York City during rough economic times could such a dump still have fetched several million bucks on the open market.

I had never met Giorgio Brahms. What I knew about him, I knew from his website. He was a theatrical agent who listed Millie McCumber as one of his clients. But just from seeing the state of his website—it hadn't been updated in a year—and his abode, I got the sense that he had probably done a lot of borrowing against the equity in the brownstone and that he had invested very little of that money back into its upkeep. I'd been wrong before, dead wrong. This time, I didn't think so. I rang the bell then knocked, and waited to find out. That the door hadn't been painted in ten years and that the bell wasn't working didn't come as a shock.

"Coming . . . coming," a man's voice called from behind the door. "Who is it?"

"Police," I lied, holding up my badge to the peephole. I'd worry about an explanation after he opened the door.

Brahms was likely a few years younger than me and considerably vainer. His website photo was either very old or had been Photoshopped to death. He'd been a very handsome man once, but he'd had the kind of work done on his face that his brownstone needed. It was a shame that the work hadn't been all that skillfully done, or it had come too late in the game. Nancy's work had been done when she was young, when there was elasticity to her skin and tone in her muscles. Giorgio's work just made him look like Saran Wrap had been too tightly stretched over his face and left there. I was kind of amazed he could move his lips or blink his eyelids. He answered the door wearing a black T-shirt over jeans and running shoes. Apparently, he kept the rest of himself in good shape through exercise and diet. As I looked him over, he did the same to me.

"A little long in the tooth to be playing a cop, don't you think?"

"I used to play one for real," I said, handing him my card. "I've been retained by Siobhan Bracken's mother."

"Yes, Nancy Lustig, the wicked witch of Old Westbury."

"Old Brookfield," I corrected, unsmiling.

"Ruins the rhythm. Come in, come in."

The interior of the brownstone—what I could see of it— though not as designer showcase–ready as Siobhan Bracken's apartment, was tidy and very nicely done up in retro '60s style. Kind of looked like a set from *Mad Men*.

"Why didn't Nancy just hop on her broom and fly over herself instead of sending a flunky?"

I laughed at that. "I like that, Mr. Brahms. I've been called a lot of things in my life, but never a flunky."

"Glad I could make your day, but could we move on . . . please?"

"Will you be taking care of the funeral arrangements for Miss McCumber?"

"Mr. Brahms, Miss McCumber . . . my, aren't you the most polite ex-cop?"

"Charm school," I said. "The funeral arrangements?"

"I will not be involved," he answered and sniffed as if offended I'd asked.

"She was good enough to rep and good enough to fuck, but not good enough to bury, huh?"

His eyes got wide. Well, as wide as the Saran Wrap would allow. And he did now seem a little frightened of me. "No, no . . . you misunderstand. I loved Millie. She'd been good to me, and I was good to her. There were times I was the only person on this earth who loved that woman, and even then it was a trial. I'm just upset because I won't be involved. She has family, though they were never there for her. They'll come out of the woodwork like rats and roaches now that she's dead, and suck up her money. They'll own her image and the rights to her story, and they'll exploit her although they abandoned her long ago. It's too ghastly to—" He stopped mid-sentence, a light seeming to click on. "Wait, you said you were hired by Nancy. So what are you doing here? And how did you know about—"

"I have my ways. I know all about the cozy little foursomes you were an occasional part of."

"The doorman, Anthony," he said, shaking his head, smiling. "Bridge and tunnel types, a real weakness of mine, but they can be awfully indiscreet." He shrugged his shoulders. "That doesn't explain why you're here, Mr. Moses Prager."

"Nancy is concerned that Siobhan is missing."

"Nancy is concerned about her daughter. Really? That's a first. She won't even call her by her name."

"Be that as it may, I've still been hired to look into it."

"Well, it's your lucky day, sunshine," he said, something resembling a smile on his face. "Siobhan went to Europe for a couple of weeks, I think. Mystery solved."

"A couple of weeks was done a couple of weeks ago. It's now been over a month since Nancy has heard from her daughter."

His smile-like expression vanished. "It has been a while, hasn't it? No biggie. Siobhan goes on lots of trips."

"But never for longer than two weeks."

He squinted his eyes and put his fists to his face in thought. "I suppose that's right. I don't know. I wouldn't worry about Siobhan. She can handle herself. Now you'll have to excuse me, Mr. Prager, but I do have to get ready to go."

I didn't know if he was full of shit or not, but I also didn't want to press him. Whereas with Dillman I assumed I'd gotten everything from him there was to get, I thought I was just scratching the surface with Brahms.

"Fine. Thanks for the cooperation. Just one thing. I know Miss McCumber was your client. Was Siobhan your client as well?"

"I'm afraid not. Siobhan was immensely gifted, but I'm not sure she even had representation anymore."

"Who was—"

"Anna Carey at ICAA Management. Now, if you'll excuse me . . . ." He gestured at the front door.

I obliged him, closing the door behind me. The deadbolt clicked into place not two seconds later.

* * *

Anna Carey was old, and if I called someone old that was saying something. Grizzled and gray-headed, she was drinking a glass of bourbon and lighting herself a cigarette by an open window when I walked into her office. She didn't appear very pleased to see me. I didn't take offense. PIs get used to that or they get out of the business. Plus, Anna Carey didn't strike me as a woman to be pleased with much of anything anymore.

"You want a drink?"

Yeah, really bad. "No, thank you. I'm—"

"Moses Prager and you're here about Siobhan. That sexy fraud, Giorgio Brahms, gave me a courtesy call. Giorgio Brahms, my wrinkly old ass. I knew him when he was a bad actor named George Abramowicz. Probably hopes I'll fuck him." She broke into hysterical laughter, baring her yellowed teeth. "They say he'll fuck just about anything with a pulse and a purse. I'd be a helluva test, don't you think?" She finished her drink and took a long drag on her cigarette. "Old Georgie says you think she's gone missing. Is that a fact?"

"Her mother thinks she might be missing. I don't have an opinion yet."

"Bullshit, Prager! Everybody's got an opinion about everything. What's yours?"

"It's suspicious. When was the last time you heard from her?"

That started her laughing again. "Agents never want to hear from their clients. It's the other way around."

"So there wasn't any work for Siobhan?"

"On the contrary . . . you sure you don't want a drink?"

I hesitated because I was strapped for the first time in months, my old snub nose .38 tucked in the clip holster at the small of my back. But I could feel Anna Carey warming to me a bit and didn't want to lose her goodwill. I held my right thumb and index finger an inch apart. "Maybe a short one," I said.

"That's more like it." She tossed the cigarette out the window. She pulled a half-empty bottle of Jim Beam and a second glass from her drawer, poured more than I wanted in the fresh glass, and twice that in her own. "Slainte."

I sipped. She gulped.

"You were saying something about Siobhan and work."

Anna Carey seemed not to have heard. "They keep me around here because I'm too old to fire. It would look bad for *dem wot sits on de frone*," she said, affecting a Cockney accent. "I'm past hanging on by my fingernails. I'm down to the cuticles, Prager. Most of my stable couldn't get arrested, let alone a gig. On the other hand, Siobhan could get all the work in the world if she wanted it. I've been in the biz in one form or the other for sixty years and I've come across a lot of hacks and a lot of talent, but there are those rare ones . . . and she's one of them. They called that drunken cunt Siobhan ran around with the next Streep, but Millie McCumber, God rest her worthless, scenery-chewing soul, didn't have the talent Siobhan has in her little finger."

"I'm missing something here. If she could have the work—"

"She doesn't want it. Whereas the rest of my clients would kill to get a second reading for a five-second, one-word bit in a local cable TV spot, Siobhan turned down juicy roles on TV, in movies, on Broadway."

"Why?"

Anna Carey finished her drink and lit up another cigarette. After a few drags, she was laughing again. "They're never the starring roles, Prager. This is a pretty girl's business. No, wait, let me amend that. This is a somewhat talented, beautiful, young, anorexic girl's business. That sound like Siobhan to you?"

"Not really."

"So, yes, she could have played the plain-faced nurse or the understanding but chubby best friend, or the dull sister, or the—"

"I get your point."

"Maybe half of it you get," she said. "The strange thing is that I do understand, completely, even if she doesn't put a nickel in my threadbare pocket. Have you ever been great at anything, Prager? I don't mean just good, or really very good. I mean great."

"No, I suppose not."

"Well, about a million years ago I was on the stage. I was pretty good, maybe very good, but I never quite got the lead. I came to think of myself as Understudy Anna."

"What happened?"

"Resentment happened. Do you know what it's like to be out on a stage, any stage, and to know you're so much better than everyone else around you? What it's like to have a minor role when you are better than the star, co-star, and the entire company? It got so bad that I could taste it, and I wasn't half the actor Siobhan Bracken is. At least I was a pretty girl, pretty enough for back then. Can you understand?"

I hadn't lied to her. I was never great at anything, but I understood resentment on a molecular level. In the spring of 1972, a little girl named Marina Conseco, the daughter of a city fireman, had gone missing in Coney Island. Several days had passed and the search shifted silently away from finding the girl to finding her remains. I was part of a search team that was covering ground that had been covered, and recovered and re-recovered over and over again, in the days since Marina had disappeared. But for some reason—I think it was exhaustion—I looked up, and when I did I saw one of those water towers on the roof of a building. It occurred to me that we hadn't searched those. We found her in the fourth or fifth one we looked in. She was near frozen, broken, and barely alive, but she lived.

I had seen other cops get gold detective shields for much less. I had been around to witness gold shields handed out as political candy, as favors, as rewards for writing a consistently high volume of traffic and parking summonses, for longevity. All I got for saving Marina Conseco's life was a slap on the back, an "atta boy" from my captain, a medal, and a commendation for my file. For years it ate at me, and then, after injuring my knee and getting retired, the resentment nearly consumed me whole. When I first became a PI, people who knew about my bitter resentment used it to manipulate me. So, yeah, I understood about Siobhan.

Anna Carey saw the answer in my eyes and didn't press me to put it to words. I asked her for a list of people she thought I might want to talk to about Siobhan's whereabouts. She gave me a few names and their contact info. When I left her office, Anna was smoking another cigarette and pouring a third glass of bourbon. When I hit the street, I realized I'd only had one sip of my drink. I looked at my hands. They didn't seem to be shaking too badly. That was progress of a sort.

Having heard the ME's theory and having read the police spokesperson's quote in the morning paper, my supposition was that Millicent McCumber's death was going to be declared the result of a heart attack or an accident. If that were so, then Siobhan's apartment would no longer be treated as a crime scene and I would be free to take a second look around. All I'd been able to do during my first visit was assess the quality of the interior design and try not to get blood on my shoes. It hadn't actually been possible for me to search for evidence concerning Siobhan's whereabouts.

My return visit to the Kremlin, I decided, would have to wait a day. I'd made a good start in getting a sense of Siobhan Bracken, but that wasn't nearly enough. I still had no idea whether or not she was actually missing. On the one hand, her taking off unannounced for parts unknown was apparently a feature of the punch-counterpunch dynamic Siobhan and Nancy seemed unable or unwilling to escape from. On the other, it was unusual for Siobhan to be gone for more than two weeks without contacting anyone. Yeah, before I did more stumbling from person to person, I needed some concrete beneath me in the form of answers.

CHAPTER FIFTEEN

Houston Street was thick with horn-blaring traffic in both directions. There was a long line out the front door of Katz's Deli. Tourists, hipsters, and neighborhood denizens zombie-marched the sidewalks. Life on the Lower East Side went on as if Millie McCumber were still alive. It went on as if she had never been born. It went on whether Siobhan Bracken was missing or simply soaking up the sun on some sandy beach. That is one of the great comforts and great horrors of New York City—it stops for no one. In my lifetime, I could recall only four times the city had even held its breath: the blackout in '65, the Summer of Sam, 9/11, and Hurricane Sandy. And still, during each of those times, the city refused to shut down. In spite of having spent my whole life here, I couldn't say whether it was the nature of my fellow citizens or something about the place itself. Maybe it was the water. Why not, right? I mean, the water's why our bagels and pizza are so good.

At least now when I approached the Kremlin I would do so armed with some notion of what Siobhan Bracken had been up to over the last month. After leaving Anna Carey's office, I'd gone home and spent most of the evening on the phone and on the computer. Between my limited Internet skills, my less limited skill at fudging the truth, my contacts in the credit card world—there were some benefits to owning a chain of wine stores—plus a long conversation with Nancy Lustig, and a favor from a friend who worked for the TSA, I had been able to patch together a rough idea of Siobhan's movements.

Rizzo, the Kremlin doorman, had been both right and wrong the other night at Grogan's Clover. Siobhan Bracken had taken an international flight—to Ireland, as it happened—but his recollection was off about when she left. Siobhan hadn't left at the very end of August. On August 23, a week earlier than Rizzo remembered, she had boarded an Aer Lingus flight to Dublin from JFK. Who knows why; maybe she liked Guinness on tap, or she'd taken her new identity to heart. Siobhan was a name, after all, with both Hebrew and Gaelic origins. As my mother had been proud to tell us, Dublin once had a Jewish mayor. But why Siobhan went or what she did there was beside the point, because she landed back at JFK on September 6. There'd also been a post-Ireland, post-Labor-Day week spent in the Hamptons at a chic motel. Yes, only in the Hamptons could a motel be chic. So I could account for her movements from late August to mid-September, but after that . . . nothing.

Anthony Rizzo didn't click up his heels at the sight of me. I hadn't imagined he would. In fact, he looked downright miserable to see me and seemed a little jumpy. I spoke to him long enough to find out if the cops had taken the tape off 5E. He said someone had been by yesterday afternoon and removed the seal and notice from the door. Entering a sealed scene was a serious offense and no matter how curious I was, I wasn't going to risk real jail time. I told him to ring my cell if the cops or anyone else came sniffing around while I was in Siobhan's apartment. He didn't click up his heels about that either, but that was just too bad for him. I handed him a twenty anyway. I was nice like that, and I wasn't stupid.

Just because it was understood that I could get his ass fired didn't mean he would ask how high when I said jump. A wise man never underestimates the power of goodwill.

This time as I got closer to 5E, it wasn't the smells of cooking nor the fainter but still present smell of death that got my attention. It was that the door to 5E was slightly ajar. The gap between jamb and door wasn't large. It didn't allow me a view of the apartment. It was as if someone had carefully closed the door without letting the locks catch. I doubted the door had been left open by the cop who'd come to remove the seal. Look, I'm the last guy on earth to give the cops a pass. Having been one, I knew how sloppy and careless they could sometimes be. A cop, even an incompetent one, would know that leaving a door unlocked like this could get him jammed up pretty bad. And this didn't have the feel of a fuck-up.

I reached under my jacket for my .38. Until my alcoholic fallout over Pam, I'd had it holstered to me every day for four-plus decades. I'd worn it to my weddings, had it on me in the delivery room when Sarah was born, and was reluctant to remove it in the hospital during chemo. It had once been part of who I was, a fifth limb. I hadn't quite felt naked without it—it was more like feeling I'd left my house and forgotten to put on one of my shoes. But when I reached for it, the old .38 was there. I slowly pulled it out of its holster, pointing the barrel at the hall ceiling. I flattened my back to the wall, willing my heart to steady and trying to calm my breathing so I could hear. For a twenty-year-old building, the Kremlin was pretty quiet and there was very little ambient street or apartment noise in the hallway. That worked for and against me. I concentrated as best I could.

I stepped to the hinge side of the threshold and very carefully pushed the door open just enough to allow me a peek inside. Even with my limited view I saw that the living room had undergone a redesign by tornado. As I legged the door open and stepped inside, I saw that the place had been totally trashed. There wasn't a chair or sofa that hadn't been cut and slashed. Foam stuffing, cotton batting, and feathers were everywhere. Every drawer was open and dumped on the floor. All the books had been wiped off the shelves, many ripped apart, pages scattered. The prints, paintings, and photos had been taken off the walls, pulled out of their frames, and hacked and torn to pieces. An antique mirror in an oak stand had been broken to bits, beads and shards of glass surrounding its wheeled feet.

I carefully made my way through the entire apartment. There didn't seem to be a thing in the place that hadn't been damaged or disturbed. The bed and carpeting, even the clothing in the closet had been sliced to shreds. The medicine vials had been opened and emptied. The endless array of hair care products, makeup, powders, potions, tonics, and toners had been dumped or poured out all over the bathroom tiles. And since I didn't know the place, I had no idea if anything was actually missing or if the place had simply been destroyed. Still, I had a look around to see if there was anything that might give me an idea about Siobhan's whereabouts.

It was a waste of time, but a few things were pretty obvious to a trained eye. The destruction wasn't done by a pro. A second-story man knows what he's looking for. He gets in, takes what he wants, and gets out. He doesn't stay a second longer than he has to. Nor was it done by a tweaker, junky, or crackhead. The things that druggies snatch for quick sale, like jewelry and electronics, still seemed to be there, if a little worse for wear. Druggies did tend to be messy, but Siobhan's apartment was several notches up from messy. For me, that left two possibilities, neither of which I liked very much. One was that there was a person out there who hated Siobhan Bracken beyond all reason, and had done this to her property because her person was unavailable. As frightening and unsettling as that thought was, the other possibility was, in a way, even more disturbing.

From the moment I had stepped into Siobhan's flat and surveyed the damage, I'd been bothered by the totality of the damage. Something wasn't kosher. Frankly, the scene seemed staged for maximum shock value, as if whoever had trashed the place wanted you to gasp at the sight of it. And there was something else, or rather the lack of something else. There was no sign of forced entry. Although the flat was on the fifth floor, I'd checked all the windows, the terrace door, and the front door. The perpetrator had used a key and had left the door open on purpose. Why leave the door open? Who would do that? When I reached what I felt was the most reasonable conclusion, I didn't care much for it, not very much at all.

CHAPTER SIXTEEN

I thought about calling it in, but was in no mood for a reunion with the detectives from the 9th Precinct. Our first meeting hadn't gone so swimmingly that I was anxious to repeat the experience. Instead, I took a minute and used my cell phone camera to document the wreck that was now the interior of Siobhan's flat. Exiting the apartment, I left the door to 5E ajar as I'd found it. I stopped by the lobby desk, but the doorman was nowhere in sight. I didn't find that particularly curious. Doormen have to answer the call of nature, too. As I walked to my car, I left a message on Rizzo's phone and described what I'd found upstairs in Siobhan's apartment. I suggested he phone it in. It wasn't like I would escape the cops' scrutiny for very long. The surveillance cameras guaranteed my presence would not go unnoticed. Once the cops saw the shambles the apartment was in, they would be going over every digitized pixel those cameras had captured. There was just something I had to attend to before facing Detectives Frovarp and Shulze again.

The drive out to Nancy Lustig's glass and concrete house took me ninety minutes. Half of that time was spent escaping from Manhattan. Oh, the joys of New York City traffic are legion. Once I managed to get through the Midtown Tunnel, it was an easy ride east along the Long Island Expressway.

The bright sun told the truth today as September fought hard to claw its way back to summer and not surrender to the calendar. It was good to ride with the windows rolled down and to let myself be fooled by the warm breeze that summer could return. In spite of the sun, the trees along the sides of the expressway denied the heat of the day and knew better than to pretend. They were still green enough, even very green, but there was a kind of exhausted yearning in the downward aspect of their leaves. I knew that downward tilt well. My shoulders had been slumped like that in surrender during the cancer.

Maybe it's cultural, or maybe it's part of the reassuring magic show we put on for those who will survive us. Even now, having gone through the horror, it's hard to know. I still wonder about the things I said in the face of my prognosis and treatment. How, after Sarah's wedding when I finally told everyone how ill I was, I went on about fighting and winning and beating the cancer as if I had a say in it. When I think back, I laugh at how I must have sounded like a losing coach's halftime pep talk to an inept high school football team. Why do we so value the magic show, the putting on of brave faces? Inside, I was just like those leaves on the trees along the expressway. All I wanted to do was give in when I knew death was coming. I became impatient for it. I wanted to tap my watch crystal with my finger and say, "Come on already. I'm here. You're late."

I found Nancy where I thought I might, out by the pool. If I had been a swimmer, it's where I would have been on such a false summer's day. She was wearing a bathing suit this time, a red Speedo one-piece that accentuated the curves she had so carefully crafted. I thought back to when we'd first met, and how she would never have dreamed of wearing such a bathing suit. How, instead of her curves, it would have highlighted her weight and rolls of fat. And for the first time since we met at the El Greco, maybe for the first time since I'd seen her thirteen years ago, I gave her a break for wanting to be an object of desire. I remembered what Sarah had said about the world being tough on girls, even the pretty ones. And I recalled what Anna Carey had said about the kinds of roles offered to Siobhan: the friend, the sister, the nurse. Never the lead. What was wrong with Nancy wanting to be the lead in her own story? Maybe it hadn't brought the happiness with it she surely hoped it would, but that wasn't for me to judge.

Her face lit up when she noticed me, and I would be lying if I said I didn't get a jolt from her smile. Men, even old ones like me, enjoy having an effect on women. Sometimes being old was like being invisible to women. Better to evoke pity or disgust than to evoke nothing at all. And since Pam's death, I'd been a little dead inside myself. It felt nice to have a flutter, even a passing one. Suddenly, it didn't seem to matter much to me how Nancy, or anyone else for that matter, had achieved their good looks. I guess I had held onto the ugly old Nancy very tightly and hadn't been willing to relax my grip.

I grabbed her towel up from the edge of the pool. "We've gotta talk."

"Sounds serious."

"Might be." I waved the towel at her. "Come on up outta there."

She frowned and swam to the steps. "It *is* serious."

I threw the towel over her shoulders. She hesitated for a second, hoping, I guess, that I might do the honors of drying her off. I was tempted. Instead, I sat down at the table near the cabana. She excused herself as she walked past me and said she'd be out in a few minutes.

Nancy returned as promised, that thick terry cloth robe cinched snug around her waist, her hair up in a towel. She stopped at the bar, poured herself a few fingers of twenty-one-year-old Glendronach.

"Want some?"

"Sure, but a short one," I said. "What's your e-mail address?"

Her face twisted in confusion. "Why?"

"I have to send you some photos for us to look at together, and my phone won't do them justice."

She put the glass down in front of me as she gave me the address. Then I forwarded the photos of the remains of Siobhan's apartment to her e-mail. She waited to drink until I was done.

"L'chaim." She touched the lip of her glass to mine. "To life."

"If you say so."

She drummed her fingers on the table. "So, you said we had to talk."

I didn't get directly to my point, choosing instead to update her on her daughter's whereabouts between August 23 and September 13. I explained how I'd pieced Sloane's travels together and how I thought I might go about filling in the holes that remained. Nancy listened with a peculiar sort of rapt disinterest: fussing with things, getting up to bring the expensive bottle of single malt back to the table with her. Yet, regardless of her practiced nonchalance, she could have repeated verbatim what I'd said; I would have bet on it. I recognized a defense mechanism when I saw one, and Nancy was displaying one writ large. God, the energy people expended on self-protection was enormous. The funny thing is that it never really works, except in the short run. And then, not always. I knew that better than most. As if to prove my point about her level of attention, Nancy interrupted.

"Did you say a motel in the Hamptons?"

"Yep. She stayed at the Stargazer Motel and Spa in Amagansett. Why?"

"Sloane always made it a point of telling me how much she detested the Hamptons. Her father has a home in East Hampton and she would never visit him there. Who knows with her? It wouldn't be the first time my daughter did something contrary to what she said. She lives to be contrary. Maybe that bitch Millie McCumber suggested it."

"That late bitch," I chided.

"Don't expect me to get all weepy over her, Moe. She was a dreadful woman who had a very bad influence on Sloane. And it was especially galling to me that she came back into Sloane's life after I thought she'd cleansed herself of that witch. Millie had the habit of getting between us, Sloane and me." Nancy poured herself a few more fingers and another for me.

"Hey, I'm a PI who owns a chain of wine stores with my brother. I'm no psychologist, but don't you think that maybe your refusal to call your daughter by her name is as much responsible for this rift between you two as Millie McCumber?"

Nancy winced. Like a careless dentist, I'd apparently hit an exposed nerve. She finished off her second drink in a gulp and looked at the glass as if she'd just swallowed a mouthful of piss. She poured herself a third. "You're right . . . you're not a psychologist."

"I talked to Siobhan's agent, Anna—"

"Sloane! Her name is Sloane."

"You call her what you want, but her professional name is Siobhan Bracken and I'm going with that. So I spoke to Anna Carey yesterday. She says that Siobhan could have all the work she wants, but won't—"

"Take the parts she's offered. I know. It's an old story, Moe."

"But—"

"Forget it. If you have a spare week sometime, I'll try and explain it to you."

No one, I thought, has a week to spare. No one. Ever. The problem is that you don't usually realize it until it's too late. "Sorry, fresh outta spare weeks."

"Then c'mon in the house," she slurred, moving toward the opening where the pool ended and the house began, bottle in hand, "and show me the photos."

Nancy took me into an impossible room—impossible, to my mind, in a house so airy and bathed in light. The room was a dark, windowless little cubical on the second floor, just off the master bedroom. Accessible only through a door in the walk-in closet, I assumed the little room was meant to be used as additional closet space if the need arose. Of course, the walk-in closet was so cavernous to begin with that I couldn't believe the need would ever arise. But I was wrong. *Imagine that.* It wasn't extra space at all. Nancy told me that she had specifically had this area built as an office. She touched something on the wall and—*poof*—there was light, not a lot, but some, anyway. I could feel cool, fresh air circulating. The little room was the most interesting one in the whole joint that I could see because, unlike the rest of the house, the office looked as if a human actually used it. It was a mess. No interior designer had gotten within a mile of it. The desk and chairs didn't match. There were photos, mostly of Nancy pre-metamorphosis, tacked to the walls. One was of Nancy in Patrick Michael Maloney's arms. She caught me staring at it.

"You married Patrick's older sister, didn't you?" Nancy asked. It sounded like an accusation more than anything else. "I'm a little drunk, so I can ask."

"Katy, yeah. We met alongside the Gowanus Canal. The cops found a floater they thought might've been Patrick. Katy was there to identify the body."

She made a face. "How romantic."

I ignored the sarcasm. "Not really. Have you ever seen a body after it's been in the water a while? It ain't pretty, Nancy. Seeing Millie the other day reminded me of that. She wasn't very pretty to look at either. Why all these photos of your old self?"

"Reminders," she said as if that somehow explained it all. I guess it did. Then she ripped the picture of her and Patrick off the wall and threw it in the trash.

"That's what this room is too, isn't it? A reminder. The ugly little core in the beautiful house."

When I turned away from the photo, Nancy was standing very close to me and there was a yearning in her eyes so deep it nearly buckled my knees. And before I could take another breath, her lips were pressing against mine. She parted her lips and I parted mine. I felt my fingers burying themselves in terry cloth. Then, from the pocket of her robe, vibration and a ringtone of The Zombies' "Time of the Season."

I stepped back.

"Ignore it," she said, but we both knew it was too late for that. The spell had been broken. She reached into her pocket, pulled out the phone, studied the screen. "It's Julian. I should take this."

"Go ahead."

When she answered, she just listened. Then, "Calm down, Julian. Yes, he told me about Sloane's apartment," she lied, shaking her head at me and giving me a look angry enough to stop time. "Uh huh, yeah, I'll have him call you. Calm down. Yes . . . uh huh . . . okay, Julian. So long." She turned to me. "Julian says that—"

"His investigator notified him that the cops got a call about Siobhan's apartment being trashed," I finished her sentence. "That's what's in the photos I e-mailed you from my phone. Except I don't think they represent what you and your husband will assume they represent."

"What the fuck is that supposed to mean?"

"Boot up your computer and I'll show you."

CHAPTER SEVENTEEN

Nancy was horrified as she clicked through the photos of her daughter's apartment. It's exactly how I expected her to react, and exactly how Julian Cantor must've reacted. I was not a fan of how they had raised their daughter, who, by the way, sounded just as responsible for her family's *mishegas* as her parents. Still, it was heartening to know that, in spite of their crazy level of dysfunction, they loved each other. But it was precisely because of Nancy's visceral reaction to the photos that I had driven here to see her and show her the photographs. What I had to say needed to be said in person.

She turned away from the screen after reviewing the photos three times. "I'm confused," she said. "You knew about this hours ago, but didn't bother to call me or mention it to me until after Julian called. We sat out by the pool and drank. We came up here and were this close to—"

"We kissed, Nancy. That's all we were doing. But yes, you're right. I didn't tell you immediately."

"Are you nuts? Why would you wait to tell me that Sloane's apartment had been ransacked?"

"You know I was a New York cop for about ten years, right?"

She seemed offended, sounded bitter. "I know all about your career and even about your saving little Marina Conseco. You must tell me about her sometime, in all her incarnations. But what does your being a cop have to do with why you didn't tell me?"

"It has everything to do with it," I said, losing my patience. "I presume that you didn't hire me only because you've been curious about being with me. That you thought I might actually find out what's going on with Siobhan." I didn't wait for her to answer. "Well, it may have been a long time since I was a cop, but I haven't lost my eye for detail or forgotten what I learned on the job."

"What's that supposed to mean?"

"It means that someone trashed your daughter's apartment on purpose, but not because they were looking to rob her. See there," I pointed at Nancy's computer screen, "her TV, her Bose system, her desktop . . . they're all still there, though now in pretty rough shape. That stuff would be worth a fortune to a junky, but it wasn't taken. I don't know Siobhan's apartment, but it doesn't look like anything's missing. Can you see anything missing that should be there?"

"No," she said. "Not from these pictures."

"Did Siobhan have a lot of jewelry? Did she keep cash on hand?"

"Jewelry wasn't her thing. She had some, but most of the time she wore what little she had. Cash . . . no, she didn't keep a lot in the apartment. Her bank is not thirty feet from her building's front door. What are you getting at? Is there a point here, Moe?"

"We're almost there. You know, beside the fact that it didn't seem to me that anything of value was taken from the flat, there was another odd thing I found when I was there."

"And that would be . . . ."

"There was not a solitary sign of forced entry at Siobhan's place. Not one. I checked and rechecked. Whoever did this had a key, or was let in by someone who had a key."

"What?"

"A key. It's a little piece of metal with ridges and grooves that—"

She flushed with anger. "This isn't funny."

"It isn't. I agree."

"All right, so nothing's missing and the person or persons that did this didn't break in. From all that you conclude, what, exactly?"

"That what happened at Siobhan's flat was bullshit. It was staged to look like a crime, but wasn't a crime at all."

"Have you lost your mind?" She was screaming at me, pointing at the screen. "Look at the damage. Thank God Sloane wasn't there."

"That's the point, Nancy. I think she was."

"She was what?"

"There."

She looked gut-punched. "You're joking."

"I think Siobhan's responsible for the damage. Maybe she had a little help. It would have been tough to wreak all that havoc by herself. And maybe I have an idea who her assistant was."

"But why? Why would she do—"

"C'mon, Nancy. Think. Look at yourself. You and your ex-husband are probably ready to walk through concrete and chew through steel if it means keeping Siobhan safe."

"That's ridiculous. You don't even know Sloane. She would never do something like this."

"All I know is that if something looks like a setup, and smells like a setup, and tastes like a setup, it's a—"

"My daughter would never do something like this to us," she repeated.

"But the Hollow Girl might."

Nancy opened her mouth, squeezed her eyes into angry slits, clenched her fists, and tensed her body as if to pounce. I felt myself flinch, but the attack never came. My words had finally seemed to penetrate her defenses. She slumped her shoulders, turning away from me.

"But why would she do it, Moe?"

"I don't know. Maybe she wanted to up the stakes or change the dynamics between you and her and her father. Maybe she just got bored and wants to try another stunt—sorry, I mean a different type of performance art. Look, Nancy, I've got enough trouble walking the high wire with my own daughter. I'm no expert. I'm not the person with the answers. I'm just giving you my opinion about what I saw at her apartment. You guys are a complicated bunch."

Nancy Lustig let out an exhausted sigh, "Well, if what you say is right, at least she's safe then. I mean, she's not really missing. I just wonder what she's really up to."

I shrugged my shoulders. "Where's your ex now?"

She faced me again. "Home."

"I think I better go have a talk with him. With your permission, of course. I work for you."

"Go," she said. "It's a good idea. He should hear what you have to say before he calls out the National Guard. You don't know Julian. He can be . . . . Let's just say he can overreact. I'll call ahead to tell him you're coming. If you're right, and I'm still dubious that you are, Sloane wants us to panic. I'm weary of it, Moe, of the drama. I'm weary of the fencing, of the thrust and parry. I don't want to play anymore. So go talk to Julian, but . . . come back when you're done, please."

"I can't."

"Because we—"

"Because we kissed? No. It should be why, but it isn't. After I talk to Julian, there's someone else who needs some talking to, maybe something a little stronger than talk."

Her eyes got big at that. "You're not going to hurt anyone, are you?"

"Scare, not hurt. I've done enough hurting. It may not even come down to scaring. Money might do the trick. It usually does. And besides, I can't avoid the cops forever. I'm gonna have to go into the 9th Precinct and clear some things up."

She clutched my forearm as I made to walk past her.

"I'll call," I said, brushing her hair back, tucking a loose strand behind her ear.

She let go of me, seeming to understand that we had gone as far as I was willing to let things go. I was glad one of us understood something about what we were doing, because I sure as hell didn't.

CHAPTER EIGHTEEN

New Mexico called itself the Land of Enchantment. Long Island was more like the land of endless strip malls surrounding pockets of wretched excess. I think Nassau County's motto is In Shopping We Trust. Not as catchy as the Land of Enchantment, I know, but probably more accurate. It's no state secret that I've never cared much for the island, and none of my experiences out here had done anything to disabuse me of my distaste for it. Most of my troubles on Long Island had been with the rich and the dead. The rich had been a varied lot; some weren't even rich, exactly. Some were semi-rich or had-been-rich or desperate-to-be-rich, but they were all money drunk. The dead were different. It's a lovely lie that we're all created equal. We are, however, all just the same in death. Liberté. Egalité. Fraternité. Mortalité. The French almost got it right. Almost.

While Nancy's house made a statement about open design and the melding of exterior and interior spaces, the only statement Julian Cantor's house made was, "You better fuckin' look at me." I looked. I had to look because I couldn't quite believe you could pack that much tastelessness into one structure. It was a muscular monstrosity of brick and stone, columns, concrete, and clapboards. It wasn't quite one of those McMansions that had sprung up all about the place. McMansions were more bland than ugly. Mostly they were too big for their lots and too much a matter of vinyl siding and silliness than of distinction. Cantor's house was a lot of things—bland not among them.

I pulled up the cobblestone driveway and parked under the triangular, capped portico that hung off the front of the house like a grandiose afterthought. The portico was held up by two massive columns that must have been pilfered from the set of *Gone with the Wind*. I noticed P EYE 7's maroon BMW parked further down the driveway. When I got out of my car, the front door to the house opened. Only it wasn't Julian Cantor who came to greet me.

"You must be Mr. Prager," she said, holding her delicate hand out to me.

I shook it. "Moe Prager, yes."

"I'm Julian's wife, Alexandra."

She was a vision. Think trophy wife. No, think "trophy for first place" wife. She was what models looked like on magazine covers, only breathing and moving. A woman of about thirty, she had long flowing dark red hair, flawless creamy skin, a perfect nose, sculpted cheekbones, and deep green eyes. She was svelte but not too thin, and her legs seemed to reach from the floor to my eyeballs. She was dressed in a white sweater and black slacks. She had to be Nancy Lustig's worst nightmare. Nancy had turned herself into a very handsome and attractive woman indeed, but Alexandra was something much beyond that. I had only ever met one other woman with the same sort of otherworldly beauty, and that was thirty years ago. I didn't like thinking about her or what had become of her.

Katerina Brightman had been married to an up-and-coming politician, Steven Brightman, whose career I helped rescue from the slush pile of once promising failures. Brightman had been cleared by the cops in connection with the disappearance of a young intern named Moira Heaton. He had, however, been tried and convicted in the court of public opinion. My initial investigation uncovered the fact that Moira had been murdered by a vicious serial killer already in police custody. In the end, though, I'd only discovered what I'd been misled to discover by a trail of false bread crumbs. The truth of what had actually happened to Moira was far more chilling. And when, out of wounded pride and vanity, I used Katerina to punish Steven Brightman for playing me as a fool, I set in motion a series of events that led to more murder and ruined several lives, Katerina's first of all.

Alexandra let go of my hand and gestured to the open door. "Come in. I should let you know that Julian is not alone."

"I can see that," I said, pointing at the BMW. "007 is here."

She giggled. "Vincent is a bit of a clod, but he's sweet."

"I'll take your word for it."

"I should also warn you that Julian is in a cross mood."

"I appreciate the heads-up. I kinda figured he would be. Daughters do that to their fathers."

She smiled coyly. "Yes, we do. It is in the nature of fathers and daughters."

"And mothers."

"But in a different way. I know that Siobhan and Nancy have a very problematic relationship. It is not so different with my mother."

"Alexandra, somehow I doubt that beauty was at the center of the battles between you and your mother."

"You would be surprised, Mr. Prager, what can come between mothers and daughters."

The interior of the house wasn't nearly as unrelenting as the outside. I supposed visitors had Alexandra to thank for that. While I wouldn't exactly call the interior design feminine, it was softer and more welcoming than the hard-nosed exterior. Although it was an Indian summer day, there was a fire going in the stone fireplace. Burning logs, the universal symbol of welcome.

"Julian's study is through the great room, up the half flight of steps, and then to the left. I will leave you men to your business."

And with that, Alexandra Cantor headed in the other direction. I had manners enough not to watch her as she walked away. Manners, and more than a little willpower.

Julian's study was something out of Dickens. Two of the walls were dedicated to built-in shelves lined with leather-bound books, and another wall was devoted to fox hunting scenes and landscapes. His desk was massive, as if honed out of a hunk of sequoia. There were green leather wing chairs, plush green carpeting, an oversized globe to one side of the grand desk, and a brass armillary with a rather threatening-looking arrow sticking out of it to the other side. It seemed a perfect place for the poor to come begging alms. A perfect place for them to be thrown out of. Cantor was seated behind his desk. Vincent, P EYE 7, was pacing about, a drink in hand.

"Prager, this is—"

"Vincent, your chief investigator," I interrupted the lawyer. With men like Julian Cantor, you had to dissuade them from bullying you right up front or they'd never stop.

Cantor shook his head. "As I was saying, this is Vincent Brock. And as you've surmised, he works for me. I take it you two have met."

"Sort of." I gave Brock's hand a perfunctory shake. He was about as thrilled with me as I was with him, which was to say not at all.

"That was real cute, that thing you pulled with the cop at Hanover Square," Vincent said, angry and spoiling for revenge. He'd been embarrassed. Men detest being embarrassed almost more than anything else. I didn't much care for it myself, but cancer treatment is a pretty humbling experience. If you can't get over the embarrassment of it, it will kill you before the disease. Because, let me tell you, a whole lot of embarrassing situations came with my treatments. Hair loss and constant nausea being the least of it.

"Yeah, well, you shoulda just introduced yourself that night at Grogan's instead of trying to play James Bond."

Vincent's face turned red. Uh oh, I'd done it again, embarrassed him in front of his employer. Apparently, he hadn't told Cantor about how he had tried to tail me the night I met Anthony Rizzo at the bar.

Cantor barked at his investigator, "What's Prager going on about?"

I figured I'd better save Vincent's tush before he got embarrassed enough to shoot me. "Nothing, Mr. Cantor. It's nothing, just a little stuff between professionals."

Vincent looked relieved, almost thankful, but Cantor didn't look especially happy.

"Well, I'm glad you gentlemen have had your fun, but what about my daughter? Nancy told me you think this is all some sort of charade. Is that right, Prager?"

"I take it you've seen the photos and Vincent here has told you what a mess the apartment was?"

"I have seen your photos and his," the lawyer said. "To me it looks like Hiroshima the day after, not like a charade."

"That's the idea. Somebody wanted to get a rise out of you and they did. Your ex reacted the same way, the way you were meant to react."

"And you think this somebody is my daughter?" Cantor asked. He knew the answer.

Why did people do that, ask questions they already knew the answers to? It made me nuts, but I kept calm and repeated what I had told Nancy about my cop-sense, about how nothing seemed to have been stolen, about how a key had been used on the front door. "Look, Mr. Cantor, whoever did that to Siobhan's apartment was good at destroying things, but not at recreating a real crime scene. If you'd been to as many crime scenes as me, you'd understand."

Cantor turned to his man. "What do you think?"

"Maybe I don't agree that it was your girl who did it, but Prager's got a point. The door wasn't jimmied and the place was a mess, but a kind of pointless mess. I guess it did feel kind of staged."

The lawyer stood and pounded his fists on top of the desk. "So where the fuck is my daughter?"

I turned my palms up. "That I can't tell you, Mr. Cantor. But Nancy didn't tell me to stop digging, so I won't."

"Vincent, give Prager your card. You help Prager any way you can."

"But—"

Cantor didn't have to say a word because the look on his face said it all. Vincent stopped his protest in order to save his job. He handed me a card. I handed him one of mine. Except for the bowing, it was like a Japanese business meeting. I didn't think we were going to be friends, but I also didn't need animosity screwing things up. It wasn't karma. It was much simpler than that. A PI's job was hard enough without having people actively working against him. Detectives Frovarp and Shulze were probably already looking for an excuse to fuck with me, and I didn't need or want Vincent working to queer things. I had enough blood on my hands because of embarrassment and acting out of a stupid sense of pride. The focus here needed to be on Siobhan, and not on some snit between Vincent and me.

"I've gotta go talk to the detectives at the 9th Precinct," I said. "But I also need to have a talk with Anthony Rizzo—"

"One of the doormen at your daughter's building," Vincent finished my sentence. Good, I thought, at least this guy wasn't totally incompetent. I'd thrown him a softball and he'd hit it out of the park in front of his boss.

"Yeah, he and Siobhan were friends." I didn't explain further. "I think he knows more about all of this than he's saying. So when I go talk to the cops, maybe Vincent can have a friendly chat with Rizzo."

But Vincent suddenly didn't look so good. I think he'd misunderstood what I meant by a friendly chat. Vincent wasn't a muscle work kind of guy. Like I said, he probably spent his days investigating sidewalk cracks and interviewing people whose wrong leg had been amputated. So I came to his aid again.

"It'll be easy," I said. "Rizzo's vain and he's addicted to cash. Just bring a pocket full of twenties with you and treat him like Pavlov's dog. You'll have him salivating at the sound of the bell in no time."

"What?"

"You weren't a psych major, huh?"

"Never mind." Cantor stomped around his desk. He pointed at Vincent. "You do what Prager says. Prager, you find what my daughter's up to."

I didn't think the timing was right to remind Julian Cantor that I wasn't working for him, so I nodded to Vincent that we should leave together. As my father might have said, Vincent was dumb, but he wasn't stupid. He got my hint and followed me out of Cantor's study. Alexandra wasn't there to bid us adieu, which was just as well. The fewer distractions, the better.

"Look, Vincent," I said, "we got off on the wrong foot here. Mainly that's on me. Cantor's a pain, but he's right, Siobhan is what we both need to be thinking about."

"Yeah, I know. You really think she fucked up her apartment like that?"

"Her or a friend. Think about it, she's got her parents jumping through hoops. Some kids grow older, but never grow up. They spend their lives trying to get the love and attention they felt robbed of as children. You ever meet Siobhan?"

Vincent flushed deep red and cleared his throat. "A few times, yeah."

He'd slept with her. That was pretty obvious.

I opened the door for him to step through if he so chose. "And . . . ."

"She was kind of sad and lonely, I guess."

"Sad how?"

"Not sad, really. More like empty, maybe. She acted like she needed to fill herself up with stuff to do or somebody to be."

Amazingly, I understood just what he meant. It seemed to jibe with the things I'd heard from Rizzo, Giorgio Brahms, Anna Carey, and Michael Dillman. The Hollow Girl, indeed.

CHAPTER NINETEEN

I called ahead to the precinct in the hopes that Frovarp and Shulze had packed it in for the day. Though I was no procrastinator, I wasn't exactly looking forward to this particular unpleasantness. Most cops gave retired cops a break, while others seemed to enjoy busting the balls of their former brethren. It was hard to figure. No one expected cops to look the other way if an ex-cop was involved in something serious—DWI, assault, spousal abuse, at least not anymore—but there were little things, small matters of courtesy that it was reasonable to expect for time served on the job. Since getting put out to pasture in '77, I'd had plenty of run-ins with members of the NYPD. Most of the time, even after a rocky start, we'd manage to find ways to work together. I'd even developed friendships with some of the cops and detectives I'd initially butted heads with. That wasn't going to happen with Frovarp and Shulze. Frovarp especially looked born to spread misery wherever she went.

Unfortunately I'd caught them on their way out the door, but they were willing to wait for me to arrive. They'd gotten a call about the destruction of Siobhan's apartment, Frovarp said, and they'd gone over enough of the Kremlin video to take note of my visit. Not my lucky day. Not a day to stop to buy scratch-off lottery tickets or bet on a horse. Frovarp's cold, gravelly monotone set my teeth on edge, so I decided that maybe strolling into the 9th Precinct wasn't in my best interests. Much easier for them to fuck with me in the precinct house than in public. I was in the middle of explaining how it would be much more to my liking if I met them on neutral turf—Grogan's or Kid Charlemagne's—than at the precinct house when my Bluetooth connection informed me that I was getting a call from Nancy Lustig. I put Frovarp on hold, no doubt endearing myself to her more than I already had.

"What's up?"

"Please come back. Hurry?" Her voice was strange, breathy and desperate.

"Nancy, I can't do this dance right now. I'm on the phone with—"

"It's not about the kiss. It's not about us."

"What then?"

"Sloane. It's Sloane."

"What about her?"

"I can't explain right now. Just come back."

She clicked off.

I almost returned to Frovarp's call, but decided that telling her I wasn't coming in after all was probably not going to improve my abysmal standing in her eyes. And this way I'd at least be able to get beyond the border of Queens before she could do something peevish like having me arrested. I killed my Bluetooth connection and shut off the phone.

* * *

Nancy Lustig's house was somewhat more ominous looking at night. Although the in-ground lights along the driveway and walk were lit, the house itself was almost completely dark. How odd,

I thought, that a place seemingly constructed on the principle of blurring the distinction between inside and out should feel so foreboding. Or maybe the foreboding was just in my head and not in the house, because I knew the hammer would fall on me when I got around to finally seeing the cops. I'd never been good with that, with waiting for bad news. If it was really bad, like when I was sick, I just wanted to face it and be done with it or have it be done with me. I wasn't good at waiting. In the Prager family we believed that bad news was always better than no news. Always.

Nancy had her front door open before I'd gotten one leg out of my car and she didn't stop there. She came running up to me, not so much to greet me as . . . I wasn't quite sure what, exactly. Obviously, something about Siobhan had been weighing on her. For the first time since the diner in Sheepshead Bay, she hadn't fancied herself up for me. The makeup wasn't perfect. The clothes weren't tight or revealing. There was only the vaguest hint of that perfume of hers. Her breath had that acidic stomach tang to it. For her to present herself to me this way, to anyone this way, meant that whatever it was, was serious. Nancy's kind of vanity, a vanity born of inferiority and self-loathing, wasn't a casual thing. It was more an occupation. I was beginning to understand that maybe it was Nancy's obsession with her appearance that had caused some of the fracturing between mother and daughter.

Nancy grabbed me by the arm and tugged me toward the house, but it wasn't like before. This wasn't about us. She wasn't a little drunk and this had nothing to do with desire. She almost seemed incapable of speech. I followed her upstairs to the master bedroom, into the walk-in closet, into her office. She pointed at the big-assed computer monitor. I didn't get it. It just looked like a Facebook page to me, not that I had been on Facebook all that much lately. Pam, in her wisdom, had made me join during my treatment.

"It'll let me message you when we can't talk," Pam had said. "It'll also give you something to do other than lying on the couch all day feeling sorry for yourself. And you might be surprised at how many people you'll find who'll support you, people who've been through the same or similar things."

She'd been right about all of it, of course. I was reluctant at first, like I always was about anything technology based, but it worked. It helped stop me from feeling so isolated. I'd rekindled a few old acquaintances and made some new friends. The irony was that my guilt over Pam's death had made me withdraw in a way that not even the cancer did, and that no amount of friend support on Facebook would heal.

"Okay, Nancy, it's a Facebook page. So what?"

"Look!" she screamed, pointing at a small ad on the right side of the screen. "Look."

There, under the blue Sponsored line with the megaphone icon, stuck in between ads for new method tennis instruction and nonsurgical facelifts, was what Nancy wanted me to see. It was another ad, this one featuring an inch-by-inch headshot of Siobhan Bracken. Above the headshot, in dark blue print, were the words: The Hollow Girl Returns Tonight at 10:00. In smaller black print below the headshot was a clickable link. I clicked on it. I was redirected to a site called "The Hollow Girl Returns." It featured a larger version of the same headshot that had appeared on the ad. Above the headshot were site destinations: History, Biography, Lost Girl/Hollow Girl Videos, Shop, Contact Me. Under the headshot in bold black print were the words: *Whatever became of the Hollow Girl? Find out tonight and every night at 10:00.* Below that, a disclaimer:

> This is performance art and is not intended for any other purpose than to entertain and to stimulate discussion. No one is under any real duress of a physical or psychological

nature. All effects in these posts are the result of makeup and digital manipulation. Do not, I repeat, do not seek to assist me in any way, shape, or form. This is a performance and should be treated as such. I accept no liability for any actions taken by the audience.

I moved the mouse to the site navigation listings, but Nancy told me not to bother.

"I've done all of that already," she said. "It's all very accurate and official looking. You were right, Moe. She set us up. She even has goddamned Hollow Girl T-shirts, sweatshirts, and baseball caps for sale."

"At least we know what she was doing and why and that she's okay. How did you find out? You don't strike me as a Facebook kinda gal."

"Oh, I'm on there, but don't spend much time on it anymore. I don't know. After you left I was still angry with you and maybe a little distracted. I decided I'd go on, answer old messages and see what my friends were up to. That's when I saw the ad. By the way, did you meet Alexandra?"

"I did."

"She's god-awful beautiful, isn't she?"

"Otherworldly, yeah."

"I wish she wasn't so fucking nice, though. It makes it hard to hate her as much as I want to."

"Why hate her at all? She's stuck with your ex," I said.

"Good point." She nodded toward the office door and walked through it. I followed. "We've got some time before my daughter plunges me back into a new mess. Pour yourself a drink downstairs. I've got Internet on the big flat screen down there." She stopped by the door to the master bath. "I'm going to go put myself back together. I'll be down in a little while."

"Okay."

"And, Moe . . . ."

"What is it?"

"I'm glad you came back . . . even if it wasn't what I wanted you to come back for. It makes me feel better about what Sloane's doing, having you here."

"Happy to do it."

Oddly enough, I was.

CHAPTER TWENTY

It was 9:50, and I had settled in on the white leather sofa in front of the flat screen. I'm not sure "settled in" is the right way to describe it, because in spite of the sofa being a stylish objet d'art, the thing wasn't quite as comfortable as stainless steel. I'd taken Nancy's suggestion, pouring myself an inch of fancy Scotch in an equally fancy crystal tumbler. I'd done likewise for her, although she had yet to make an appearance. I was a rotten alcoholic. Just a few cycles off the day-long benders I had been indulging in for weeks, and I was barely shaky. I could casually take a sip here and there without sucking at the bottle like a starving baby. I guess I had Nancy to thank for that. Unintended consequences make the world go 'round.

Then there was Pam. I'd been able to think of her again just lately without wanting to light a match to my guilt and burst into flames. For the past two months, all I pictured of her during my waking hours was her body protruding from under the front end of Holly D'Angelo's Jeep. That or Pam in her coffin, cold, eyes forever closed, her face utterly neutral and damning. But since the day Aaron shook me out of my stupor and lost his patience with me, I'd been able to remember Pam apart from my culpability in her death. It was a relief to have Pam restored to me as something other than a source of pain. I suppose I had Nancy to thank for that, too.

As if on cue, she came down the stairs dressed much like Alexandra Cantor had been dressed earlier in the day—only there was so much more calculation in Nancy's choices. The neckline of her white sweater fairly swooped down and her slacks looked painted on rather than slipped into. Everything about her was now just so: her crushed herb perfume evident, but not overwhelming, her hair shining, falling perfectly on either side of her shoulders. Even her decision to come down in bare feet seemed like something she'd taken time to debate. I pictured her in front of a mirror with ten pairs of shoes, trying each pair on, considering which would have the desired effect. When she said she had to put herself together, she wasn't being figurative. Though I knew that not even a woman as breathtakingly beautiful as Alexandra simply fell out of bed looking like an airbrushed goddess, she had fewer steps to take than a woman who had constructed her appearance. I wondered if Nancy still thought all the effort was worth it. I wasn't complaining.

She sat down on the sofa and fiddled with the controller, picked up her drink, and took a sip. She turned, wearing her smile as a mask. Nancy was trying very hard to hold herself together, but there were cracks in her veneer. She was hoping those cracks wouldn't turn into fissures after watching whatever it was her daughter had gotten up to. Nancy hit the refresh button on the controller when the satellite box indicated it was 10:00. Nothing.

"I called Julian to let him know," she said, voice strained. "He'd already gotten calls about it."

"He have any ideas about what's going on?"

"No, he's as nervous as I am."

She hit the refresh again. A black rectangle appeared center screen with Siobhan's now familiar headshot. It was a fairly recent photo and while she hadn't suddenly blossomed into Alexandra, she was indeed much more attractive than Nancy had been when she was younger. Still not pretty, per se, but her face had thinned out some and it made up nicely. Not nicely enough to get a lead role, apparently. Nancy enlarged the box to full screen and pressed the play arrow. When she did, the disclaimer that was on the website appeared, superimposed over Siobhan's headshot. Then, after enough time elapsed for viewers to have read the disclaimer, someone did a voice-over of it.

"That's Sloane. That's her voice," Nancy fairly shouted, happy and relieved to hear her daughter's voice.

As Siobhan read it, each word on the screen changed from black to yellow to black again. The screen faded to black. Five seconds later, the void was replaced by Siobhan. Not her headshot, by her.

She was wearing an outfit not unlike what she had worn in the "Suicide Posting" on Valentine's Day, 1999: a plain white T-shirt, ripped jeans. For all I knew, it might've been the same outfit. She'd lost some weight and the clothes hung loosely on her. There were dark stains on the tee over where the fake stitches that closed the false, self-inflicted stab wound had been. She seemed to be sitting on the same stool she had sat on all those years ago. The room and backdrop looked exactly the same, though I knew that wasn't possible. Siobhan—Sloane then—had done the posts from her bedroom and the basement of a house that no longer existed. I was sitting in the house that had been built where the old one had stood.

The shock was evident on Nancy's face. I could see her asking herself: *How can that be?*

Siobhan stretched her neck and waggled her arms as if to shake the tension out of her body. Then she spoke:

I'm Siobhan Bracken. My name used to be Sloane Cantor, but most of you viewing this know me or knew me as the Hollow Girl or, at the beginning, as the Lost Girl. For those of you who knew me then, this place should look familiar and [Lifting shirt to reveal perfect replicas of the blood and stitches that had been there on Valentine's Day fourteen years earlier.] *so should these. All that stuff back then, they were just an ugly girl's lies spun out of her anger and her fantasies. I was an angry, hurt, confused little girl who loved acting more than anything in the world. I hurt a lot of people back then and I'm very sorry for it, but, like I said, I was a little girl who didn't understand that other people could hurt like I could hurt.*

I'm a woman now, though not much less ugly than I was when I was in high school. The world isn't a very nice place for ugly girls and fat boys, is it? So, okay, no more bullshit personas for me. It's all lies and make-believe. What I tell you here, what I'll show you here every day will be false. It will be art, but maybe it will speak to you now that I'm telling you the truth that it's all lies. I've lied to myself since I could think. How about you? How many lies do you tell yourself in a single day? It's how I've gotten through every day of my life.

Tomorrow, we're going to talk about where the lies began. [Reaches below camera view. Comes back into view holding two white rectangles.] *Here's a hint.* [Turns rectangles around. Photos of Nancy Lustig: one taken sometime in the late '70s, the other recent.] *She's where the lies began.*

Till tomorrow.

The screen faded to black. The disclaimer came back up, followed by something about all posts being archived and then available on YouTube, and asking viewers to "Like" The Hollow Girl on Facebook and follow @TheHollowGirl on Twitter.

And that was that. Nancy sat frozen in place. Her mouth moved, but nothing came out of it. Her phone began vibrating within a second of the post ending. Her arm moved, as if disconnected from her body, reached for the iPhone on the couch next to her and shut it off. I didn't move or say a word. I can't think what I would have said that wouldn't have just made it all worse. After another minute, Nancy reached for her Scotch and drained it. I poured her another and she drained that one, too.

She finally turned to me as if coming back into her own body, black, mascara-fucked tears flooding over her cheeks. Her mouth moved some more, but still nothing would come out. I didn't need to hear the words. I knew what they would have been, so I took her by the hand and led her upstairs into her bedroom. There was nothing I could do for Pam any longer, but someone needed my help just then, and it was help I could give.

CHAPTER TWENTY-ONE

No one had to say the words, This wasn't how I'd pictured it. The darkness fairly screamed it. But there is something liberating about desperate, wounded sex. Even an old man can recall how it is to succumb to pain and hunger. How it removes the specters of expectation and disappointment from the equation. And Nancy, by her own account, had thirty-five years' worth of fantasies and expectations about what had just happened between us. Thank God that wasn't the baggage I'd carried up the stairs and through the bedroom door. When I'd taken her to bed, I thought it had been all about Nancy and her freshly opened scars. I was wrong, of course. Siobhan's scalpel cut her mother deep, yet Nancy's distress was a portal through which I eagerly swam. I had a lifetime full of my own disasters, great and small. A life full of small victories and guilty defeats. Wounds, desperation, and sex make a potent, explosive cocktail. I hoped this one wouldn't blow up in our faces. Tick . . . tick . . . tick . . . .

There was no tenderness, no gentle embraces in the wake of the breathlessness and clawing. The sighs, screams, and moaning that filled up the room had been replaced by a chasm across the bed and an aching, uncomfortable silence. It got so that the sounds of a passing car along 107 felt like a reprieve from the governor.

I couldn't begin to speculate at all the bad places Nancy might be going to in her head. I didn't know her well enough, frankly. One bit of relief for me was that I no longer wasted time on judging my performance in bed. At my age, unaided by modern pharmacology, I was glad to have been able to perform at all, thank you very much. I was a little saddened that our lovemaking had closed the door on the distant kind of love I had clung to for ugly-beautiful old Nancy. That kind of love breeds only in a vacuum, not the bedroom.

Eventually, we both inched our ways to the middle of the bed and Nancy quietly nestled under my left arm, resting her right cheek on my chest. Still silent, she traced the scar on my abdomen with her index finger.

"Did it hurt?" she whispered, finally.

I took a second to consider if she was asking only about the surgery or if it was a broader question. I decided it was about the scar.

"I was unconscious," I said.

She rose up and punched me in the arm. "Idiot! I know you were unconscious when they operated." There was a smile in her voice. I was glad to hear it. I felt like I could finally exhale.

"You know, that whole year's a bit of a blur, Nancy. I went through so much. They weren't going to do surgery at first, but the tumor started bleeding and they had to go in. That's what I got for delaying treatment until after Sarah's wedding."

"Is she happy . . . Sarah?"

"Happy, what's that? I never know how to answer those kinds of questions. Is anyone happy?"

"Talk about not answering a question."

"She has a busy practice, a husband who loves her, a new son, and a father who disappoints her."

Nancy kissed me softly on the lips. "You didn't disappoint me. I knew you wouldn't," she whispered, sliding her mouth down along my skinny old body.

I wasn't going to pick a fight with her, not then.

* * *

When I woke up, the dark foreboding of the house at night was gone, Nancy with it. Sun streamed in, but I could tell that autumn had taken back its rightful place on the calendar. The warmth of the previous days had vanished. At first, after the chemo and radiation, my body's thermostat had gone haywire. There seemed to be no relationship between the ambient temperature and my sensation of heat or cold. I could sweat through my shirt in mid-February on the boardwalk or be bone cold in the sauna at the gym. But in recent months I'd been transformed into a human weather station. I could just feel that it would be crisp outside before ever stepping outdoors. I could smell the chill, though the air in the bedroom was still redolent with the scents of Nancy and me.

Nancy had told me she was going to play tennis. Good for her, I thought. What the hell was she supposed to do, sit around the house all day fielding gossipy phone calls? Was she supposed to eat her guts out, waiting for Siobhan to drop the next bomb on her head? I also had selfish motives for being glad she was gone.

There was a note in the kitchen, thanking me for last night, and telling me to help myself to anything I wanted for breakfast. She hadn't come right out with it, but I got the sense she expected or at least hoped that I'd be there when she got back. That wasn't going to happen. Pleased as I was about what had gone on between us last night in the wake of the Hollow Girl's reemergence, I wasn't vaguely ready to set up shop. In some ways, Nancy and I falling into bed out of circumstance gave us license to enjoy the experience. It saved us both the strain of circling and circling each other. I wasn't about to push the limits beyond that. I wasn't sure I wanted to. Sometimes, one night together is all that's meant to be.

Out of the shower and dressed in yesterday's clothes, I went to check my phone messages before heading back into the city. Only then did I remember that I'd shut the phone off on my way over. It didn't quite light up like a Christmas tree, but I had lots of messages. I didn't check them, not then. I wanted, needed, to get out of there before Nancy returned. Any "morning after" scenario comes with its share of potential awkwardness. When your morning after is three and a half decades in the making, awkwardness is the least of it. There were land mines everywhere, and I wasn't up for eggshell-walking. I jotted down a quick note of my own beneath the note Nancy had left me. The note itself was quick. The thinking about it wasn't. I didn't have all the words to express what I felt—whatever that was—and decided that less was definitely more. "Will call later. Moe," was the best I could do. I hoped I'd come up with something better than that by the time I actually called.

When I got to the front seat of my car, I listened to the messages. Not unexpectedly, two were from Frovarp and were of the *Fuck-you-Prager-I'm-gonna-fry-your-ass-for-hangin'-up-on-me* variety. The rest of the messages were from Vincent Brock, two from the night before and one that morning. In all the previous evening's turmoil, I'd forgotten about Vincent and the task I'd assigned him. Given that Siobhan had resurfaced, I wasn't all that curious about what had happened between him and Anthony Rizzo. I listened to the messages anyway and when I did, I wished I hadn't.

I got Vincent on the phone as I pulled out of Nancy's driveway and headed down to the Long Island Expressway.

"What do you mean, Rizzo split?" I asked.

"Yeah, and good morning to you, Prager."

"Sorry I hurt your feelings. Good morning. So . . . ."

"It means what it means. The doorman is in the wind. When I went to talk to your pal Anthony, I found Jesus Chavez there instead. Chavez is one of the other two doormen at the building. He was pretty pissed off because he got called in early. Seems Rizzo called the cops, then just walked off his post without notifying anyone he was leaving. You know how touchy people in the city get about paying those ridiculous rents and not having the doorman around. So I tried Rizzo's phone a few times. No luck. Straight to voicemail. Then I took a drive up to the Bronx to have a little visit with him, but he wasn't there, either. I staked out his place all night. He never showed."

"I don't like it."

"Doesn't matter anyway," he said. "The boss's daughter is back."

"Your boss, not mine."

"Whatever."

"I still don't like it."

"Look, Prager, I get that you think I don't know my ass from my elbow."

"Colorfully phrased, but accurate enough."

Vincent shrugged it off. "But Rizzo splitting makes sense. Obviously, Siobhan—I mean, Mr. Cantor's daughter paid the guy off to trash the apartment. He realized he was going to get exposed, probably shitcanned, and maybe even arrested. So he splits until things calm down a little. The cops might be hot to arrest him now, but a few weeks from now no one will care. A few days from now, no one will care. No one cares about anything for very long anymore."

"Pretty philosophical for a guy who rides around in a red BMW with vanity plates, but maybe you're right."

"No maybe about it. Rizzo's out of here. You don't think he just decided to use his back vacation time, do you?"

"I don't like it."

"So you keep saying. What is it with you? You think you're like Sherlock fucking Holmes?"

"No, Brock, but you'll have to forgive me if I don't swallow shit whole and smile about it just because someone says it's veal."

"What's that supposed to mean?"

"Nothing. Forget it. I'm just cranky. It's one of the great privileges and pleasures of old age."

"Yeah, whatever."

He clicked off.

I *was* cranky. That much was true. And I really didn't like the fact that Rizzo had so conveniently vanished. But my crankiness had nothing to do with Anthony Rizzo or Vincent or Frovarp and Shulze. It probably didn't even have much to do with Nancy and me sleeping together. My crankiness had to do with what lay ahead of me. Searching for Siobhan Bracken had given me back something I'd needed: a sense of purpose. Purpose had given me a reason not to drink and not to pray at the altar of my own guilt. The new incarnation of the Hollow Girl had pretty much pulled the rug out from under all of that. I didn't want to think about how long it would take for the prayers and drinking to resume.

CHAPTER TWENTY-TWO

The 9th Precinct was on East 5th Street, not too far from Grogan's. Inside the NYPD, it was known as the Fighting Ninth. Perfect, I thought, given the ornery natures of Detectives Frovarp and Shulze. They had no doubt begged to be assigned there. I hadn't been to the 9th since the old shithole had been knocked down and rebuilt. Though the truth is that after a few years, a station house, no matter how brightly painted or designed, turns bleak. It grows dreary and takes on a distinct odor. It's more than simply the institutional tang of ammonia or chemical pine cleaners. It's also part sweat sock and vomit, part too-sweet perfume and cigarette smoke. Doesn't matter that smoking is verboten. It's as if the tar rides in on the backs of the skells the way fog comes in on little cat feet.

I asked for the squad room and told the uniform manning the desk that I was there to see Detectives Frovarp and Shulze. He smirked, shook his head, and buzzed me through.

"Good luck with that," he said as I walked on.

I'd decided on my way in from Nancy's house that I wanted to get this confrontation out of the way. The longer I put it off, the worse it would get. That's why I didn't usually procrastinate. Putting shit off almost never improves the situation. I'd also abandoned the idea of trying to do this outside the precinct house. The way I figured it was that even if Frovarp and Shulze had a legitimate gripe with me—which, I suppose, they did—the reappearance of the Hollow Girl worked in my favor. Assholes though they might be, they were still detectives and would have a hard time denying that there really wasn't much substance here. I'd left the Kremlin the day I discovered Millie McCumber's body. And Siobhan's flat had been trashed as a gimmick. They couldn't very well break my horns for not calling in a B and E if no one actually broke in. Nor could they toss my ass in jail for screwing up a crime scene if there was no crime. I also realized that I was taking rationalization to new heights.

Except for the addition of computers, squad rooms hadn't changed much in thirty-five years. There was more estrogen in them and less polyester than in my day, but they looked the same, felt the same, smelled the same. The thing was that they were less busy these days. There had been 1,557 homicides in New York City in 1977, the last year I was on the job. In 1990 there had been over 2,600. There were 414 in 2012. Maybe that's why Frovarp and Shulze had spare time to fuck with me. Whatever the reason, I was about to find out.

Frovarp had a scowl on her face even before she noticed me. When I got her attention she showed me her teeth.

"Hey, Gary," she shouted across the squad room to Shulze.

"Yeah, Pat, what is it?"

"Come and see what washed up out of the sewer."

Shulze turned around from the file cabinet he was resting his coffee on. He had that aw-shucks grin on his face. "The box?" he asked his partner.

"Sounds good to me. Interrogation room one, Prager," she said, pointing over my right shoulder.

Suddenly it occurred to me that maybe I should reconsider procrastination as a viable option in the future. I didn't bother protesting and headed straight to where Frovarp pointed. I sat down in the metal perp seat without needing to be told. I was smart like that. The two detectives followed me in and Shulze slammed the door behind him.

Frovarp turned to her partner and said, "Cuff him."

I opened my mouth to say something, then thought better of it. Sometimes you just gotta let kids have their fun even if it comes at your expense. Shulze snapped one cuff around my left wrist and clicked the other cuff around the long, U-shaped metal bar bolted to the table. This wasn't going to be good cop/bad cop. It was going to be bad cop/worse cop.

"All right, asshole," Frovarp started, "what the fuck was that bullshit the other day, you walking away from a crime scene?"

"You heard the ME. I heard the ME. It wasn't a crime scene. She had a heart attack."

"The ME doesn't run the crime scene, shitbird. We do. There was a dead woman in that apartment and until things are all official-like, we treat it as a crime scene. You know that. What happened since you got off the job, you get stupid or something? Oh, that's right, when you were on the job, they used smoke signals to communicate. You don't ever walk away until we tell you to walk away."

"Okay. I get the point. I'm sorry. You're right. I should've waited around."

"Where'd you go after you walked away?"

That question surprised me. "You're kidding me, right?"

"Read him his rights, Gary. I have no time for this bullshit."

"What the fuck? You're arresting me on what charges?"

"We'll think of something."

I reached into my pocket with my right hand and pulled out my cell phone. I knew I shouldn't have done it, but I was getting equal parts angry and worried. Frovarp was quick and slapped the phone out of my hand and sent it crashing against the wall.

Frovarp shook her head at me. "You try something like that again, Prager, and it won't be your phone smashing against the wall. Pretty fucking stupid of you to reach in your pocket like that."

As pissed off as I was, I didn't want to bring up that I was currently the only armed person in the room. The two of them had neglected to pat me down and my old .38 was still holstered in the nook between my belt and the small of my back. I hadn't thought about it until then and mentioning it now might actually get me arrested for real.

"I went to my bank after leaving the Kremlin, the day I found Millicent McCumber's body."

Shulze nodded. "That's more like it. And what was so important at the bank that you had to leave a crime scene?"

"Understand, I'm really trying not to be a smartass, but I didn't know you were still treating it like a crime scene. I needed to get some cash because . . . well, I needed cash."

I could see that neither of them liked that answer much. Whether they liked it or not, I hadn't left them much room to work with. Still, I didn't figure they were just going to throw up their hands in frustration and let me walk out of there. Not yet, anyway. I was right.

"Did you have contact with any employees from the Kremlin between the time you left the building and when you returned days later?"

I considered lying, but the form of the question suggested they already knew the answer.

"The doorman, Anthony Rizzo. We had a few conversations."

"About what?" Frovarp asked.

I realized I was on the threshold of losing my patience soon and that I had to do something before I got to that point.

"Okay, look, you guys are pissed at me. I get that. So why don't we let's stop going at this piecemeal. Gimme the big picture. Tell me what you want?"

Frovarp and Shulze stared at each other like two cats deciding if they should keep playing with their prey or just eat it.

Frovarp had tallied the silent vote and said, "Don't bullshit us."

"I won't. Scout's honor."

"Uncuff him, Gary."

Shulze looked disappointed, but it was clear who the junior partner was in this team. He unlocked the handcuff. I rubbed my wrist.

"Here's our problem, Prager," Frovarp began, her voice a belligerent whisper. "We got one has-been actress dead in an apartment one day. Then that same apartment is trashed. We—"

"Yeah, the apartment's a wreck," I interrupted, "but it's staged. It was all for show."

Shulze agreed. "Yep, Prager. We figured that out in about two seconds. We're real detectives. We've got shields and guns and everything."

"Sorry."

Frovarp began again. "So, we got a stiff. The apartment gets tossed, but nothing is missing that we can tell. We try and contact the renter, Siobhan Bracken, and get nowhere. We call her phone, goes straight to voicemail. We send her e-mails, no reply. We text her, nothing. Then, lo and behold, she pops up on the fucking Internet last night. We wanna know what the fuck is going on here. We don't like looking stupid, and we hate it even more when our CO thinks our looking stupid makes him look stupid."

There are times as a PI you really have to stick to your guns about privileged information and client confidentiality. This wasn't one of those times. I explained about how I'd gotten involved in the case and how Nancy Lustig had been just as interested in locating her daughter as they were. I told them about the Lost Girl, the Hollow Girl, the name change, and pretty much everything else except about my sleeping with Nancy and the more titillating details of Siobhan's relationships with Millie McCumber, Anthony Rizzo, and Giorgio Brahms. I didn't see the point.

"I figure the apartment was trashed to get a rise out of her parents, or it was an aborted attempt at whipping up publicity for her reappearance as the Hollow Girl. My best guess is that Siobhan did it herself or she paid someone to do it for her."

"Someone like Rizzo, you think?" Frovarp offered.

"That's exactly who I'm thinking. But I'm curious why *you* think it's him?" I asked.

Shulze looked at Frovarp for permission. She nodded. "Because there are some gaps in the surveillance records and the building management tells us the doormen have access to the video feeds. We checked, and the wiring's been fucked with."

I shrugged my shoulders. "Well, go have a talk with Anthony. I have his address," I said, nodding my chin at my smashed phone. "Well, I used to have it."

"Never mind. We know his address. Problem is, he didn't go home last night and he's not answering his phone. He didn't show up at work this morning."

"Maybe he wasn't in the mood to get reamed a new asshole or to get fired. I don't know what else to tell you."

"You don't know where he is, Prager?" Shulze wanted to know.

"Not a clue, and it's not my concern anymore. Since Siobhan turned up, I don't have a case to work anymore. Can I go now?"

Shulze picked the pieces of my phone off the floor and handed them to me. He didn't bother apologizing for his partner. I doubted Frovarp was acquainted with the word *sorry*, so I didn't hold my breath.

"All right, Prager," Frovarp said, leaning in toward me. "Here's the deal. Siobhan Bracken shows up on your radar, your first call is to us. Not to her mommy or daddy. To us! You hear from this Rizzo asshole or you find him—"

"I get it, but like I told you, there's no case for me. The only thing I'm going to be looking for now is my bed."

Shulze was skeptical. "Yeah, yeah, yeah, whatever. That's not an answer. Just remember what my partner said. We find out you—"

"Can you two take it easy on the threats for five minutes? I find out how to get in touch with either Siobhan or Rizzo, I'll call you."

"First!" Frovarp barked.

"I'll call you first."

"Okay, Prager, get the fuck outta here." Shulze gestured with his arm. "And sorry about the phone." That dumb hangdog smile on his face said otherwise.

I didn't wait to be told twice, and left the Fighting Ninth behind.

As I drove home, a niggling thought crept into my head. I knew that Frovarp and Shulze were unfriendly, belligerent bastards. That they didn't like looking stupid in front of their commanding officer. I wasn't swallowing it. They were too hungry, too adamant about incidents that barely amounted to cases worthy of their time. Why the fuck should they care about finding Siobhan or Rizzo? It made me think I was missing something, but what?

CHAPTER TWENTY-THREE

Everybody needs to unwind after work. The world would be a better, less bloody place if everyone got an hour to decompress after punching the clock. But even if that was the case, there were certain jobs, adrenaline-fueled jobs, that required something beyond a passive, stress-free hour. Just ask any cop, nurse, or firefighter. My generation of cop did it the old-fashioned way—we drank ourselves blind. Me, I used to be the one to stop short of blindness, the one to drive the other guys home or to put them in cabs. I was no saint, mind you. It wasn't like that. For me, drunkenness, especially public drunkenness, caused far more stress than it diminished. It caused me shame.

Not that I grew up in a religious Jewish home—quite the opposite, really—but when it came to the consumption of alcohol, we became magically observant. In the Prager household, drinking as an activity outside of ritual was frowned upon. Between my father's failures and my mother's pessimism, frowning had been turned into high art. Public drunkenness was totally taboo. *That's for the goyim.* Getting drunk was what gentiles did. I guess it was a means for us Jews to nurture a sense of superiority in lands that were never our own and in which we were always a tiny minority. Even peoples who lived with boots on their necks needed a way to feel empowered. So it was no small irony that Aaron and I should come to own a chain of wine shops. Still, shame at the thought of drunkenness, public or otherwise, had kept me in check for most of my life. I supposed it would have to again.

That's what I was thinking as I walked through the door of my condo. At that moment, it was probably the worst place I could have gone. Worse than a bar, much worse. It was really too bad that I had nowhere else to go, now that I had subjected myself to Frovarp and Shulze and that the Hollow Girl had punched the clock for me. My work was done, and it was time to unwind. It didn't help that my place smelled like the inside of a fucking Dewar's bottle. Whether that was in my head or actually in the air was beside the point. And if that wasn't hard enough to cope with, it felt like a magnet was drawing me to the front window. That same magnet seemed bent on tilting my head down and to the right, my eyes focusing on the spot on the asphalt where Pam had been killed. Nothing like a little self-flagellation and guilt to get a thirst going. Less than twenty-four hours ago I'd been able to calmly sip Scotch on Nancy's sofa without any compulsion to chug the bottle. Yet here I was in my condo, itching for bottle diving like a desperate rummy.

I took another shower to get the stink of the 9th Precinct off me and out of my nostrils. Once, a lifetime ago, I had gone to identify a friend's body at the now defunct Fountain Avenue dump. The body turned out not to be my friend's, but the stench of the dump had stayed with me for hours. It did more than just stay with me. It filled me up, coated me, covered my skin like a film. I couldn't help but wonder if our memories ever let us get clean. Forgetfulness was a skill I had never completely mastered, because though I could no longer smell the 9th Precinct on me, I could still smell the dump. I would until the day I died.

After the shower, after dressing, my thirst was not quite as powerful as it had been when I first stepped through the apartment door. Nor did the living room seem as saturated with Scotch vapors as it had earlier. Even as my computer booted up, I studied the pieces of my cell phone and thought that maybe its loss was something short of tragedy. I recalled that once being free was freer than it was now. There were times when you were unreachable, unaccounted for, unconnected to a cyberlife. A time when your actual, living breathing life was more important, when the details of what you were saying and doing and thinking and feeling at any particular moment was all that there was of you. No more.

The shower and the fresh clothes hadn't washed away my curiosity. I still hadn't been able to figure out just what it was that Frovarp and Shulze were so keen on. I'd tried to convince myself that they really were just such assholes and bulldogs that they couldn't let anything go. That getting me into the interrogation room was payback for pissing them off. I was unconvinced. They had a hunch, and "interviewing" me was an attempt to test it out. Problem was I couldn't reverse engineer what their hunch was from the questions they had asked me. So I sat at my computer and let Google do some walking for me. I read everything there was to read on the discovery of Millicent McCumber's body. I watched all the TV reports, read all the entertainment news commentaries on her life and career.

There was nothing latent there that I could see. Her story was a familiar one. Young, talented, beautiful—she had once been stunning—actress gets famous and full of herself. Then came the boyfriends and girlfriends, the drugs and the drinking, the DWIs and DUIs, the community service and the rehab, the late-night punch lines and jail time. The parts disappeared, as did she from the public consciousness. In fact, there was a five-year stretch, from 2008 until this year, when she'd seemed to have fallen off the face of the earth. Then in April, Millie's name began popping up in online blogs and in some celebrity columns. Nothing big, just a two-line mention here and there about her wanting to get back in the game.

The reincarnation of the Hollow Girl had, however, sparked more than a one-line mention here and there. Several online articles about Sloane Cantor/Siobhan Bracken's comeback had appeared since 10:00 P.M. the night before. Most were recapitulations of the original Lost Girl/Hollow Girl phenomenon and the fallout from the infamous "suicide" posting. Michael C. Dillman wasn't going to be pleased. That was for damn sure, because there in a photo array, next to an old photo of Siobhan and the more recent headshot of her that appeared on the website, was a photo of the teenage Michael Dillman. The caption read *Michael C. Dillman, "Lionel."* His innocent consent to let a high school friend use his photo was about to blow his world up yet again. Once, only memories kept our bad choices alive. Now cyberspace had the power to grant them eternal life.

There was also mention of Millicent McCumber's body having been found in Siobhan Bracken's apartment. Well, Millie might not have been able to get her own career going again, but her death had surely given a boost to the Hollow Girl's comeback. Confidential sources had "implied" that Millie and Siobhan had been lovers and that there might be photos of orgies that had taken place in Siobhan's apartment. Nothing like a few salacious details to get people's attention. If those photos did exist, I had a pretty good idea of who had taken them. At least now I had a sense of what Anthony Rizzo had gotten up to. He was a complete toad, but you had to admire his entrepreneurial instincts. In the end, though, it was Siobhan who had expertly pulled off this masterful manipulation. If the numbers on YouTube could be believed,

Siobhan had made a smashing success of the Hollow Girl's rebirth, and she had done it while embarrassing her mother to potentially devastating effect. But in the new millennium, it was more difficult to keep people's attention than it once had been. Recalling what Siobhan had done in 1999, I got a chill thinking about what the Hollow Girl might be willing to do in order to grow her audience this time around.

The house phone rang. Caller ID: *Private Number*. I let it ring until it went to the cable system's voicemail. I didn't have to be clairvoyant to know it was Nancy. When I got my cell phone replaced, I had no doubt there would be several messages from Nancy waiting for me. And when the current message had finished, I saw that the little red light on my cordless phone was madly blinking. I would have to talk to Nancy eventually, just not until I sorted out my own feelings about having slept with her. That was the thing about desperate, wounded sex: It may make falling into bed that much easier, but it makes the morning after that much more difficult. There was something else I knew I couldn't do, and that was to stay where I was.

CHAPTER TWENTY-FOUR

The Coney Island boardwalk at dusk could be a desolate place. Once fall opened its arms to the heartless Atlantic winds, the death of the season was at hand. When those cruel winds whistled through the salt-rusted bones of the dinosaur rides, when they picked at the flaked paint and plywood scabs of shuttered food stands, hope was exposed as folly. I suppose that deep within me I loved its desolation more than the mirage of hope that was Coney Island in summer. This, I thought, looking out over the guardrail at the empty beach and cold, blackening ocean beyond, is what lay ahead of us all. Not summer. Not crowded beaches and sun block and teenagers riding the waves wreathed in seaweed and children shrieking on rides. This.

Carmella Melendez—my second ex-wife and former business partner—once said that this was where I should be buried or where my ashes should be spread. She was right, of course. I had left it in my will for Sarah to spread my ashes here. Not in the ocean or on the beach, but on the boardwalk near the Cyclone in the fall at dusk. I wasn't sure why it should have mattered to me as I believed in death more strongly than I ever believed in God. Dead was dead. I would be beyond caring or knowing. I'd understood why Mr. Roth had wanted his ashes spread at Auschwitz. Because although he had survived the camps and lived a long life, he had never really been set free. He'd been a prisoner there his whole life. The strange thing is, he'd never been explicit in his instructions. He'd never once mentioned Auschwitz by name. He said that when the time came, I would know where to place him. The only other thing he'd ever said on the subject was that he didn't want to be cold in the ground. "Kaddish and ashes, Mr. Moe. Kaddish and ashes." And so it would be for me, the mourner's prayer optional. But Coney Island for me was not so much prison as womb.

The boardwalk was not desolate, exactly. Starting in the mid '70s, Russian and Ukrainian Jews had resettled this area of Brooklyn. They were a hearty, stubborn bunch. They had to be. The older émigrés, the ones who had had rough lives back home, viewed New York City's climate kind of like how they viewed American prisons. *Is nothing. Like country club.* So yeah, these days when the Atlantic winds came in with fall, there were plenty of old Russians strolling the boardwalk. There was someone else coming onto the boardwalk, too, someone I'd asked to be there.

Detective Jean Jacques Fuqua's handsome black face was making a feeble attempt at a smile as he came up the Stillwell Avenue steps to greet me, the smell of Nathan's Famous french fries bubbling in oil overwhelming the sea air. We shook hands, and walked to the guardrail on the beach side of the boardwalk, Fuqua rubbing his palms together, cupping them, blowing warm breath into them as he went.

"How do you cope with this weather, *ami?*" he asked, only a hint of Port-au-Prince in his voice. "I have lived here for many many years, but I find the cold unbearable."

"Ask one of the ninety-year-old Russian ladies for a transfusion."

"You are an amusing fellow, Moses, but most of all amusing, I think, to yourself."

"May well be," I said. "May well be."

He turned away from the beach and took a long look at me. I tried not to stare him down. We'd met a few years back under very unusual circumstances. Soon after I received my cancer diagnosis and only a few weeks before Sarah's wedding, Carmella had come to me in desperation. She asked me to look into the murder of her estranged sister, Alta, who had been stabbed to death in Gravesend. It was an ugly affair all around and Jean Jacques Fuqua was the unlucky detective who'd caught the case. We'd worked together to get to the truth of things, taking some pretty unethical risks in the process. When the smoke cleared, he'd gotten the bump to detective first. But Fuqua, a proud, up-by-the-bootstraps Haitian immigrant, had never gotten over the ethical compromises he'd made in order to solve the case. I guess I was past caring about compromises and pride. So although I'd helped get him his promotion, he regarded me with strong mixed feelings. In spite of his calling me *ami*, I knew the appellation came with reservations. Maybe that's why I trusted him to tell me the truth.

"You are not looking so well, *ami, non?*"

"You are quite the charmer, Jean Jacques. You're looking good."

"Are you ill again, Moses?"

I laughed. "No, it's nothing like that."

"Then what?"

Alcohol. I could not bring myself to say it. The shame was still there. Maybe not as strong as guilt, it was still plenty strong. "I'm just tired."

"I do not believe you, but I am too cold to argue. Why did you call me here?"

"You worked in the 9th Precinct before you got transferred to Brooklyn South Homicide, right?"

"I did, yes."

"Did you know Frovarp and Shulze?"

That seemed to fully get his attention. He stood erect. Only then did I remember what an imposing figure Fuqua cut. He had shoulders like a linebacker dressed in his pads and he had a body builder's torso. "Why do you ask?"

"I'm working a case, and let's just say I have been forced to cross paths with Frovarp and Shulze."

"I thought you were not working cases any longer. You said you were going to enjoy your life and your grandchild."

"I wasn't lying when I said it."

"You are being evasive today, Moses."

"If it will make you feel better, think of me as doing God's work."

"God's work? Have you turned in your wine stores for angel wings?"

I was getting tired of avoiding Fuqua's questions, so I explained about the Hollow Girl and Nancy and my involvement in the case. Though much younger and way more tech savvy than myself, he hadn't ever heard of the Hollow Girl in either her old or new incarnation. I detected a kind of revulsion in him—if not revulsion, then a cross between bewilderment and condescension. It was something like I felt about it. I was going to say as much when he beat me to it.

"It is why the world hates us, *non*? Our obsession with ourselves; the inflation of our small lives into objects of public fascination. It is not our bombs or our constant flag waving in their faces that they so much detest, I think, as our petty obsessions. The world wants our country to care about important things, but instead we care about *Dancing with the Stars*. We know the bra size of Lady Gaga and we have TV shows that sexualize little girls as beauty queens, but how many of us can name even a single country in West Africa, or know who is the president of Russia? Our lack of perspective is what makes us hated.

"I am a proud American, Moses, but I am also Haitian. I can see us in a way that maybe you cannot, but that your grandparents might have. Like your grandparents, who had a homeland to look back to and remember the hardships and the struggles, I can see my new country with such eyes as theirs. Haiti was destroyed by an earthquake not so long ago. There has been famine and disease. As you are aware, there has always been political turmoil. The United States has done very much to help Haiti, but is it not very difficult to reconcile Port-au-Prince in ruins and Honey Boo Boo?"

"Christ, Fuqua, the Hollow Girl is just a gimmick, the product of a talented and complicated woman, not the benchmark for the decline of Western civilization."

"I am not so sure of that as you, but what is it that you wish of me?"

"You still have people you're close to at the 9th, people who talk to you?"

"Naturally, I have many friends who are there."

"Do me a favor, have those friends of yours keep an eye out for Frovarp and Shulze."

"How so, Moses?"

I gave a shrug. "I don't know. See if they are acting edgier than normal? Do they seem obsessed with any one case? If so, which case? Are they putting in a lot of overtime? Stuff like that."

"I will see what can be done."

I held out my hand to him. "*Merci beaucoup*, Jean Jacques."

He shook it. "*De rien.* I repay my debts."

"Forget the bump. You would have made detective first without me."

"But not so quickly." He was fast to react.

"Maybe not, but I am asking you to do this thing for me as a favor to a friend, not as repayment. I want to be clear on this. If you think you owe me some debt for what happened with

Alta's murder and the blackmailing, forget it. You don't owe me anything, nor do you have to fear that I would share any details of what we had to do."

"Very well, Moses, as you say, a favor for a friend."

"And a case of that Bordeaux you like."

That got a smile from him, at last. "That, *ami*, is a reason I can embrace."

"I'll hear from you, then?"

"Yes." I let go of his hand and made to step away, but he would not release my hand. And his hand was far stronger than my will. He stared directly into my eyes. "As a friend, Moses, take some advice. Go away for a few days, please. You do not look well. Brooklyn will still be here when you return. I am sure of it."

And with that he let go of me, retreating back down the Stillwell Avenue steps. I watched him get smaller and smaller as he walked toward Surf Avenue. I checked my watch and saw that I still had time to get to the phone store. I needed to get that done with, because I meant to take Jean Jacques Fuqua's advice.

CHAPTER TWENTY-FIVE

I stopped by the phone store and told the young woman to salvage the data as best she could.

"Don't you want your new phone? It'll only take a few minutes for us to transfer the—"

"No," I said. "I really don't. I'll pick it up in a couple of days."

It was to laugh, the expression on her face. She seemed to view the very concept of removing one's self from the world of Angry Birds and Yelp and Google Maps as a cross between heresy and psychosis. Maybe she was right. Maybe I'd go home and make a bonfire of my Kindle, iPod, Roku box, flat screen, DVR, and computer. After that I'd move to a cave in the woods and bay at the moon. *OW-OW-OWOOOOO! OW-OW-OWOOOOO!*

Untethering myself from the world that way was a small gesture, I know, barely more than a nod or a wink in the scheme of things. I'd never been a fan of the grand gesture. Those things seemed like façade and artifice, brightly colored balloons—bloated, pretty objects meant to distract, to capture your attention, but ultimately empty and quickly forgotten. In my life, it had always been the little things that stayed with me. My memory wasn't full with fancy gold watch moments or the fanfare of trumpets. My memory was filled up with the little things. The things, good and bad, that occurred by chance, by serendipity and happenstance, not by plan. The sun filtering through Andrea Cotter's hair on the boardwalk. Bobby Friedman's smile. Rico Tripoli's '70s polyester leisure suits. The unexpected kiss. The panicked dream. The first wisps of Sarah's red hair as she was born.

Before getting on the road, I went home to throw a few things in a bag. When the house phone rang, I almost regretted not making that bonfire. I was confident it was Nancy even before I checked caller ID. And when I noticed it was 9:55, all doubt was erased. Given that we'd slept together and that I had deposited her five thousand dollar check, I owed it to her to pick up. More than that, I owed it to myself.

"Hey."

"Were you ever going to call?" Her voice was cracked and brittle.

I confessed, "Not tonight. I wanted to give it a few days."

"For what? To forget? Was it that bad, fucking me?"

"No, it was that good," I heard someone say in my voice, not quite believing I'd admitted it to her, let alone to myself.

"Then why—"

"Because I was afraid it was more about the circumstances than the players. I'm still not sure that wasn't the case."

"In English, please, Moe."

"I think you understand. Last night was kind of a perfect storm."

"I guess it was," she said.

"I just wanted to give it a few days and I realized there are some things I need to take care of."

"What things?"

"Things that don't concern you, Nancy. Things that I haven't been up to facing until now. I will be out of touch for a few days."

"I've waited for you since I was nineteen years old. I can wait a little—Wait . . . Sloane's coming on. Are you watching?"

"No, I was about to leave and my computer isn't booted up."

"I wonder how badly she's going to slam me tonight."

"Maybe it won't be as bad as you imagine it will be. Who knows, maybe she'll turn on her dad," I said without much conviction.

"Maybe. Go do what you have to do."

I wasn't going to argue with her. I had a long drive ahead of me.

CHAPTER TWENTY-SIX

I had been as surprised as anyone that Pam had willed me her Vermont house. Until the moment I walked through the door, I had, with the help of Dewar's, avoided dealing with what owning it entailed. The place smelled of must and sorrow, not of death. There were no bodies here, just memories, and only some of them mine. Pam and I had grown into love as opposed to falling into it. Falling is so much more exciting than growing. Falling is all about the manic blur of obsession, the ache of separation, the joy in the exclusion of everything else but love as so much noise. Even at my age, the thought of falling could still make me dizzy. But gravity dictates that falling is always followed by a crash. Gravity is funny that way. Sometimes, like with my first wife, Katy, the crash could be twenty years in coming: inexorable and inevitable.

Pam and I had done it in reverse. We literally started with a crash; the front end of her car meeting the back end of mine in the shadow of the Brooklyn Bridge. It made me laugh to remember that we had done many things in reverse. For not only did our love begin with a crash, it began with lies. Mary Lambert, an IT consultant from Boston, is who Pam claimed to be when I got out of my car to confront the idiot driver who'd rear-ended me. None of it was true. Even the accident was a convenient lie meant to catch me off guard. She was actually Pamela Osteen, a Vermont-based PI sent to investigate a paternity issue involving my old precinct mate, the long-dead Rico Tripoli. Eventually I got past the lies. I think the fact that she once saved my life kind of helped cut through the bullshit and endeared her to me. Besides, who was I to be indignant about lies? I had lied to Katy about her brother's disappearance for twenty years. I had spent so much of my life lying to protect secrets—my own, yes, but mostly other people's—that I feared losing the ability to sort out the truth. For some reason, the truth had become increasingly important to me the closer I got to the grave.

I switched on a light and noticed that my footsteps had kicked up a panic of dust, motes swirling madly in the shaft of light. Everything I touched was covered in a downy gray layer of dust. But instead of brushing it away, I found I was smiling at the notion that bits of Pam and I were mingled together in the dust. That even the most thorough cleaning in the world wouldn't get rid of all of it, not ever. That even after I sold the place, we would remain here together forever. Forever, that was another thing Pam and I had done ass backwards. Having both taken wrong turns up the aisle, we'd pretty much started our relationship by declaring open warfare on marriage. Yet when I asked her to marry me, she couldn't say yes fast enough. I rubbed my fingers in the dust. I didn't believe in heaven, but I believed in dust. I could hear Mr. Roth tsk-tsking me, pictured him wagging his finger at me. *Oy, Mr. Moe. Are you ever gonna learn?* I looked up at the dark ceiling and said aloud, "I guess not, Izzy. In the end, ashes and dust aren't all that different."

I turned on some more lights and my eyes went immediately to the wall of framed photos above the sofa. There were photos of us together, of me taken by Pam, and of Pam taken by me. I took one off the wall, one I'd taken of her only a month before she was killed. She was seated on the deck, her head thrown back against an Adirondack chair, her left hand shielding her eyes from the setting sun, a glass of red wine in her right hand. I was shocked to see that she had let her hair go gray. Funny, I hadn't noticed. She'd never seemed to have aged, to me. I guess you stop seeing things after a while. When we first met, her hair was mostly black with only a strand of gray here and there. I wondered if it was me who'd turned her hair gray? Had my sickness aged us both? No, she was happy. I believed that just as much as I believed in dust. And I wasn't going to beat myself up over this. I had done enough of that.

There were other pictures, too: Sarah and Paul, the newborn Ruben. But like I said, there were memories here that weren't mine, but were now my responsibility. Memories that were wholly Pam's. I knew that in a cabinet somewhere there was a first wedding album, and high school photo albums with pictures of old friends long forgotten. There were knickknacks and mementos, awards and certificates, old love letters and jewelry, an attic full of things I had never seen. There were a thousand stories here that would remain untold. That was the true robbery, the cheat in death. Not the things shared, but the stories left untold, the unshared details that had been someone's life. What else do we amount to but what we leave of ourselves with others?

Unshared details. Suddenly I remembered a detail of my life I had vowed to share with Sarah that had somehow fallen through the cracks. It was perfectly understandable how it would have gotten lost in the joy over Ruben's birth and the turmoil in the wake of Pam's death. When Sarah was pregnant and had driven down to New York to take me to Bobby Friedman's funeral, she had asked me to tell her the story of how I'd become a cop in the first place. It'd taken the better part of a night to explain how and why I'd made the leap from the Brooklyn College campus to the police academy in the course of only a very few months. And in the telling there had been one thing she had seemed desperate to want to know, as I had been desperate to know myself many years earlier. I patted my pocket for my cell phone. Shit! It was in pieces in a phone store in Brooklyn. Maybe the woman behind the counter had been right to think me psychotic for willingly taking myself off the grid.

I picked up the phone in Pam's kitchen. Nothing, not even a dial tone. Apparently the local cable company was a little bit more diligent about cutting off service than the local electric utility. I actually took a few steps back toward the door, thinking that Sarah and Paul's house wasn't more than a half-hour drive away. Then I looked at my watch and noticed it was near two in the morning. It dawned on me that if Sarah had waited this long to hear that one detail of my life, she could probably wait a few hours longer. In the meantime, I got busy building a fire.

CHAPTER TWENTY-SEVEN

The look on Sarah's face was priceless, something between abject horror and joy. I took it and ran, abject horror notwithstanding. Maybe I was willing to accept the bad with the good because I was freezing my flat Jewish ass off and would have done just about anything to get inside. I'd dressed for late September in New York City, not late September in Vermont. Act on impulse and that's what you get.

"What the fuck, Dad?" Unlike her father, Sarah almost never cursed.

"They can take my girl out of Brooklyn, but not the Brooklyn out of my girl. Hey, kiddo. You gonna make me stand out here in the cold?"

"Come in."

"You sure you don't wanna give me a Breathalyzer first?"

"Dad!"

I stepped inside and followed Sarah to the kitchen. For a people reputed to be dreadful cooks, Jews always congregated in the kitchen. Maybe we hoped God would make himself known to us there.

"Where's my grandson?"

"Paul's got the day off. He and Ruben are out running errands and having a little father and son time. I'm going into the office later. What are you doing here, Dad?"

"It was the name of a horse," I blurted out.

Sarah's eyes got wide and she tilted her head at me in confusion. "What? What was the name of a horse? Dad, are you—"

"No, kiddo, I'm not drunk. I swear."

"If you say so."

"Remember last year when you came to Brooklyn to take me to Bobby Friedman's funeral?"

"Of course."

"And you asked me to tell you how I became a cop."

"I remember, Dad."

"I promised to tell you how the Onion Street Pub got its name?"

She was still confused. "What does a horse have to do with it?"

"The cop who owned the place bet his paycheck on a forty-to-one long shot named Onion Street Blues at Aqueduct, and the horse came in. He used the money he won to buy the bar. So since he won the money on a horse named Onion Street Blues, he decided to call the place—"

"The Onion Street Pub. Jesus, Dad, you drove all the way up here to tell me that?"

"No, I drove over from Pam's house to tell me that," I said. "I drove up here to take care of the things I haven't been able to face since she was killed. And one of those things is to apologize to you for the way I treated you that day in August."

"You apologized already."

"Not in person, I didn't." I reached my hand across the table and took her right hand in mine. "I'm sorry, kiddo. I was really lost and you were right, I was wallowing. I was feeling sorry for myself."

"But you're okay now?" Sarah asked, pulling my hand up to her face and resting her cheek against it.

"If you mean, am I still drinking . . . I've pretty much stopped drinking like I was, yeah. I made a bad drunk. The pain never went away, and all the drinking did was to make it easier not to deal with stuff like selling Pam's house."

"Why sell it at all? Why not move up here? You've never liked the wine business anyway. This way you wouldn't have to feel you were underfoot living with us, but you could spend time with your grandkids—"

"Grandkids! Are you—"

"Pregnant? Not yet, Dad, but Paul and I want more kids, lots of them. We're gonna have more of our own and maybe adopt some."

"Because Paul was adopted?"

"Because Paul was adopted. Because I was an only child. For a hundred reasons."

"Okay, I'll think about moving up here," I said, disbelieving. "Did I just say that?"

The smile on my daughter's face was answer enough.

We had a cup of coffee, Sarah catching me up on her family's progress. She discussed her vet practice—growing steadily—and Paul's cases: mostly boring stuff. She showed me the most recent pictures of Ruben. Then Sarah shifted the conversation around to me.

"So, how's the case with Sloane Cantor going?"

"There is no case," I said. "When she showed up on the Internet two nights ago . . . it kinda put an end to my job."

"Too bad."

"For me, yeah, maybe. I was having fun working a case again. But it's better that she's not missing. I'm not so sure her mother's enjoying it much."

"Tell me about it. God, Dad, she crucified her mom yesterday."

I must have gotten a sick look on my face because Sarah asked me if I was feeling all right and did I need to lie down.

"I'm fine. I'm fine." But I wasn't fine. I felt the sting for Nancy. I didn't want to. I didn't want to feel a connection to her like that. I didn't want to feel a connection like that to anyone. Maybe only to Sarah and Ruben. Then I said another thing I wasn't sure I could believe I was saying. "Listen, kiddo, do you think I can use your computer to see the post from last night?"

"Sure, the computer's on in my office."

Sarah was not prone to exaggeration and she hadn't exaggerated about the Hollow Girl's treatment of Nancy. It was more than nasty, crossing way over the double yellow line to cruelty. Somehow, Siobhan had gotten hold of Nancy's medical records, of her pre- and post-surgery photos. They were hard to look at. Siobhan was so cold, her assessment of her mother so callous that it was difficult to listen to. I squirmed in my seat. The tirade was about how Siobhan viewed her mother as a coward for not being willing to deal with life as it had been gifted to her. Didn't ugly people just have to deal with their ugliness? And how could someone who had made herself pretty through artificial means be so cruel as to have children?

That was the crux of it, I realized. Siobhan's rant wasn't really about Nancy at all, but about herself. It was about how the plain-looking girl would never land the leading role regardless of her being the most talented actor in the room. About how there would always be more big roles available to half-talented sluts like her late friend and lover Millie McCumber than there would ever be for her. Surely Nancy would understand that this wasn't really about her. She was so smart and perceptive, but she was human, and I supposed they didn't make armor thick enough to protect a mother from a daughter attacking her this way. What I knew was that when Sarah shut me out for years after Katy had been killed, I lived in perpetual ache. Sometimes the ache was a dull one and whole weeks, sometimes months, would pass without a sharp pain. Then again, Sarah wasn't torturing me by the day on the Internet.

Immediately after the Hollow Girl signed off for the night, a different video came up. It was another disclaimer, this one featuring Siobhan. She was smiling, though she held a pretty scary-looking bayonet in her hand. As she spoke, she brushed the tip of the blade along her palm.

Hey, guys, just a reminder. The stuff you see here is performance art. It's make-believe. Please, please remember that. Don't go calling 911 when you see stuff like this happen. [Drives bayonet into her shirt above heart. Holds bayonet in place. Blood soaks shirt. She laughs.] *It's special effects.* [Removes blade from chest. Slowly shoves bayonet into palm.] *The blade is a prop. It recedes into the handle. Listen to the spring.* [Lifts shirt to reveal plastic blood pack taped to chest and tucked partially under bra cup.] *Remember, it's art.*

With that last line, Siobhan Bracken faded to black. I didn't quite get the need for all the disclaimers, especially since the only person getting cut up in all this was Nancy Lustig and then only by her daughter's wicked tongue. I felt awful for Nancy, but she'd manage. I would have enough on my own plate over the next few days without trying to salve someone else's wounds.

CHAPTER TWENTY-EIGHT

I stayed the weekend. It had been a good few days. The best days I'd had since late June. I'd spent a lot of catch-up time with Ruben and let Sarah and Paul get out for dinner on Saturday night. What can I tell you, besides being incredibly handsome, my grandson displayed genius tendencies and laughed at practically everything I did. He was a particular fan of me tickling his belly and playing peek-a-boo. On Sunday, Sarah came over to Pam's house and helped me organize the paperwork that needed taking care of. We looked through some of Pam's stuff, her old stuff that predated me. Mostly Sarah and I laughed as we filled in invisible thought balloons and made up dialogue for the people in Pam's high school yearbook and in her photo albums. It was good to be happy again at the sight of Pam and to see her so young, pretty, and smiling. That's how I wanted to remember her, not as a body sticking out from under the front end of a Jeep.

We made a deal, my daughter and me. If I promised not to sell Pam's house immediately, Sarah would come over once or twice a week and sort through Pam's clothing and papers. She would send me the paperwork that needed seeing to, would bundle up and donate the clothing, the books, all that kind of stuff. She would go through the attic, garage, and basement, and put aside things for me she thought I might want to keep or sell. I was good with that on many levels. I loved my daughter, but she did have a bit of her Uncle Aaron in her. She had a head for organization that had always escaped me.

Now the weekend was over and Monday morning was at hand. Time to head back home to deal with the world again. It would be both the same world I'd left behind and a different world. Although there was no longer a case to work, I would still have to deal with Nancy. I couldn't dismiss as simple human empathy the sting I'd felt for her as I watched Siobhan rip her to pieces. There were feelings there, and I would have to make sense of them. And I would have to face the world without drinking. I suspected that would be far less complicated than dealing with Nancy Lustig. With a few days' worth of perspective I'd come to realize that heavy drinking was like most self-destructive activities—far more romantic from the outside looking in. Most importantly, there was something else that needed doing when I got back into the city, something, I realized, that had needed doing for many years.

I locked the front door behind me, but stopped in my tracks as I noticed Sarah's Subaru—almost everyone in Vermont, it seemed, drove a Subaru—kicking up clouds of dirt as it flew up the driveway towards me. My heart jumped into my throat because Sarah, Paul, Ruben, and I had said our goodbyes after dinner the night before. I couldn't imagine what reason she could have for rushing to see me like this. I couldn't imagine it was for anything good. I heard my mom's ghost whispering to me, *When things are good, watch out.* And when I saw the look on Sarah's face as she got out of her car, I heard my mother's ghost clap her hands together and laugh with joy at being right.

"What is it, kiddo? What's wrong?"

Sarah handed me her cell phone. "Some guy named Vincent Brock called and left a message with my service. He says it's urgent that you call him. Something about a guy named Rizzo."

"Anthony Rizzo," I mumbled to myself, screwing up my face.

"What is it, Dad?"

"Anthony Rizzo," I repeated, louder this time. "He used to be the doorman at Siob—at Sloane Cantor's building."

"Well, I thought you ought to know. Here, call him." She handed me the phone. "I wrote down his number if you need it."

"That's okay, I've got it."

I took his card out of my wallet and tapped in the number. Vincent picked up after one ring.

"Yeah, Prager, Jesus, where have you been? I've had to turn over your family tree to find you."

"You know where I am. I'm in Vermont. What's so—"

"The Nassau County cops found Anthony Rizzo's car yesterday."

"This is why you tracked me down and frightened my daughter, to tell me that the Nassau—"

"They also found him."

"And . . . ."

"They found him in his car in the trunk."

"Dead?"

"Very dead. His head was smashed in like a grapefruit dropped off the Empire State Building."

"Nice image."

"What do you think it means?" Vincent wanted to know.

"I don't know, but I don't like it."

"You say that a lot."

"What?"

"*I don't like it.* You say that a lot."

"I'll remember that. I don't know what Rizzo getting his head bashed in means. You met him. He was the type of guy who was good at pissing people off. Maybe he pissed someone off past the breaking point."

"Well, duh."

"Vincent, do me a favor, don't bust my balls. I'm not the schmuck who drives around in a neon car with vanity plates that scream 'Hey, look at me' or can't find his own dick in the dark. I'm sure you're good at what you do, but you're not good at what I do. I'll check in with you when I get back into New York."

"That's big of you, asshole." His voice cracked with anger.

"Who knows? I mean, about the doorman?"

"I had to tell Cantor."

"His ex, does she know?"

"No clue."

"Shit!"

I clicked off and handed the phone back to Sarah.

"Do you always talk to people like that?" she asked, smiling, yet a little bit horrified.

"Only when they deserve it, and even then, not always."

"Is it trouble?"

"Murder is always trouble for somebody, kiddo. I just don't know if it's my trouble. I gotta get going."

I hugged Sarah tight and kissed her forehead. Then I turned and looked at Pam's house and wondered if I could really ever call it home.

CHAPTER TWENTY-NINE

Nancy had left a few messages, but none were about Rizzo. She was mostly just curious about when I was getting back and if I had seen Sloane's recent posts. There was an odd kind of glee in her voice that seemed disconnected from the question, but I didn't turn myself inside out trying to make sense of it. I would be seeing her soon enough. Most of the messages were from Julian Cantor and his tone of voice was pretty far removed from gleeful. Mostly he was gruff, alternating between rude and frantic. He wondered if I'd seen what his daughter had been up to. Wondered what I thought about Rizzo's murder. Wondered why the hell I wasn't calling him back. Urged me to call him back. Demanded that I call him back. Threatened me that I'd better call him back.

Listening to cell messages after being out of the loop for a few days was like reading through your mail after returning from vacation. Neither was much fun, and both reminded you that all respites were temporary. But before I dealt with Cantor, I had to check in with Frovarp and Shulze to make sure they knew that I hadn't been screwing them around. I got Shulze on the line. He didn't even bother giving me a hard time. He assured me they knew all about Rizzo being dead, and Shulze actually sounded as if he believed me when I explained that I'd been out of town.

When I asked him if he thought Rizzo's homicide had any larger implications, Shulze laughed that goofy, malevolent laugh of his and said he would have to look up the word *implications* in the dictionary. Of course he couldn't let me go without a little bit of unpleasantness, making sure to threaten me if I didn't alert him to anything new that I might hear in connection with Rizzo's murder. Everyone seemed intent on threatening me.

I put in a call to a Nassau County detective I'd met about six years back when the art prodigy Sashi Bluntstone had been kidnapped from near her home in Sea Cliff, Long Island. Detective Jordan McKenna and I weren't exactly close, but we'd found Sashi alive and mostly intact. That had made him look pretty good in the eyes of the brass and, like with Fuqua, had earned him a promotion and a medal. So I was more than a little disappointed to hear that McKenna had chosen to take a week's vacation.

"Prager, P-r-a-g-e-r," the guy repeated as he took down the message. "Hey, wait, I know that name. Aren't you the old guy who dived in the fucking canal in Babylon to save that Bluntstone girl? Man, it took some pair of balls to jump in that water in the middle of winter."

It's not quite how I would have described myself. "Yeah, that was me—Old Frozen Nuts Prager."

He liked that. "Sure. We met at McKenna's promotion party. I'm McKenna's partner, Mike . . . Mike Bursaw."

"Right. Right. Mystery Mike."

"That's me. Shit, you remember that, huh? I'm impressed. I couldn't remember which way was up the next day, I was so hammered."

"Listen, Detective Bursaw—"

"Call me Mike, okay?"

"Okay. Listen, Mike, I heard that your uniforms found a guy from the city stuffed in his car trunk yesterday."

"We did indeed. Hold on a second." I could hear him tapping on a keyboard. "Yeah, here it is. The vic's name was Anthony—"

"Rizzo."

"You knew him?"

"Sort of. Listen, Mike, could I buy you a drink tonight after your shift? I think we might be able to do each other some good."

"How about maybe breakfast tomorrow? These days coffee suits my habits better, if you hear what I'm saying."

"Loud and clear. You know Barb and Rob's Pantry in Roslyn?" I asked.

"Sure. Tomorrow at 6:30."

"See you there."

I picked up the phone to call Cantor back, but decided to watch the last few posts from the Hollow Girl before dealing with him. Before you step into a minefield, it's good to know what kinds of mines were buried there. The last post I'd seen was the one I'd watched the day I showed up on Sarah's doorstep. After that, I hadn't been willing to let the Hollow Girl inject her particular brand of *mishegas* into my life. I was too busy enjoying my time with my own daughter's family to allow Siobhan's anger and pain to rob me of my pleasure.

The posts I missed were more of the same, but with a different flavor. During Sunday's post, the Hollow Girl turned her focus away from Nancy and aimed it directly at Julian Cantor. Although Cantor's sins were more diffuse than Nancy's, he was portrayed by his daughter as a little man—weak, insecure, consumed by petty jealousies and vanities. She claimed that her father had married her mother only as a means to gain access to his father-in-law's money and influence. That he was a serial cheater both in his marriage and in his law practice. This post, like the ones about Nancy's surgeries, came with a photo display. This time, however, the photos were of Cantor's alleged mistresses. A few, apparently, were the wives of friends and business associates. One of the photos was of Alexandra Cantor. Neither the gleeful tone in Nancy's voice nor Julian Cantor's frantic one were mysteries to me any longer.

I took joy in none of it. It was getting ugly, and harder to watch. Given how she had carved up Nancy and trashed her father's reputation, the new disclaimer with the fake blood and bayonet seemed strangely appropriate. Viewing the Hollow Girl's recent posts was like watching a slasher movie with family members as all the victims. It was bloody and vicious, and there seemed to be no thought given to collateral damage. Would any family, I wondered, have withstood this kind of perverse scrutiny? Mine surely couldn't have. It was like that PBS show from the '70s, *An American Family*, but this was worse because here there was only one voice, one perspective, one opinion, one knife. There was no other side of the story, no one to tell it, no defense, no rebuttal. Siobhan was determined to show the world what had made the Hollow Girl hollow.

I couldn't help but hear Fuqua's words in my head. *It is why the world hates us, our obsession with ourselves. The inflation of our small lives into objects of public fascination.* And with the huge number of hits these posts had gotten, it would have been hard to argue that Fuqua was wrong. The level of interest was bizarre. Then again, I'd never watched a single episode of anything labeled reality TV. *Reality TV*, now there was an oxymoron if I ever heard one. Just the fact that people knew they were being observed distorted reality. When I thought about it, I realized that the Hollow Girl had a point, too: Reality TV was nothing more than performance art.

I called Nancy on my way out to Long Island and told her I'd see her in a few hours. That seemed to placate her. She hadn't mentioned Rizzo to me, so I didn't mention his murder to her. That kind of issue was always best discussed face to face. Besides, I didn't want to interfere with her schadenfreude over the treatment her ex had received at the hands of the Hollow Girl.

I wanted to believe Rizzo's murder had no connection to Siobhan Bracken's life, to the trashing of her apartment, to Millie McCumber's death, to the Hollow Girl's reincarnation as an avenging angel—that Rizzo's demise and the rest of those other incidents were simply isolated dots connected in my mind by lines of proximity and coincidence. I argued with myself that even in a cold and random universe, things sometimes got clustered together by chance. I tried hard to make myself believe, but it was a waste of time. I couldn't ignore what a lifetime of experience had taught me. That's why I was going to meet with Detective Bursaw in the morning. Maybe he could convince me of what I could not convince myself, that the connection was only in my head.

CHAPTER THIRTY

The sky was overcast, the warm air heavy with moisture, and still, deathly still. The trees along the expressway seemed a little less green today, their leaves hanging inert from their stems as if holding their breath. I could not escape the sense that an invisible wind was howling, blowing through the lives of Nancy, her ex, and their daughter. Something dark, insidious, and more destructive than the sum of its parts. I thought I could almost hear it whistling as it blew through the cranky metal bones and creaky wooden beams of the old rides in Coney Island. It was a familiar song to me, not a siren's song. Nothing so sweetly torturous as that. Not this whistling. This was a high-pitched whine of ragged edges that only old ears could hear. It's hard to explain, but a closeness to death had increased my sensitivities to the darker frequencies.

Julian Cantor's house looked more gothic than ugly under the overcast skies. I couldn't imagine how a thunderstorm might further enhance its appearance. Not unexpectedly, Vincent Brock's BMW was parked where it had been the last time I visited. But as my arrival was unexpected, Alexandra hadn't come out to greet me. I knew that in spite of the calm exterior, things would not be nearly so calm inside the house. It was tough to do damage control when your own daughter was your accuser. I knew a little something about that. And whether she was telling the truth about her father or not was almost beside the point. People would believe her because, in our culture, the worst of someone was always easier to believe.

What the Hollow Girl had done to Cantor was different than what she'd done to Nancy. I'm not saying that what she had done to Nancy wasn't cruel. It *was* cruel, and hurtful and largely pointless to my way of thinking. But I imagine that many of the people who viewed the posts about Nancy came away feeling some level of mixed feelings for her. Maybe a measure of empathy, possibly sympathy, even admiration for recreating herself. After having some time to digest the content and tenor of the posts about her mother, I think it was Siobhan, not Nancy, who came off as the ogre. That wouldn't be the case with Julian Cantor. No one was going to be feeling sorry for him except Alexandra, and I'm not sure even that was a lock.

I rapped my knuckles on the front door. It took a moment for someone to answer and that someone was Vincent "P EYE 7" Brock. He looked mighty unhappy. No doubt Cantor had made Vincent's life a misery since last night's Hollow Girl post. Men like Cantor needed whipping boys. I'd recognized that in him the minute we'd met. As Vincent had now discovered, being the teacher's pet didn't make you bulletproof. It didn't protect you from people like Cantor. I had known many ambitious men in my life and, while they weren't all the same, they shared certain common traits. For them, loyalty was a two-way street only to a point. They expected you to stand by them straight down the line. Their obligation to you, on the other hand, was situational and subject to change. Loyalty for them was a calculation, not a commitment.

"I wouldn't wanna trade places with you today," I said to Vincent, stepping inside the house. "Your boss must be a real pleasure to be around."

We stepped into the great room.

"Yeah, Prager, a real joy. Think Hitler's last days in the bunker."

"That bad?"

"Worse. He's been fielding some pretty nasty phone calls from all sides—angry husbands, POed ex-mistresses, and his law partners."

"Where's the wife?"

Brock looked at his watch. "Probably halfway to Sydney by now. After last night, the boss thought it would be a good idea for everybody if Mrs. Cantor got far out of Dodge until things settled down some."

"Yesterday couldn't have been too much fun around here either."

"It didn't help that you were nowhere to be found."

"Look, Vincent, I understand you're under a lot of pressure, but try to remember that I don't work for Cantor. You called me an asshole this morning. Okay, I get that. I get that he's giving you all the shit you can handle, but don't push me."

But Vincent had had enough and push me is exactly what he did. He clapped his right hand on my left shoulder and shoved. "Listen, you old prick. You may think you're smarter than the average bear and that I can't . . . what was it you said this morning, that I couldn't find my own dick in the dark?"

"Something like that, yeah."

"Well, if you say another word to me, I'll put my hands around your scrawny-assed old neck and snap it like a chicken bone."

"Get your hand off me, Vincent. Get it off me right now," I said, cool as could be. I wasn't the one spoiling for a fight.

"And what if I don't?"

I guess I could have just answered him. Instead, I decided that showing was better than telling. I clasped my right hand on his wrist to lock it in place, swung my left arm over his right, and stepped forward. When he tumbled to the floor, I locked up his thumb so that he was on his knees in front of me. His face turned a bright red and spit flew out of his mouth as he cursed in pain. I reached under my jacket, grabbed my .38, and pressed the muzzle to the tip of Vincent's nose.

"Now, I've been threatened enough for one day. You call me old, or insult me or threaten me again, and I'll snap your thumb off your fucking hand. You understand me?"

He hissed something through his clenched teeth that sounded a lot like, "Fuck you!"

That was when I clicked back the hammer on the .38. If nothing else I'd said or done had gotten Vincent's attention, that sure did. He got the shakes bad. His eyes grew big and scared.

"Okay, okay, okay. I get it," he said.

"What the fuck is this?" Cantor screamed as he came stomping into the great room, his eyes pouched and puffy, face creased with stress.

I pointed the gun away from Vincent and let his thumb go before he pissed his pants or worse. He fell back, grabbing his hand and wrist, trying to rub out the pain. I uncocked the .38 and holstered it.

"You didn't answer me, Prager," Cantor shouted again.

"Look, Mr. Cantor, I'll tell you what I told Vincent here before he decided he was gonna act like a tough guy and threaten a card-carrying member of AARP. I don't work for you. I don't even technically work for your ex anymore, either," I said, pulling a check out of my inside jacket pocket. "This is a refund of most of her retainer. I'm here out of courtesy, and because I'm worried."

"Worried about what?" he asked.

"Not about you or your reputation, if that's what you're thinking. Like I explained to Vincent this morning, this thing with Rizzo . . . I don't like it. The whole way here I tried to talk myself into believing that there's no connection between what your daughter's doing and Rizzo getting murdered."

Cantor snickered. "And how did that work for you?"

"It didn't."

"Maybe you needed a good lawyer to argue the case."

"Do you know one?" I said.

"Very funny, Prager, but—"

"Like I said, Mr. Cantor, I'm here as a courtesy. I think there's some stuff I know about Rizzo and your daughter that maybe you and Vincent need to hear."

"Such as?"

"Yeah, like what?" Vincent echoed his boss.

"It's not pretty. I think maybe you'll want a drink to help wash it down."

"Maybe I do." The lawyer nodded. "You want one?"

"No, thanks," I said. "I'm good."

"Vincent, go pour me a bourbon and get back in here."

But Vincent stayed down on the floor. He didn't seem so keen on getting ordered around like a houseboy in a '30s black-and-white movie.

"Did Prager break your legs when he wounded your pride?" Cantor barked.

Vincent looked about ready to blow again, but held it together this time. I think maybe he realized making payments on his fancy BMW wouldn't be quite so easy without a job. He stood up, glared at me as he walked past, then turned to his boss. "On the rocks?"

"Neat," Cantor said dismissively, then waved at the sofa. "Sit, Prager. Sit."

I sat. As Vincent left to get his master's drink, the phone rang. Cantor didn't move.

"Aren't you going to get that?" I asked.

He raised his voice to be heard over the ringing. "I've been doing that all day long, answering the fucking phone. I've had a bellyful of phony, indignant bitching and whining, thank you very much. The husbands are the worst, so fucking hypocritical. I know most of them are banging women at the office or waitresses at the club. They're all rubbing their hands together because they think they can use me as their get-out-of-marriage-free card. But all they've got is my daughter's angry rantings and a bunch of photographs. I mean, for chrissakes, there are a million disclaimers before and after her posts about the shit Sloane says just being performance art."

"Doesn't mean she's lying," I reminded him.

He snickered again. "Well, good thing you need more than that in court."

That's when Vincent came back into the room, handing a tall pour of bourbon to Julian Cantor. I smiled, wondering if Brock had spit in his boss's drink. What's the old restaurant rule? *Never piss off the waiter before he serves the food.* Cantor either didn't have similar reservations or didn't care. He gunned down the Kentucky honey in a gulp.

"Okay, Prager, now tell me."

He was a man who enjoyed giving orders and the more he gave the more I wanted to get this over with and get going.

"Your daughter had an arrangement with Rizzo. She used to pay him two hundred bucks a throw to service her. His words, not mine. He told me this was going on for about a year, and that they had averaged about one encounter a month. When Millie McCumber came back into the picture, the frequency increased.

Your daughter would pay him to be the third, and sometimes there was a fourth involved, an agent named Giorgio Brahms."

The expression that flashed across Cantor's weary face was difficult to describe. It was a jumble of disappointment, defeat, disgust, but largely guilt. I knew that look. I'd seen it in the mirror a lot over the last few months. It seemed as if hearing about the arrangement between the doorman and his daughter wasn't so much a surprise to Cantor as a confirmation of his worst fears. I could almost hear him thinking: *What else could I have expected from my daughter? I have no moral compass, so how could she?* The look on Vincent Brock's face was much less complicated, much easier to read. He was angry and jealous.

"Get the fuck outta here!" Brock screamed in spite of himself. "She wouldn't have anything to do with that piece of shit."

Cantor jerked his head around toward his investigator, apparently taken aback by the vehemence of Brock's reaction. Maybe he was a little upset with himself for not coming to his daughter's defense, or maybe he understood what Vincent's reaction might have meant. Or maybe he was just surprised to see Vincent grow a pair of balls before his eyes.

"I'm only telling you what Rizzo told me," I said. "The guy was an obnoxious, conceited prick and I bet there wasn't much he wouldn't have done for a few hundred bucks. It's easy enough to confirm with bank records. Believe me, I know Rizzo was a total skell, but he also had no reason to bullshit me."

"He had the best reason: money." Vincent jumped to the defense again.

"What about it? Just because the guy took money from me doesn't mean he was lying and you know it, Brock. This is one area of the business you know as well as me, maybe better. You depose people in personal injury cases all the time. You know the sound of bullshit when you hear it. Plus he gave me info, like about this Giorgio guy, that didn't exactly make him look good, and it checked out. I'm not saying that Rizzo wouldn't've lied if there was money in it for him. What I'm saying is that just because he was a scumbag didn't mean everything he said was crap."

Now Cantor, whose eyes had turned inward for a moment, rejoined the fray. "Let us suppose that what you're saying is true, Prager, that this piece of shit Rizzo was involved with my girl. Why do you think there's a connection between his murder and what's going on with Sloane?"

"I don't know that there is for sure. There's just a lot of little things. Too many incidents, too much coincidence. First your daughter falls off the radar screen for a month so that your ex comes to me. I find Millie dead in Siobhan's apartment. Two days later, her apartment is trashed and it's trashed in a silly, theatrical way. When does it happen? The trashing takes place conveniently between the time the cops take down the crime scene notice and when I show up. Rizzo walks away from the Kremlin before I get back downstairs from Siobhan's apartment. Then that night, voilà, the Hollow Girl reappears after a fourteen-year hiatus. A few days later Rizzo turns up in the trunk of his car on Long Island with his head caved in. I just have a feeling, is all. Call it instinct."

"I call it bullshit," Vincent was shouting again. "I don't know what this guy is up to, Mr. Cantor, but—"

"Hear the man out, Vincent," Cantor said. "There's no harm in that."

"There's only one more thing I have to say and then I'll be out of your hair for good. Why hasn't anyone heard from Siobhan? I don't mean the posts from the Hollow Girl. I mean a phone call, an e-mail, a text, something."

Vincent answered, "Because she knows how hurt and angry her parents will be at what she's doing."

Cantor agreed. "He makes a good point, Prager."

"Maybe. If not you or Nancy, why hasn't she gotten in touch with her friends, or you, Vincent?"

Vincent had an answer for that, too. "Maybe she has been in touch with her friends and we just don't know about it."

"Maybe," I conceded. "I don't know her friends, but you guys do. Do some checking and see what you find."

The lawyer waved his empty glass at Vincent. "Another. Prager, you sure you don't want—"

"No, thanks."

Vincent grabbed the empty glass and headed for the study. When he was out of earshot, Cantor whispered, "Look, Prager, I know that Vincent and my daughter have been . . . together. I'm not certain that he is aware that I am aware. I've been okay with it as long as I felt it made Sloane happy. Do you think that Vincent is in any way mixed up in this? That is, if there is a *this*."

"Like I said, I'm not sure there is anything here more than a hunch. Besides, Vincent is clearly in love with your daughter. I don't think he'd do anything to hurt her or risk his job. So the short answer is no."

"Prager, have you discussed any of this with Nancy?"

"Not yet, no. I'm not sure I will, at least not as starkly as I have with you and Vincent."

Cantor snickered that increasingly annoying snicker of his. Suddenly, the puffy eyes and the stress lines seemed to vanish from his face completely. He smiled as if he was a cat that had just eaten a sizeable and most delicious canary. "I knew it. You've fucked her. I told you she'd fuck you, didn't I? That's one more thing she can mark off on her checklist."

I wasn't sure whether to kick him in the groin or to congratulate him on his powers of prediction. Vincent prevented me from having to make the choice by coming back into the room, bourbon in hand. As he did, the phone rang again. Cantor was too preoccupied with the glory of being right to notice that Vincent had grabbed the receiver.

"Hello, Cantor resi—" Vincent's face went blank as he listened, then he, too, was smiling. "Sorry, Nancy, I think he must have been on another call. What's that? That's great news. Great news! Yeah, I'll tell him. Okay, Nancy, it was good to speak to you, too." He put the receiver back in its cradle.

Everybody was smiling except me and I was beginning to feel left out.

"What was that about?" Cantor asked.

"It was about the genius detective here getting his instincts and hunches and having them shoved up his ass. That was your ex. She just heard from your daughter and she's fine."

Now I was smiling, too, sort of. Unlike Cantor and his ersatz son-in-law, I would need some more details before I broke out the party balloons and confetti. When I excused myself and left the house, I'm not sure either one of them noticed or cared. Not that I blamed them.

CHAPTER THIRTY-ONE

My heart beat pretty hard at the sight of Nancy, and I was glad of it. She really was something to look at and when she came close to me, the smell of her raw, crushed herb perfume—which, I'd discovered, was a perfect match to her natural scent and taste— was intoxicating. And when she dispensed with a formal greeting, placing her hands on my cheeks and pulling my lips toward hers, I surrendered to the moment. We kissed there in front of her house for five minutes, maybe more, and when we were done, she was cradled in my arms. She felt good there, pressed against me. Still, I wasn't prepared to take a knee and declare everlasting love. I was just relieved to not feel a kind of awkward dread at seeing her again. With Nancy and me, there was so much baggage. Circumstance had let us postpone dealing with it for a little while, but that delay was probably at an end. She took me by the hand and led me into the house. She didn't let go of my hand until we fell into bed together.

I must have fallen asleep because when I woke up, the room was dark. This time, Nancy was still there with me. We weren't tangled together, but I could see her naked back, hear her breathing. I reached out, pulled her close, wrapping my arms around her. She made sleepy, satisfied sounds. It was still an odd thing, being close to her like this. For a brief moment I wondered what it was like for her, then got that out of my head. I'd learned a long time ago not to go there.

"Sorry I fell asleep," I whispered. "I've had a long day with lots of driving."

She spun around and reached her fingers up to my lips to shush me. "Don't worry about it. You did your manly duties well enough," she said with a hint of a laugh, her voice raspy and thick from sleep. "And you seem to have tired me out as well. I don't want to talk anymore." She kissed my neck.

I stopped her and gently forced her to look up at me. "We need to talk."

"Don't ruin it, Moe, please. I don't want to talk about why we're here. Isn't it enough that it's so good?"

"Not about that. Not about us."

I felt her tense in my arms. "Then what?"

"I was at Julian's when you called about Siobhan."

"So? I gave you permission to—"

"I know, but it wasn't strictly ethical, me going to him first with my concerns about your daughter."

"God, please, I've had enough of Sloane for now. Can you please just kiss me?"

I obliged her and myself, and we forgot all about the Hollow Girl.

Afterwards, we showered. I went down to the kitchen to cook omelets while Nancy did herself up for presentation. I didn't know that I would ever get used to her need to show herself to me only as her perfectly made-up self. I didn't know that I would have the chance, or if I wanted the chance. I only knew that it felt good to breathe again and to feel I wasn't living a guilty betrayal. I was determined to do a very rare thing for me, to take things as they came with Nancy.

Barefooted and wrapped in white terry cloth, she made her entrance into the kitchen. We didn't talk. She sat at the black soapstone island and watched me make asparagus, red pepper, and cheddar omelets. I served them with a bottle of Pinot Noir I found in her wine rack.

"This is great," she said, taking a big forkful.

"The trick is to keep moving the pan while you're making the omelet. It cooks the eggs through without browning them or making them hard."

"Ummm. A man who can fuck and cook."

I didn't go anywhere near that line. "I left a check for most of the retainer by your other papers."

"That wasn't necessary."

"It's absolutely necessary."

She stopped eating and put her hand on mine. "Moe, I know I was the one who didn't want to talk about this, but now I feel like I have to. Do you feel it's wrong?"

"What's wrong?"

"Us. This. Being here together. Please don't be mad at me for saying this, but Pam is only dead a few months. Are you going to get all guilty and—"

"I don't know what's going to happen two minutes from now, so I can't answer about that. But what I can say is that Pam would want me to be happy. A year and a half ago, I was pretty close to dead, and that taught me a few lessons. Life is too short and then you're dead forever. I've spent way too much of my life keeping score of my sins and keeping secrets. If we can make each other happy, even for a few minutes, we should do it. Now, can we please finish eating?"

She didn't answer, but simply took another bite of her omelet. When we were done eating and after Nancy cleaned up, I finally got around to asking her about the conversation she'd had with her daughter.

"It wasn't a conversation. It was a message. It was on voicemail when I got back from tennis. She just said that she was fine and that she didn't mean to worry me or make me angry. She just needed to get stuff out of her system and behind her. And she promised that it would all make sense soon enough."

Nancy must have seen the look on my face, because her relief morphed into a reflection of my concern. I didn't try to pretend that I was anything less than thrilled that her daughter's "all clear" had come as a phone message and not as a conversation. It was too late to pretend, anyway.

"A message, huh?"

She popped out of her seat, grabbed the house phone, tapped in her message code, and pressed a button on the base unit. "Here. Listen to it."

Nancy had very accurately described what I heard coming out of the speaker. First thing I was encouraged to hear was that it was definitely Siobhan Bracken on the message. She had a resonant, distinctive voice with an accent that still showed faint traces of upscale Long Island. The second thing was that her tone was upbeat and unstressed. The words flowed smoothly, but not too smoothly. She was conversational and she didn't seem to be doing a recitation from a script. I also liked that she sounded genuine in her sentiments. Of course, there were aspects I didn't much care for. I wasn't happy that she hadn't mentioned anything about where she actually was. Nor did I love the fact that she was less than specific about the "stuff" she needed to get out of her system or about how "it" would all make sense soon. But I was willing to let it go for the night and I smiled up at Nancy.

"You must have clicked your tennis shoes together when you got this."

"Pretty much. When this Hollow Girl stuff is sorted out, I want to make things right with her. Having you here makes me think I can do it. I guess that's silly."

"No, making things right with your daughter isn't silly at all. I speak from experience. It's almost ten," I said. "Do you wan—"

"No. Not tonight. All I want to do tonight is to go upstairs and put my head against your chest."

"Sounds like a plan."

An hour later, she was asleep and curled up on the other side of the bed. Me, I was setting the alarm clock on my phone for 5:45 and worrying about the things Siobhan Bracken hadn't said.

CHAPTER THIRTY-TWO

Barb and Rob's Pantry was a local institution. Aaron and I used to interview our applicants there as it was only about five minutes away from Red, White, and You. It was only ten minutes away from Nancy's house. They did breakfast right. If you liked New York–style breakfast, with bagels and bialys, they had those brought in fresh from the city every morning. If you liked your breakfast Southern style, they actually did grits and biscuits with gravy. Rob used to say he was from the South . . . the South Bronx. Barb was a Southerner, too—from the South Side of Chicago. And it goes without saying that they did eggs, bacon, hash, sausage, ham, pancakes, waffles, et al. quite well.

Detective Bursaw was already seated at a two-top, drinking a cup of coffee, when I walked in. It took me a few minutes to get to his table because both Barb and Rob made it a point to harangue me for not having darkened their door in a very long time. They didn't seem to care that I hadn't worked out of Red, White, and You for many, many years. They weren't interested in excuses, just hugs, handshakes, and chop-busting.

Bursaw was a tall man with thinning hair, wire-rim glasses, a disarming smile, and too much Old Spice for so early in the morning. He stood to greet me, giving my hand the death grip and patting my left bicep like an old friend.

"Mystery Mike, how you doin'?"

He let go of my hand and said, "I stopped calling myself that when I gave up alcohol. Man, that stuff used to make me think I was Superman. Only in my own head, though, only in my own head. These days I'm just Mike."

"Just Mike it is."

We sat. Barb came over and took our orders. Bursaw and I made some small talk about family and the job. Then we got to business.

"You know, Moe, this isn't my case, but if you think you've got something that will help the department . . . ."

"I'm not sure I've got anything solid. In fact, I know I don't."

"Then what do you have?"

"A bad feeling."

He laughed. "Shit, if bad feelings made you powerful, I'd rule the world."

"A hunch, then."

"Now you're talking," he said. "Your hunches worked out good for that Bluntstone kid and my partner. So, tell me."

I had the presentation pretty well prepared before I got out of Nancy's bed that morning. When I gave it voice, however, it didn't sound quite as convincing as it had in my head. But it didn't sound ridiculous either. I laid out the history of the Hollow Girl and my history with her mother. I explained about why Nancy had come to me, explained the various connections between Siobhan and Rizzo, between them and the late Millicent McCumber. I explained about the trashed apartment, and my less than amicable relationship with Frovarp and Shulze. I confessed that my suspicion, linking Siobhan's disappearance and the subsequent reappearance as the Hollow Girl to Anthony Rizzo's homicide, was somewhere between tenuous and amorphous.

He took it all in, straight-faced and quiet. When I was done, he rubbed his cheek with his right hand, weighing his options. He took his hand away from his cheek, reached under his chair, and came up with an unmarked folder. He placed it on the table and slid it across to me. "Have a look."

Vincent Brock must have had his own good sources inside the Nassau County PD because his description of the late Anthony Rizzo's head as looking like a grapefruit dropped off the Empire State Building was spot on. The human skull can withstand a lot of force, but once it cracks . . . . Although the photos before me showed me a body I knew to be Anthony Rizzo's, his face and head had been remade into something only Picasso's mother could have loved. I didn't envy the mortician who had to try to piece the doorman's head back together.

"Jesus, Mike, talk about a candidate for a closed coffin . . . somebody was really angry at this guy here," I said. "This wasn't one mistaken blow with a blunt object. Whoever killed him had rage in him, a lot of rage."

"No shit," Bursaw agreed. "Looks like the Yankees took batting practice on him."

"Well, he *was* from the Bronx."

Bursaw was laughing again. "If it had been the Mets, he probably would've walked away without a scratch."

Now it was my turn to laugh. "Spoken like a true Mets fan."

"Penance for my past drinking."

"God just doesn't like me. He made me a Jets, Mets, Knicks, and Rangers fan so he could enjoy my pain."

Cop humor, you gotta love it. Here we were looking at photos of a man's head so crushed that it was barely recognizable as human, yet we were laughing. When you get on the job, you either adopt laughter as a defense mechanism, or you get off the job. And once you learn it, the reflex never leaves you. I put the photos away before Barb served breakfast.

"There's not much blood in the trunk, so he must've been killed outside the car," I said.

"He was. There was splatter on the rear fender and trunk, but none on the ground around where the uniforms came upon the car."

"So Rizzo was killed elsewhere, dumped in the trunk, and moved. Means the killer had an accomplice or felt comfortable enough to walk back to wherever."

"Shit, Prager, you almost sound like you know what you're doing."

"Don't be fooled. Did you find his cell phone on him?"

"Everything but: wallet, jewelry, some coke. No phone."

"Maybe the killer thought Rizzo wasn't dead enough, or that someone would think to track him down by GPS."

"Fair assumption. We'll get the phone records anyway."

I took out my cell phone, a pen, and wrote some stuff down on a napkin for Bursaw. "That's the cell number I had for Rizzo. That other number and address is for a guy named Giorgio Brahms. I doubt he had anything to do with the murder, but he was intimate with all the actors in this little passion play."

Bursaw raised his eyebrows at that. "Intimate?"

"Yeah, Anthony Rizzo would do just about anything for a few bucks and he was a vain bastard. He enjoyed being wanted, from what I could tell, anyway. And he was a kid from the boroughs. You know how it is. He was impressed by people with brains and taste. So, Mike, not for nothing, but why are you being generous with a case file that's not yours to be generous with?"

"Honestly, Moe?"

"Probably a good idea to tell me the truth."

"I dug some deep holes for myself with my drinking and got jammed up a few times too many. I'm just sort of hanging onto my shield by the skin of my ass. I could use a little magic to pull my bee-hind out of the fire."

"Hey, enlightened self-interest makes the world go around. But let's be clear on this, my self-interest is important here, too. So I will share with you as long as you share with me. I get something about Rizzo, you're gonna hear it. You hear anything about the case, anything, I wanna hear about it."

He put his hand out to me. "Sounds fair."

We got done handshaking just as Barbara showed up with breakfast.

After he'd taken a few bites of his omelet, he asked me the question I knew was on his mind. It was on my mind, too.

"Moe, I gotta ask. Do you think this Siobhan Bracken coulda been angry enough with Rizzo to have done that to him? She calls him up to meet her. She catches him with one swing of an aluminum baseball bat and he's down and helpless. Then when he's down she beats his brains out."

"I don't know her. My instinct is no, but that's based more on hope than anything else. I only knew about their relationship from him. When it comes to sex and money, anything is possible."

"You know if the detectives don't come up with anything soon, I'm gonna have to—"

"I know, Mike, you'll have to point them toward Siobhan. Just do me a favor, give it a few days before you go that route, okay? Try letting the catching detective get there on his own, if you can. Besides, I have no clue where she is. I swear."

He looked skeptical, but promised to give it a few days as I asked.

Detective Bursaw left first. I stayed, savoring my bialy, slowly sipping at my third cup of coffee. I loved Barb and Rob's. Truthfully, though, I wasn't exactly anxious to rush to my next appointment.

CHAPTER THIRTY-THREE

Aaron eyed me suspiciously as I walked into the small office in the back of Red, White, and You. I didn't blame him given our last encounter, but it pissed me off just the same. I would never get used to my big brother's judgmental nature. My whole life, I'd felt like Aaron had a red pencil and a report card with my name on it in his pocket. He always made me feel as if I was only as good as my last fuck-up. Just lately, I had to admit, I'd pretty much earned that red F Aaron seemed determined to someday give me. I hadn't spoken to him since the morning this all began, when he let himself into my condo and shook me out of my drunken stupor.

"You look clear-eyed and sober. You look good," he said from his seat behind the desk. But he quickly followed it up with, "Did you close the front door behind you?"

"Shit, Aaron, I used to run this store." I sat in a folding chair opposite him. "I've been your partner going on thirty-five years. I'd think you would trust me to shut the front door before store hours."

"These days, I don't trust you to do much of anything except get shitfaced."

"I guess I deserved that."

"I guess you did." He was only too happy to agree, but he didn't go for the red pencil. "So, you're here, I'm here. Now what?"

"You were right last week. I hated it, but you were right. What you said about you being the responsible one. You *were* the one who did the right thing, the responsible thing. If it wasn't for you, I don't know what would've become of me after I hurt my knee."

Aaron's face turned from his defensive smugness to worry. "You're sick again. You made yourself sick again with the drinking."

"You're worried about me."

"Of course I'm worried about you. You're my little brother. It's my job to worry about you."

I shook my head at him. "No, shithead. That stopped being your job a long time ago. But you don't need to worry. I'm not sick, and I'm not drinking the way I was."

"Then what?"

"I'm done with this, with the stores. You were right about that, too, Aaron. I came to appreciate the wine itself, even came to love it, but I have never liked the business."

He was crestfallen, slumping down in his chair. "Not any of it."

"The business part, no, big brother, not any of it. But being around you, seeing you shine and be such a big success, that made it worth it. Hanging around with Klaus and Kosta and all the people who we gave jobs to. And I never would've met John Lennon, or all the other famous and not-so-famous customers who came through our doors. I liked the money well enough, and I have you to thank for that. Dad would've been so proud of you."

"Us! Dad would've been proud of us, Moe."

"Okay. Us." I smiled at my brother. "You know, I think I'm a little offended that you haven't tried to talk me out of it. You didn't say, 'We can't do it without you.' Or, 'What am I gonna do without you?'"

"Well, little brother, we've kind of done it without you for the last few months."

"I know that, you prick, but you're not supposed to say it."

Aaron stood up from his desk and gave me a big hug. When we both let go, I saw that he was crying. I didn't say anything about the tears for fear it would get me going, too.

He sat back down behind the desk. "So, what are you gonna do, move down to Boca and investigate the thefts of scooters, canes, and hearing aids?"

"Was that an attempt at humor from my big brother?"

"Fuck you, Moe."

"No, I'm thinking of maybe moving up to Vermont to be close to the kids. I'd live in Pam's house so that I wouldn't be underfoot."

"You sure about that?"

"No, but I'm gonna do it anyway. I had my stint as a PI with Carm, and I'm getting too old for that stuff anyway. Besides, I've wasted too much time in my life already. I wish I'd realized sooner that we don't have any to waste, not even a minute."

"How do you want to handle things, business-wise? Do you want me to buy you out?"

"I trust you, Aaron. I always have. You're an honorable man. However you wanna do it is good with me."

"You sure about that, little brother?"

"I've never been more sure of anything in my life," I said, turning to go. "I'll call you in a few days and you can tell me what you've figured out."

Then I walked out of the office, out of that store, and didn't look back.

CHAPTER THIRTY-FOUR

That Sunday evening at 10:00 P.M., the world wobbled on its axis. Yet in the intervening days between the time I left Aaron sitting at the desk and 9:59 P.M. on Sunday, life had kind of settled into a nice rhythm with few hints of what might be coming. I'd taken Nancy out to dinner and a play—*The Book of Mormon*—in the city. We'd established that we got along better than fine in the bedroom, but we needed to find out if there was something more between us than sex and a long history of yearning. We needed to expose our relationship to the open air and to the light. Things were less smooth and easy for us out in public, though by the time the play let out the discomfort seemed to have faded away with the laughter. We went for a drink and then back to my condo.

My guilt and Pam's lingering presence there made things a bit awkward. Sensing the problem, Nancy took a photo off the wall and asked me to tell her about Pam. Talking about Pam, telling Nancy about how Pam and I had met, about how we'd grown into love, about how she'd willed me to survive, didn't quite exorcise her ghost. I don't suppose I really wanted it to be exorcised, not completely. Somehow, Nancy had the trick of helping to bring Pam back to me, not of pushing her away. If nothing else came of us, I would be grateful for that.

When I drove Nancy home the following morning, there was another voicemail message from Siobhan. It was similar to the first one, sweet and reassuring. *Everything was fine. Everything would be revealed. Everything would be explained.* In fact, there were messages like it every day including Sunday. They made Nancy happy. Apparently these voicemails were the most civil and kind words her daughter had spoken to her in many years. Even the Hollow Girl's posts had taken a sharp turn away from parent-bashing territory. She had instead taken aim at casting directors and the cruelty of life in theater, film, and television. The savagery of these posts made her stuff about her parents seem almost like puff pieces. Her audience ate it up. Her numbers appeared to be growing exponentially, surpassing her original Hollow Girl audience by a hundred thousand.

Aaron had wasted no time in setting up appointments for us with our lawyer and accountant. To an outsider it might have looked like he couldn't shed me as a partner fast enough. That wasn't it at all. He knew that once I'd decided to get out I wasn't going to change my mind about the business. He was shocked I'd lasted as long as I had. I'd also heard back from Jean Jacques Fuqua. According to him, there were no rumors or whispers around the 9th Precinct indicating that Detectives Frovarp and Shulze were up to anything suspicious. Their particular distaste for me seemed to simply be a matter of bad chemistry: They were both malevolent pricks and I just got under their skins.

I got a few calls from Mike Bursaw. Every time I hung up with him, I got a familiar knot in my gut or, as my bubbeh—my Yiddish-speaking grandmother—might have said, in my *kishkas*. Over the years I had come to think of that knot in my *kishkas* as the physical manifestation of my mother's pervasive, cloying pessimism. I hated to admit it, but that knot had saved lives, my own and others, on more than once occasion. I'd found that to ignore it was to do so at my own peril. Problem this time around was that the knot wasn't linked to anything concrete, nothing specific. In fact, most of what Bursaw had to say was encouraging.

"Yeah, Moe, the detectives working the case are looking at these two mobbed-up Russian brothers from the Bronx who deal 'roids to juicers at gyms all over the city. Seems like Rizzo used to do some distributing for them and they had a falling out. Someone must've tipped the Russians off because the comrade brothers have split to parts unknown. So it doesn't look like I'm gonna need to go to them about Siobhan," he said, his voice tinged with disappointment.

I didn't hold his disappointment against him. "I'm glad for that, but it's too bad I couldn't help you out on this. I guess my hunches failed you this time. Sorry about that."

"Hey, what can you do? Maybe next time." His voice trailed off.

"Yeah, Mike, next time."

But even as I said "next time" to Bursaw, I knew that this time wasn't over yet. That knot in my gut was tightening. I should have been happy about where things were. I just wasn't. When I thought about it, I realized Siobhan's messages bothered me. They bothered me a lot. Somehow she never managed to catch Nancy at home. To me it felt like Siobhan knew when her mother would be out so she might slyly avoid having a real conversation with Nancy. Then there was the similarity between the messages. They were sweet and hopeful, but there was very little actual substance to them. Siobhan didn't say where she was, or why she was doing what she was doing, or why she had gone about doing it the way she had. She always promised answers were coming without supplying any. And lastly, she never left a call-back number or indicated that she'd like Nancy to call back.

On Thursday, I'd asked Nancy why she hadn't tried to return any of her daughter's calls.

"Please, Moe, I'm done pushing her. This is the most respect and conviviality Sloane has shown me in ten years. Why would I want to mess it up? For this one time, I'm going to let her come halfway home to me. When she gets there, I'll go the other half."

Although I understood her reluctance to rock the boat, I found myself wishing she would have displayed more of the impatient, demanding, narcissistic Nancy I'd encountered back in 2000. That Nancy would have been a bulldog. She would have been pushing for answers.

I guess the other thing that tightened the knot was the incredible emphasis on the disclaimers both before and following the Hollow Girl's posts. I knew it was a craziness, but I couldn't help feeling that the posts themselves seemed more like vehicles for the disclaimers than the other way around. It was like all disclaimers all the time. They appeared to be preparing viewers, inuring us. In spite of the pleasant rhythm of the days, that knot in my *kishkas* got to feeling Shakespearean. Something wicked this way was coming. I just didn't know what.

CHAPTER THIRTY-FIVE

At 10:00 P.M. the form of the current evil revealed itself to Nancy and me, and to the several hundred thousand viewers who watched the Hollow Girl's Sunday post. I have little doubt many of them gasped in horror the way Nancy Lustig had, but only Nancy was the Hollow Girl's mother.

Siobhan, naked as far as I could tell, had her back to a steel lally column. She was tied to the column with heavy, straw-colored rope, wound tightly from her ankles, her legs, her body, her arms, to her neck. She was bound so tightly that it seemed she could barely breathe, let alone wriggle. The rope was coarse and bit hard into her skin, so hard that it appeared to chafe and cut her. Rivulets of something that looked a lot like blood dripped down the rope toward the floor. A piece of gray duct tape was wrapped around her forehead so that it held the back of her head to the steel pole. She had a black leather and orange plastic ball gag in her mouth. Her face looked puffy and there were dark purple bags under her eyes.

As bad as seeing her bound, gagged, and seeming to bleed was, it wasn't the worst of it. The utter stillness of the camera, never panning in or pulling out, the unblinking, unflinching focus of the lens on the Hollow Girl as she wiggled against the ropes was excruciating to watch. Harder to take were the sounds she made:

her gasping for breath, her gurgling, her desperate struggle to speak with the plastic ball pressing against her tongue. If Siobhan's intent had been to create compelling viewing, she'd done it. *Bravo!* But at what cost, I wondered, at what cost?

Propped up against her bare feet and roped shins was a framed photograph, an eight-by-eleven color headshot of a woman or a girl. It might even have been a photograph of the Hollow Girl, but it was difficult to tell. First, because the camera shot of Siobhan was a wide-angle view, and the photo was only one small element in the composition. The second thing that made identifying the person in the photo impossible was the lines of shiny black electrical tape plastered across the subject's face. Across her eyes, her nose, her mouth, her chin, jawline, and forehead. The tape was strung across her face at odd angles, so that it looked like a piece of Warholian art. It almost seemed to be more about the tape than the face of the woman or girl beneath it.

That was it. Fifteen minutes of that one wide shot of the Hollow Girl, bound, gagged, bleeding, a photo at her feet. But it wasn't real. I wasn't much of an artist, my only attempt at art consisting of one high school poem of unrequited love. My previous experience in the art world had taught me little. I admired artists, yet I couldn't begin to understand what made them do the things they did. When I was working to find Sashi Bluntstone, I felt like I was swimming through a sewer pipe. The charisma of the artist and how much patrons and collectors were willing to pay mattered more than the art. The art seemed almost secondary. And now with Siobhan, it was impossible not to wonder what she was trying to say.

My cell phone, Nancy's cell, Nancy's house phone were vibrating and ringing not a minute into the post. Listening to Nancy's "Time of the Season" ring tone made me think she'd picked the wrong Zombies song. "She's Not There" now seemed the more appropriate choice. I kept that thought to myself, as the phones didn't stop ringing until we shut our cells off and took the house phone off the hook.

"Look at the fear in her eyes, Moe?" Nancy repeated over and over again as we stared, transfixed by the image on the screen. "Look at the fear in her eyes."

"Everybody says she's such a good actress: you, her agent, everybody," I said, holding Nancy close to me, stroking her hair.

"I know. I know, but look at her eyes."

She was right and she was wrong. The fear in the Hollow Girl's eyes seemed real enough to me. I had seen real fear in people's eyes up close as a cop and PI, and Siobhan's eyes had the same look, but so too did the eyes of the victims in the B-movies I watched on Netflix when I couldn't sleep. I couldn't tell them apart. I wasn't going to argue the point too hard.

"That lally column she was tied to, did you have one of those in your—"

"Yes, a few. It was an older house," Nancy said, glad I wasn't trying to talk her out of her fears. "I always thought they were ugly."

"Ugly but necessary. Did you recognize the woman in the photograph at Siobhan's feet?"

"It wasn't Sloane. I could tell that. A mother knows that."

"But did you recognize who she is?"

"No. Why, do you think it means something?" Nancy asked, grasping at straws.

"It means something, but I'm not sure what. It might be symbolic, some artistic statement Siobhan's making about appearances or your surgeries. It's hard to know. Or it might mean something very different."

"Different how?"

"If she really is in danger—"

Nancy blurted, "What do you mean, if? Didn't you just see that? Didn't you just see her tied up and bleeding, for chrissakes?"

"The disclaimers, Nancy. You're forgetting the disclaimers and her history and her talent. She knew people would react the way you're reacting . . . well, maybe not quite the way you are, but close to it. Look, I'm going to find her whether she's really in danger or if this is just bullshit. I promise. So don't worry about that."

She kissed me on the cheek. "I don't think you can understand how much better that makes me feel. After we first met, even thinking about you used to make me feel safe. Just knowing you were out in the world somewhere . . . I don't know how to explain it."

I put my finger across her lips. "Then don't try."

"I'm sorry, you were talking about the photograph."

"Right. Like I was saying, if she is in danger, the photo wasn't put there by her. And if it wasn't put there by her, it has meaning to whoever has her."

"Has her! Oh my God, Moe. I—"

"Calm down, calm down. It's my job to think this way, not yours. I'm just thinking out loud. One thing is pretty clear, though. Your daughter isn't alone. The gag she could have put in her mouth herself, but she couldn't have done the rest of it alone. She couldn't have tied herself up like that, certainly not so tightly. She couldn't have placed the photo by her feet after she was tied up. Someone else had to do that. What I have to find out is whether this other person did it for her, or to her."

Nancy reached into the pocket of her jeans, pulled out her phone, and switched it back on.

"What are you doing?"

"Calling the cops," she said.

I stopped her. "Not yet, Nancy. Not yet. Trust me, in spite of the disclaimers, the cops'll be getting plenty of calls tonight. It's just the way people are. They don't read instructions and they ignore warnings. You don't want your voice lost in all of it. You also don't wanna be accused of crying wolf. When we call the cops, we want them to listen."

She put the phone down. I could tell she wasn't happy to do it. If I'd thought Sarah or Ruben were in danger, I wouldn't've been happy to do it either, no matter what was said or who said it. But Nancy had yet to be so overwhelmed by fear that she'd lost touch with her rational self. Then there was hope. Hope was often a person's worst enemy. The persistence of hope, only second to love, caused people to make terrible decisions, or worse, it stopped them from making decisions at all. This time, hope worked in my favor. As long as Nancy clung to even the slightest hope that this really was just some elaborate charade, it stopped her from doing something counterproductive. I laughed at myself because I found I was hoping I was right to stop Nancy from calling the cops. If I was wrong and things turned out badly, I wasn't sure I could withstand another prolonged bout of guilt.

"Pack a bag," I said. "You're coming to stay with me."

"What? No. What if—"

"This place is going to be inundated by the press. The phones won't stop ringing. The paparazzi will be climbing the walls. Satellite news vans will be lined up across 107 and news helicopters will be flying overhead. Believe me, I know how it works. I've seen it destroy people. Do you really want to deal with all that now? You'll be harder to find at my place."

"I'll follow you in my car. I need to be mobile. I don't want to be trapped in Sheepshead Bay if Sloane needs me."

"Okay, as long as we get out of here soon."

A half-hour later I was heading south on Glen Cove Road toward the Long Island Expressway, a red Porsche Cayman trailing close behind.

Newsday
Monday, October 7, 2013
DANGEROUS STUNT REDUX
Media Columnist Linda Brown

Last evening marked another bizarre twist in the tale of the Internet phenomenon known as the Hollow Girl. The fifteen-minute single shot of the semi-naked Hollow Girl bound to a pole with rope, an orange ball gag in her mouth, and covered in fake blood is testament to the extent people desperate to breathe life into flagging careers are willing to go. Given her history of this sort of outrageous stunt, one would have hoped that this now-grown woman would have learned her lesson. But the obviously phony panic in her cynical blue eyes showed only a continuing pattern of condescension and contempt for the viewers who, since her return, have been flocking to watch her posts.

In the waning years of the last century, a lonely, nondescript girl became one of the first Internet stars by posting a video diary that purported to describe her daily adventures as a college freshman. She would remain anonymous and would be known to viewers only as the Lost Girl. The Lost Girl's posts attracted a wide viewership over the span of several months during 1998 and 1999. The postings ranged from the mundane to the salacious. The Lost Girl was just as apt to describe poetry class with a boring professor as she was to detail her abusive relationship with her boyfriend Lionel or her intense sexual attraction to her roommate Victoria.

Only after posting a particularly graphic entry on Valentine's Day 1999 in which the eponymous Lost Girl detailed witnessing a traumatic sexual encounter between the two objects of her desire did the lie begin to unravel. During the now-infamous Valentine's Day post, the Lost Girl, calling herself the Hollow Girl, feigned suicide by overdosing on red wine and pills. The post caused quite an uproar as the "dying" Hollow Girl pleaded for help. 911 call centers, suicide hotlines, and hospitals were inundated by pleas from desperate fans in a panic to save the Hollow Girl's life. Squad cars, ambulances, and emergency personnel were dispatched throughout the country, throughout the world, and several innocent people were injured as a result of traffic mishaps.

The Lost, or, as she would thereafter be known, Hollow Girl, was subsequently revealed to be a precocious high school senior and aspiring actress named Sloane Cantor. She has since legally changed her identity. She had perpetrated the entire hoax—which she claimed was simply performance art—from the basement and bedroom of her parents' lavish home in a very well-to-do Long Island suburb. Although her viewership expanded after the Valentine's Day post and the revelations about her true identity, the Hollow Girl could not survive the threats of criminal action and civil suits that followed in the wake of the "Suicide" posting. She somehow managed to come out the other end of it relatively unscathed, though she left much collateral damage behind her. Not only were people physically injured, but lives and reputations were ruined.

In spite of her past history, the Hollow Girl recently resurrected herself in a somewhat new form. Until last evening's post, I'd found the latest incarnation of the Hollow Girl rather snarky and claustrophobic. Now, regardless of the myriad disclaimers and false sanctimony about performance art, she has done it again. The Suffolk County Police reported a twenty-three percent increase in 911 calls in the aftermath of last night's "S&M" post. Nassau County Police reported a similar increase. This time, at least, no cars were dispatched and no one was injured. Maybe Warhol was correct, and we shall all have fifteen minutes of fame. I hope that if it comes to me it does not come at the cost of fifteen minutes of shame, as displayed by the Hollow Girl last evening. But this must stop. I urge you not to watch, because to watch is to reinforce this kind of behavior, and this kind of behavior will breed copycats. Only your refusal to be part of the performance will close the show. Please, close the show.

BitterArtBitches.com
Monday, October 7, 2013
by Cilla

Last night we bore witness to an ascendancy the likes of which we are not apt to see again in many years. The Hollow Girl officially said Get the fuck outta here to poseurs like PSY, a chubby no-talent who wasted our time and whose only wisdom was Whop. Whop Whop. Whop Whop. I was totally gobsmacked by the Hollow Girl, who changed course from her intensely personal, parent-inflicted self-hating rants to a kind of still life, masochistic Kabuki. Her brilliant fucking use of clichéd symbolism was outstanding. The metal pole as phallus. The rope and tape as the restraints of a male-dominated society still bent on the subjugation of women. The ball gag to shut up those who would fight the power and as a reference to the male preference for women as exclusively sexual objects: silent, pliant, obedient. The fiercely tight rope a sign of male desperation at the sense of loss of control. The blood as the blood of a martyr, as menstrual blood, as blood of the whipped slave. But by far the most intriguing and poignant bit of theater was the detail of the photo at her bound feet. The woman in the photo, her identity, her true nature obscured by strips of black tape. The tape cannot be removed, her nature cannot be revealed until the Hollow Girl herself is freed from the restraints of male dominance. Is the identity of the woman in the photograph of any importance? Maybe not, but I confess to a desperate need to know who she is and to see her face. Some day I hope to kneel before the Hollow Girl and kiss her rope-burned thighs. I am hers.

CHAPTER THIRTY-SIX

The sun hung low in the sky over the eastern jaws of Long Island, a veil of haze cooling its bright orange to a sickly, pale yellow. Here at the western tip of the island, in the other world that was Brooklyn, my breath made white smoke in the crisp morning air. A sad chorus line of freshly fallen leaves cartwheeled past my shoes as I stepped to my car. In the hum of the cars along the Belt Parkway and in the pier-slapping waters of the bay I thought I could hear the faint, unpleasant snarling of winter. But I think I woke up looking for omens.

I'd gotten out of the condo before Nancy got out of bed so I could go down to my car and check the messages on my phone. I'd made a promise to Nancy to find her daughter no matter what. I was apparently untrainable. I should have known not to make promises, that promises were quicksand and swampland. I figured I might find some sign in my messages that would give me a sense of how deep the swamp was into which I was about to wade. I prayed it wasn't much more than shin deep. At my age, with my knees, I didn't even do that well on dry land.

There were a series of increasingly angry and desperate calls from Julian Cantor. The three calls from Vincent Brock were just desperate. Man, the guy really had it bad for Siobhan. I didn't know Siobhan except as the Hollow Girl. I didn't much like her. I was willing to bet she had slept with Vincent to prove a point to her father. Sex as an oblique weapon often seems like such a good idea, though it rarely is. The person you're trying to injure usually walks away untouched and, in the end, it's always the innocents who bear the scars. That was certainly the case here. Cantor had admitted to me that he knew all about Vincent and his daughter. Once Siobhan found out that her father was okay with her bedding his whipping boy, Vincent would be shit out of luck. I almost felt sorry for the poor schmo. I didn't call either Vincent or his boss back. Allaying their fears was low on my list of priorities.

There were other calls, too. One from my daughter Sarah. She had seen the post. Suddenly she didn't sound quite as happy about her dad playing PI again as she had been last Monday when we'd said our so longs. I wasn't happy about having made a promise to Nancy, but I couldn't say that about the rest of it. The soul-numbing, suffocating routine of the wine business had always heightened the pleasure of working a case. That was the corollary to the knot in my gut: the excitement, the stumbling around in the darkness. Not all the money I'd made nor the success I'd achieved as a shopkeeper could touch that. None of it could even touch the shifts I'd spent walking a beat on the boardwalk in the heart of winter, pellets of wind-whipped sleet gnawing at my face, the smell of Nathan's hot dogs beckoning. I remembered that during the worst of the chemo and radiation, when I could barely raise my head to vomit, that I would have given anything to be back there, back on the boardwalk, alone in the sleet.

The other call I got was the one I hadn't expected. It was from Siobhan's agent, the tough old bird, Anna Carey. Her voice made me smile. I liked thinking about her there in her office, drinking and smoking, too old and stubborn to give up her job or bad habits. I used to hate stubbornness in people. Now I found that I admired it. She needed to talk to me, to see me and pronto. I had to call her back. Well, no, I didn't, but since I was going into the city anyway, I'd add her to the list of people I meant to see while I was there.

* * *

I hadn't been to the offices of D&D Security and Investigations, Inc. in many years. Although they now did the security for our New York City and Long Island stores, I hadn't had much need to pay them a visit. D&D was established by two of my former employees at Prager & Melendez Investigations, the firm Carmella and I ran out of 40 Court Street in Brooklyn. When our marriage dissolved the business melted away with it. Brian Doyle—an ex-NYPD detective with great instincts and a bad tendency to take shortcuts—and Devo—Devereaux Okum, a Zen-like high-tech wizard—had set up their own shop in Lower Manhattan near the courthouses and federal buildings.

Doyle was a night owl, but Devo was there when I stepped out of the elevator into their offices. He bowed to me slightly, showing the shiny black skin atop his perfectly shaven head. Although he had put on a few pounds in the years since we'd first met, Devo was still nearly two-dimensional. And when he gestured with his willowy arm toward his office, it was more a tree branch swaying in a gentle breeze.

"Boss," he said, nodding for me to sit in the chair across from him. Neither he nor Doyle had ever gotten out of the habit of calling me "Boss," and I have to say I was honored by it. "What do you wish of me?"

"First, I need to tell you I'm leaving the wine business. The details have yet to be worked out between Aaron and me, but you guys have no need to worry. I'll make sure Aaron keeps you on."

"Are you ill again?"

"It's not that, Devo. It's just my time to go."

"As you say. I will inform Brian. But this is not why you've come today."

"Have you ever heard of the Hollow Girl?"

Devo's eyes, large and hypnotic, grew wide with curiosity. His eyebrows tilted. "I have."

I slid the envelope Nancy had given to me across his desk. "I need deep background on all the people listed there. They are all connected in one way or another to the Hollow Girl."

The corners of his lips curled up in what passed for Devo's broadest smile. "And by deep you mean—"

"Deep." This was our code word for accessing things that weren't strictly kosher to access. "Very deep. Especially those names I highlighted. I also need background on the fallout from the Hollow Girl's 1999 Valentine's Day post where she faked her own suicide. I did some preliminary digging, but only what I could get from a Google search. Did you see last evening's Hollow Girl post?"

"Indeed. Disturbing."

"To her mother, especially."

"I can imagine so."

"But top priority is for you to give the Full Monty to—"

He raised his hand to stop me. "What is a 'Full Monty'?"

Sometimes I swore Devo had been abandoned on earth by a UFO. Maybe they didn't show British movies on his home planet. I was just happy not to have to explain who the Hollow Girl was.

"It means to give it your full treatment. Do your magic," I said. "About the posts themselves, is there anything about the set or the room or anything that gives any indication of where it was shot? Can you see who manufactures the rope? Stuff like that."

"Go on."

"That photograph at the Hollow Girl's feet. I need you to see if you can identify the woman beneath the tape."

"That would truly be magic, Boss. The tape was strategically placed to cover precisely those features that facial recognition software is designed to focus on. The photo was also placed at an angle to the camera, which makes identification more challenging. The camera, at least, was of high quality."

"And, Devo . . . ."

"Yes."

"I need it all like yesterday."

"Do you believe the Hollow Girl is in danger?"

"Remember when you worked for me, those knots I used to get in my *kishkas?*"

"Say no more." He stood up, shooing me out of his office.

There were no goodbyes. That was fine. Devo had work to do.

As I left Devo's office, other employees were filtering in to work, but Brian Doyle's office was still dark. It was comforting to know that some things never changed.

CHAPTER THIRTY-SEVEN

I got the sense that Giorgio Brahms would've been more pleased to see his bookie's legbreaker at the door than me. I was forced to divine his displeasure from the grump in his voice because his Saran Wrap surgery had severely limited his subtlety of expression. Unhappy to see me or not, he was polite enough to let me in. Again, I was surprised by the stark contrast between the Battle of the Bulge condition of the brownstone's exterior, and the nicely furnished and appointed front parlor.

"Coffee?" he asked.

"Sure," I said, following him into the kitchen.

The kitchen was caught between the condition of the parlor and the brownstone's façade. The old plaster and lath construction had been torn off two walls and taken expertly down to the studs. Some new wiring and plumbing had been started but left unfinished.

Giorgio tipped over his French press. "How do you take it?"

"Milk, no sugar."

"Well, there is something we have in common," he said, grumpiness still in his voice.

I didn't take the bait, just the coffee and thanked him. Sipped. I nodded my approval. We sat at the rickety kitchen table.

"So, I suppose I have you to thank for siccing the police on me."

I didn't bother denying it. "I suppose you're right. You had a connection to the guy, Giorgio. I wasn't gonna withhold evidence from the cops for you. You sure as shit wouldn't do it for me. But I did tell the Nassau cops I was pretty sure you had no connection to Anthony's murder."

"Well, I guess I should be grateful for that. Let me kiss your ring," he said, bitchy as could be.

I waved my hands at him. "No rings. Too bad."

"So what are you doing here?"

"Did you see Siobhan's post last night?"

"Pardon me, but no. I have a life. I'm not some prepubescent twelve-year-old girl, sitting by her computer, glued to the fucking Internet. Why do you ask?" As he posed the question, his eyes drifted over to the stripped walls. Unconsciously, he shook his head in a kind of disgust. He had retreated into his own world and mumbled something to himself.

"What?"

"Oh, sorry. I was just thinking aloud."

"Yeah," I said, "I noticed, but what about?"

"Those damned walls. I hate them that way. If I knew how things were going to turn out, I wouldn't have started the work in here."

"Have the work finished."

He turned his left palm up, rubbing his thumb across his other fingers. "You need money to do that and my source . . . forget it. Forget it. So, what do you want to know?"

I asked him some more questions about Siobhan.

No, he hadn't seen Siobhan's posts. No, he didn't know where she was, nor did he care. His involvement with her had been facilitated by Millie McCumber. Yes, he confessed to wishing she had been his client and admitted that he had tried to persuade her to leave Anna Carey for him. But with Millie dead, he had lost interest in Siobhan. The more he talked about Millie, the angrier he seemed to get. He didn't know anything about Anthony Rizzo except that he preferred catching to pitching and that the minute he orgasmed, he had his hand out for money. He didn't know anything about any steroids or mobbed-up Russian brothers. What he did know was that he wanted me to finish my coffee and get out of his house. Even as he made that sentiment known to me, he couldn't take his eyes off the walls.

Back in my car, I called Michael Dillman's office. When Giorgio was talking about his lack of funds to finish the construction, an image of Dillman in his fancy office came into my head. It struck me that when I'd spoken to Dillman the first time, I'd been way too quick to take as gospel his version of events. And I was curious to hear his reaction to the Hollow Girl's latest stunt. Me, I wasn't much of a grudge holder. Grudges were like jealousy: They ate away at the grudge holder, not at the person you held the grudge against. On a TV show once, I heard a character say that jealousy was like you swallowing the poison, but waiting for the other person to die. *A-fuckin'-men!* But I knew I was an exception, that some people, maybe most people, just couldn't let shit go. And as far as justification went, Dillman had plenty of it to continue to carry a grudge against the girl he'd known as Sloane Cantor. He and his family had paid a big price for the simple gesture of letting a friend use a photograph in an art project.

And seeing Brahms looking at his kitchen walls had reminded me that a copious amount of money was a great resource. That someone with a lot of money could afford to buy an expensive camera and recreate the rooms from Sloane's old house. That if someone was holding the Hollow Girl against her will, a vacation home would come in mighty handy. That if you didn't want to use your vacation home, then having the money to rent space would come in even handier. Then when I got the receptionist at Dillman's firm on the line, the knot in my gut tightened so that it nearly strangled me.

"I'm sorry, Mr. Dillman has taken a leave of absence," she said, her voice cold. "May I put you in touch with the person now handling his clients?"

Leave of absence, my ass. I may not have been a player, but I spoke the language. Michael Dillman was out on the street. You had to love Wall Street firms. No one with a title gets fired. That would make the firm look bad. Instead, they take leaves of absence or new positions elsewhere, or they just go walkabout.

"That won't be necessary. May I please speak to Mike's secretary?"

The receptionist did everything but offer me eternal life to try and dissuade me from speaking to Dillman's former secretary. In the end she relented for fear of having to confess that Dillman had been shitcanned or quit. The secretary was more polite than the receptionist, but equally unwilling to discuss the truth of Dillman's departure.

"I'm sorry," I said. "I'm an old friend of Mike's from high school and I've been in London for many years. Do you know, is he at his vacation house?" His secretary's momentary hesitation was answer enough. *Yes.* I pushed. "Do you know, is it the house his dad used to have in East Hampton?"

There was no hesitation this time. "I'm afraid it's against company policy for me to give out personal information, but I would be glad to forward any messages to Mr. Dillman."

"That's okay." I thanked her for her help and clicked off.

Next call was to Devo.

"Among the highlighted names, put Michael Dillman at the top of the list. I need to know if he has a second residence, a vacation house somewhere. I need to know soon, and I need to know where."

"Got it."

Devo was good, the best, but he really wasn't magical. He might call me back in five minutes, or five hours, or five days. It all depended on where the vacation house was, whose name was on the deed, things like that. I decided to keep pushing forward as I had intended until I heard back from Devo. I was no good at just sitting around and waiting. Anything was better than waiting.

* * *

Anna Carey wasn't very good at hiding her emotions. Maybe she had been when she was younger and an actress, but one of the privileges of age is impatience, and she took full advantage of it.

"I thought I told you to call me!" she barked, throwing her lit cigarette at my feet. "You want a drink?"

"Not today, thanks."

"Well, son, fuck you, then." She winked at me and smirked. She poured herself a few fingers of bourbon.

"Okay, I'm here. Now that you've told me to go fuck myself, can you tell me what's so urgent?"

"Learn the lines right, boyo. I said fuck you. I didn't tell you to go fuck yourself."

"Sorry, poetic license."

She let out a shriek of laughter, lit herself another cigarette, and sipped her bourbon. I was helpless to do anything but wait until she deigned to speak again. It was chilly and noisy in her office, due to her window being wide open, and I did a little dance, hopping from foot to foot to keep warm. Then she tossed the cigarette down onto the street and closed the window. She walked over to her desk and picked up five pink message slips.

"You want to know what's so urgent? These!" She waved the slips in my face. "These are just the messages from the five casting directors I was too busy to talk to. She's done it. That ugly broad is a fucking genius."

I took the "ugly broad" as a reference to Siobhan. Even I could do simple math, and I was a licensed private investigator and everything. "What has Siobhan done, and why is she a genius?"

Anna Carey went back to her desk, put the slips down, and picked up three bound documents. She threw them at me. I caught them, though not very gracefully. My knees were for shit, but I always had good hands and reflexes.

"Scripts. Three scripts messengered over this morning alone. They were waiting out front when I got in. Leading roles, Prager. Leading fucking roles. That bit last night with the blood and the ropes did it." Anna grabbed her right breast. "I tried every trick in my book to get that gal a role she deserved and I came up dry as an eighty-year-old—"

"I get the picture. Trust me, I get the picture."

"And so will Siobhan Bracken get a picture, or a Broadway play or a TV series, if you can find her. Now get your ass outta here and find that girl. She's gonna be rich and famous. Me, I'm gonna take my money and pay old Giorgio Brahms to spend a week with me in Cabo. I'll ride that dumb, talentless shit halfway to Texas."

There was an image I could have really done without. I put the scripts down on her desk and left. As I got in my car and headed out to New Jersey, I tried not to think of the perversity of a world in which being bound by ropes and made to bleed was considered a breakout performance.

CHAPTER THIRTY-EIGHT

I'd been in Hallworth before, in the 1980s, and not for any good reason. The last time I'd driven there was with my late friend, the Pulitzer Prize–winning author and journalist, Yancy Whittle Fenn. Wit, as the world knew him, was a rare bird, a mix of Truman Capote, Dominick Dunne, and the devil. Wit had helped me get to the truth of what had happened to Moira Heaton, Steven Brightman's murdered intern. Her murder was in fact rooted in another murder that had taken place decades earlier. In the course of finding Moira's killer, I had solved the earlier crime as well. That last time I'd driven here with Wit, I'd come to reveal the truth of the first murder to the victim's mother. The victim had been just a little boy when he was killed. When I got out of my car and saw the boy's mother raking leaves in front of her house, I stopped, turned around, and drove away because I couldn't bring myself to tell her the truth. I couldn't make her relive it all over again.

I was weak that way, weak in the face of painful truths. I always had been. It had been my experience that truth wasn't the great emancipator, not the great tonic and elixir everyone touted it to be. I'd often found the opposite was the reality, that truth could be toxic, that it sometimes made everything worse. I'd also found that the effects of truth, good or bad, had as much to do with when you told it as the truth itself. I was haunted by some truths I hadn't told soon enough, or not at all. I still had the occasional sleepless night thinking about what would have happened had I had the strength to tell Katy the truth about her brother Patrick's disappearance. The universe might not have changed, but our little world certainly would have.

Hallworth hadn't changed much either in the thirty years since my last visit, nor had it changed much in the nearly sixty years since the first murder. It was the kind of beautiful, wealthy suburb where the good parts of the 1950s seemed frozen in time. The streets were tree lined, the lawns were big and green and beautifully kept. Being house-proud was a virtue, as was being quiet and being civil. The only things that had seemed to change at all were the cars in the driveways. I was fine until I drove past the block where the first victim's mother had lived. I sped up. I didn't stop to see if she was still there.

Valerie Biemann lived at 6 Mystic Street in a lovely Georgian style home. The gates and brick walls surrounding the house were ivy covered, but not overgrown with it. I walked past a white Range Rover in the driveway as I made my way to the front door. I used the knocker. Did anyone knock on doors anymore?

"Coming. I'll be right there," shouted a woman from inside the house. The door opened. "That was quick," she said, pulling a wallet out of her Coach bag. "How much do I—" She stopped when she looked up and noticed I wasn't who I was supposed to be.

Valerie Biemann was a very attractive woman in much the same mold as Nancy had used to remake herself. She had streaked dark blond hair, blue eyes, a button nose, a pursed mouth. She was taller than Nancy, about five ten, and a bit less curvy, but the rest of her, from perfume to simple but expensive clothing, was right out of the Nancy book of design. The thing is, she was more like

Nancy-in-training than Nancy, because Valerie was about twenty-five years her junior. While I recognized her, she had no idea about me except that I wasn't the delivery man.

I handed her a card and said, "I'm here about Sloane Cantor." That did the trick. She read my card, frowned, sighed. "I've been waiting for somebody to find me. It was only a matter of time once Sloane started this nightmare all over again for someone to come have a talk with the infamous Victoria."

"I won't bite, I promise. I'm not interested in spreading the word of your whereabouts. Her mother is concerned, that's all."

"How is Mrs. Cantor? I liked her," Valerie asked, smiling with genuine affection.

"Sloane's parents are divorced."

"That's too bad. I'm sorry to hear that."

"But you're even more sorry about the resurrection of the Hollow Girl."

"I am, Mr. Prager. Dave, my husband, he doesn't know about all that."

"He won't hear about it from me."

"For some reason, I believe you," she said.

"When you're old, Mrs. Biemann, people believe you."

She laughed, told me to call her Valerie, and invited me in. We walked through the house into a solarium. She got me some sparkling water with lime, and she drank water out of a square plastic bottle.

"Have you been to see Mike Dillman yet?" Valerie asked, sitting on a big rattan chair.

"Funny you should mention that."

"*Funny* isn't the word I would use. Sloane really fucked up Mike's life, and it pretty much ended our relationship."

"You and Mike were an item?"

"We were in love, Mr. Prager. You know, that sick to your stomach, top of the world, intense first love. That was us. It wouldn't have lasted. It never does, but it really hurt for it to end the way it did. I think that's what Sloane had in mind. She got my photo the same way she got Mike's. I had no idea what she meant to use it for."

"So you're saying—"

"You know the Hollow Girl's sad adventures didn't just materialize out of her ass. I'm sorry, that was rude. But I find I'm angry all over again. Sloane always had a thing for Mike because of the time they spent in drama club together, and she also had a—" Valerie cleared her throat and squirmed in her chair. "She also had a thing for me."

"Did you return her interest?"

Now Valerie was squirming up a storm. "Yes, a little. Once. I was curious and I thought it was safe with Sloane. She made it pretty obvious that she was attracted to me, so I didn't have to worry about putting the moves on some other girl who might reject me and then tell the whole universe. I guess I got that wrong, huh? Anyway, Sloane may have not been so pretty, but there was something attractive about her. The artist thing, maybe. I don't have an ounce of art in me, but people who do . . . there's just something about them. You know?"

An image of my high school crush, Andrea Cotter, popped into my head. She had been an amazing poet. "I do. So this one time . . . ."

"I invited myself over to her house one night when her folks weren't home." Valerie blushed intense red. "And we had some beers and we went down to her basement and . . . we . . . . It was okay. It really was, all very exciting. Sloane was really, really into it. Me . . . I kinda liked it, but it scratched my itch, you know? I was curious about skydiving, too, but I've also only done that once."

"I understand."

"Well, Sloane didn't. You know how high school girls can get. First, she followed me around all over, kept calling me and e-mailing. Then one time she cornered me and begged me to be with her, just once more. When I said that I'd think about it, she cried, then she got touchy. But by then I was so turned off by her puppy dog act that . . . I guess I was pretty mean to her afterwards. So she turned me into the Hollow Girl's Victoria to punish me. But it didn't screw up my life like it did Mike's. It was the '90s, and no one thought it was freaky for girls to experiment with other girls. But Mike was black, you know. His dad may have been rich and powerful, but Sloane played to some vicious stereotypes. It was cruel of her to do that to Mike. Some stuff just never goes away."

"No, it gets better with time, but there are things that persist. So, have you kept in touch with Mike?"

"Not really. It's just too painful, and I don't want to have to explain that part of my life to Dave. I'll hear about Mike occasionally from some old high school friend."

"Do you think he'd carry the grudge this long? Do you think he'd hurt Sloane?"

That took her aback. "Mike? I mean, it still hurts me, what Sloane did, so I wouldn't be surprised if Mike was unforgiving. That order of protection thing, that really went too far. Would he hurt Sloane now?" She shrugged. "He was angry enough to have strangled her then, but so was I. I'm not sure he'd be up to it now, anyway, with what's going on in his life."

I was confused. "How's that? You just got done telling me that you didn't keep in touch."

"Patrick Millikin, he went to school with all of us and he keeps in touch with Mike. I heard from him just a few days ago."

"What did he say?"

Valerie tensed. For the first time she was having reservations about me. "I thought you said you'd spoken to Mike."

"I did, weeks back, in his office at Hanover Square."

She relaxed. "Oh, I see. Did you know about the divorce?"

"Divorce? No, he didn't mention it." I stopped there.

"It's terrible, a real messy divorce and a custody battle. Patrick said Mike was a basket case and things at work were . . . well, they weren't great."

I finished my sparkling water and thanked Valerie for being so helpful. She wished me well and asked me to please keep our conversation confidential. I vowed that I would. She wished me luck in my search for Sloane.

"I don't think I'll ever be able to forgive her for what she did. It still hurts, Mr. Prager, but I find myself thinking about her sometimes. She could be really empty sometimes, and so attractive at others. Does that make any sense?"

"More and more."

The front doorbell rang as we headed that way.

"There's the dry cleaning guy," she said. "That's who I thought you were when you knocked."

"One more thing, Valerie, and then I'll go."

"Sure."

"Did Mike's family have a vacation home on the island, or in Connecticut?"

"Yes, on the North Fork, in Orient. A big, old white farmhouse. We made good use of it." She blushed again.

"Do you remember the address?"

"I'm not sure I ever knew it, and it was so long ago. All I can remember was that you could see Gardiners Bay or some body of water out the bedroom windows."

I shook her hand and left, the dry cleaner giving me a funny look as I walked past him. Hallworth may have seemed a perfect town, but it wasn't immune from gossip. I was confident that Valerie would survive the whispers about the old guy who'd come out of her house on Monday afternoon. I wondered if she would fare so well if the gossip concerned her high school exploits.

You don't race through a town like Hallworth, but I did. One thing a badge and a PBA card do for you is get you out of tickets. I called Devo as I drove out of town. Conversations with Devo tended not to last very long, and this one involved him saying one word (*Hello*) and me saying seven (*Dillman's father had a house in Orient*). That was it. If I knew Devo, that would be enough information for him to get me the answer I was looking for.

CHAPTER THIRTY-NINE

It was only when I walked into the bedroom and saw her bag was missing that I became concerned about Nancy. I found the note in the bathroom. Made sense, really. When you want a man my age to find something, leave it in the bathroom. Even if he misses it the first time, don't sweat it. He'll be back in less than an hour. When I returned from New Jersey, Nancy's car was gone from the visitor's parking spot in the condo's lot. That didn't necessarily raise any red flags. She'd said that she didn't want to feel trapped in my apartment. I didn't blame her. My condo was spacious enough for me, but I could see how Nancy might find it confining: no pool, no cabana, no sauna, only four rooms. If you included her walk-in closet, Nancy's master suite was probably larger than my entire condo. And it wasn't like she didn't have a lot on her mind. I figured that she went for a drive to clear her head or to get something to eat. Eating, now, that sounded like a good idea. I'd called her cell from the parking lot, but it went straight to voicemail. I asked her to call me back if she was at a restaurant, that I was pretty hungry myself.

Upstairs, it hadn't taken me a minute to discover the note. None of what she'd written surprised me. I can't say that it pleased me. It just didn't surprise. She said that she might have lasted longer had I been around to keep her from climbing the walls. She understood that I was out trying to find Sloane, to do what I'd been hired to do in the first place, but that sitting there alone just gave her too much time to think about things. That she couldn't get last night's post out of her head. She hoped that I wouldn't be too angry with her. That I would understand, she just had to be at home in case Sloane needed her. I understood. I wasn't mad. Who was I to judge her?

I never thought she would last very long at my place, anyway. It was a short-term fix that I expected to last maybe two days at best. I got it wrong by a day and a half. So what? I tried her phone a second time. Straight to voicemail again. I told her I'd gotten her note, that I wasn't mad, that I was coming out to her house, and that I might have a lead. I washed up, threw some clean clothes in a gym bag, grabbed an energy bar, and headed back down to my car. I stopped by a gas station on Knapp Street to fill up and headed back to Long Island with the sun now at my back.

As I drove east, the Belt Parkway moving at a crawl, the events of the day came back to me in flashes. If Siobhan Bracken wasn't doing the Hollow Girl of her own free will and somebody had her, I thought I had a pretty good idea of who that somebody was. Everything pointed to Michael Dillman. He appeared to be the poster model for MMO: Means, Motive, and Opportunity. But strangely, it wasn't Dillman or Anna Carey or Valerie Biemann I couldn't get out of my head. It was Giorgio Brahms. More specifically, it was the disgust he displayed over the open walls in his kitchen. Some people took stuff very personally, and he seemed to be inordinately angry about his unfinished construction. The entire time I was there, he could not take his eyes off those walls. Those walls even had him muttering to himself. Why I should be thinking of that, I couldn't say. It's funny what you think about sometimes. Poor Giorgio was in a tough spot. If he didn't find a source of revenue soon, he might actually have to go to Cabo with Anna Carey.

When I hit Exit 32 on the LIE, my car announced that I had a phone call. I still hadn't gotten used to the whole smart car, smartphone, GPS thing. I recognized the number.

"Hey, Nancy."

"God, it's good to hear your voice. I got your messages. If you're close to my house, forget it. Don't go there. It's not as crazy as you expected, but it's pretty bad. I had to get out of there." Her voice was a tired whisper. "I had one of my girlfriends come over, and I hid in the trunk of her car as she drove out."

"Very sneaky. That's two house escapes in one day."

"I'm sorry about leaving your place like I did, but—"

"I'm teasing. Don't worry about it."

"Moe, there was another message from Sloane waiting when I got back home."

"Let me guess. She said not to worry, that no matter what you saw on the post last night, everything was fine and everything would be explained soon enough."

After a long painful silence from her end, she said, "It's a lie, isn't it, Moe?"

"Maybe. I don't know anything for sure."

"You said something about a lead."

"We'll talk when I see you. Where are you?"

"At Maggie's house in Crocus Valley."

"Gimme the address. I'll be there in a half hour."

Just as she finished giving me the address, my car told me that I had another call. Devo. I got off the phone with Nancy as calmly and as quickly as I could manage.

"The house was, until last week, still in his father's name," Devo said. "Once the deed was amended, the house was immediately put on the market."

"No surprise there. He lost his job and he's just gone through a messy divorce. It's an old story."

"And one too familiar in our business. Now all his recent banking activity makes sense. Mr. Dillman has very little cash in reserve, Boss."

"Listen, Devo, I'm gonna hang up in a minute. When I do, text me all the details you have. I need you to do me another favor. I need you to make a phone call for me." I gave him Nancy's number.

"What should I say to her?"

"As little as possible."

I hung up, pulled off the expressway, and waited for Devo's text to arrive.

CHAPTER FORTY

We were almost there. Bursaw riding up front with me. Vincent Brock in the backseat, nervous as a cat. I didn't begrudge him his anxiety. It had been a long ride to the northernmost tip of the island, a long ride and a dark one. The North Fork of Long Island was the unfashionable, countrified counterpoint to the Hamptons on the South Fork. The forks were separated by only a few miles of bays, sounds, and inlets with quaint names, but might as well have been on different continents.

Orient was a tiny humpbacked wedge of land northeast of Shelter Island that sat out in between Gardiners Bay and where Long Island Sound met the Atlantic Ocean. It was also only a few scant miles from Plum Island, where the government had established an animal disease laboratory in the 1950s to study lovely things like anthrax. The only reason anyone outside of Long Island knew about Plum Island was because Nelson DeMille had written a thriller novel set there and so titled. The island had also gotten a nod in *The Silence of the Lambs*. But the drama we were about to engage in wasn't just words on a page or lines spoken in a movie.

Both Bursaw and Brock had their separate motivations for joining me in what had the potential to be a fool's errand. Bursaw, because he loved the job and was willing to do just about anything to stay on it. Brock's motivation was both more complicated and simpler. He loved Siobhan, and he worked for her father. When he agreed to come, I'd been tempted to talk him out of it by giving him a cold shower of the truth. Siobhan was unlikely to ever return his affection, whether she needed rescuing or not. But like I said, I had a dicey relationship with hard truths. I was also a pragmatic son of a bitch. Sometimes, three guns are better than two. I'd called Bursaw first because I needed a cop's opinion about Dillman. He agreed with me that Dillman was the perfect candidate to go off the deep end and pull a stunt like this.

"I went through a messy divorce, too, Moe. I didn't lose my kids or my job, not yet, anyhow, but trust me, it was *ugh-lee*. My credit got completely fucked. They repoed my car. I had to sell everything I had, including stuff I'd inherited from my dad. I also lost half my friends. There were a few times I almost ate my gun. And when I wasn't trying to get up the balls to kill myself, I wanted revenge. It wasn't even on my ex all the time. It was her lawyer, the judge, my in-laws. Sometimes it was just a guy in the car next to me because I didn't like the way he looked, or a woman texting while she was driving. This guy, Dillman . . . shit! You throw in losing your kids and your job . . . forget about it! Plus, I'm sure he's held a grudge for years. He probably said, fuck it, if I'm going down, I ain't going down alone. I'm taking that Sloane bitch with me."

Even though Bursaw's rant made it pretty clear he was far from over his own divorce, his logic jibed with mine. Dillman was perfect. He got even more perfect when I received Devo's text. It seemed Dillman's house in Orient had undergone an update about a year ago during which the basement had been expanded and refinished. And—this was what sealed the deal—he had purchased an expensive digital camera a few weeks back. I didn't know how Devo got that kind of information. I didn't want to know.

The one decision we'd put off until we got off the LIE for the last substantial leg of the trip—through wine country— was whether or not to call the cops. No knock on the Town of Southhold PD, the department with jurisdictional responsibility for Orient, but neither Detective Bursaw nor I had much faith that such a small department would have a lot of experience in hostage situations. If we had been sure the Suffolk County cops—who we knew were prepared to handle this sort of thing—would be called in immediately, we would have alerted the Southhold PD. But one thing I knew as an ex-cop, and one thing Bursaw knew as an active one, was that cops are as territorial as lions. I wasn't willing to take that gamble with Siobhan's life, whether I cared for her or not. Besides, there was no catching anyone by surprise when you had two police departments involved in anything.

"Okay," I said as we headed across the slim thread of highway over the water between East Marion and Orient, "so we all know what the plan is, right?"

Bursaw nodded yes. He was calm. Vincent, not so much. I hoped his nerves would work in our favor since it was up to him to distract Dillman. There was that word again, *hope*. Always trouble. We didn't have much choice. Dillman knew my face. Bursaw was the steadiest gun hand, and had the most training at handling potentially dangerous situations.

"Vincent?" I prodded.

"Yeah. I drive the car up to the house, get Dillman to the door, and act like I'm totally lost and say that I'm having car trouble."

"Right. You say you're lost and your car won't restart. Ask him for a boost. I've got cables in the trunk. Just get him away from the house for as long as you can, but nothing stupid. Don't pull your gun on him or anything. No hero shit. We just need him away from the house long enough to break in through the back."

"I got it. I got it."

At the point where we had to turn off Village Lane onto Orchard, I stopped the car.

"Two minutes for us to get into position," Bursaw said, turning around to Vincent, holding up his right middle and index fingers. "Two minutes."

"I got it, for chrissakes! I got it."

Vincent switched places with me. Bursaw and I got out of the car, closing the doors silently behind us. Neither Bursaw nor I asked Vincent if he was okay before we took off for the big white farmhouse on the hill. He was so clearly not okay that we were afraid of setting him off completely and blowing any chance we had for surprise. It was chilly and deathly still this far out on the island. Even in the dark, it was obvious why some people chose to live or summer out here—all the water and the fresh air and the quiet.

We made it to the back of the house in about ninety seconds. There hadn't been any tall fences between the lots. We sat behind a low hedge that lined the back of the Dillman property. The house was pretty big, but the lot was only about a half acre. The ground and second floors of the house were completely dark. At one side of the house, there was a drop in elevation that afforded a scenic view from the basement. Apparently, a window had been built into the foundation at that point to take advantage of the view. But it was the light leaking out of the basement into the night, and not the view from the basement, that encouraged us.

Bursaw checked his watch. I checked mine. We nodded to each other as we heard Vincent pull my car up in front of the house and screech to a halt. So far, so good. He was doing really well, stomping up the granite block steps that led to the front door from the street below. He rang the bell, patiently waited, and rang again. Bursaw and I heard the bell's chiming drift through the walls of the house into the silence of the night. But that's when it started going wrong. Vincent pounded on the door. Not knocked, pounded, and there was no more patient waiting. There was just more pounding. Harder and harder. Louder and louder.

Bursaw and I shrugged our shoulders at one another. Even if this was a deviation from the plan, it was no doubt distracting. Dillman wouldn't be paying much attention to the back door of his soon-to-be former vacation home with crazy Vincent trying to punch down his front door. So we walked, guns drawn, slowly, quietly, to opposite ends of the back wall of the house. Then we took measured steps toward one another until only the width of the back door separated us. That's when Vincent just lost it.

"Open up, dammit! My fucking car broke down," he screamed between pounding. "Open up."

It wouldn't be long before neighbors got curious. I knew it. Bursaw knew it. He shrugged again and I nodded for him to go ahead.

"Your guy's sure there's no alarm, right?" Bursaw whispered.

"If he says there's no alarm, there's no alarm."

Bursaw holstered his Glock, turned toward the back of the property, and then jerked his right arm so his elbow punched a hole in the glass of the back door. He calmly reached inside, undid the deadbolt, and unlatched the door lock. His Glock was back in his hand before we were even inside.

"Oh, shit!" we said in unison.

"Only one thing smells like that," I said.

"I hope we only find one body, not two."

I agreed. "And I hope the one is his."

"Go open the front door for that asshole and tell him to wait in the car," Bursaw ordered, shifting into detective mode. "I'll make sure we're not dealing with one body and one living nut with a gun."

I ran to the door, did what Bursaw asked, but Vincent wasn't about to wait in the car. I wasn't going to waste time arguing with him either. Bursaw needed backup, and I meant to give it to him.

"Keep your weapon holstered and keep far behind me," I growled at Vincent. Then he caught a mouthful of air, made sense of the smell, and got weak in the legs. I grabbed him. "It's okay. It's okay. You'll get used to it," I lied. "Shallow breaths. Shallow breaths."

I hurried to find the steps to the basement, heard Bursaw's steps on the stairs. Then, "Fuck! Fuck! Clear. It's clear. Come down, Moe. Come on down."

When we got down to the basement, we didn't find exact replicas of Sloane's teenage basement and bedroom. We didn't find ropes or a photograph covered in strips of black electrical tape. We didn't find Sloane or Siobhan or the Hollow Girl. What we found was a beautifully finished basement and a huge flat screen TV with Bang and Olufsen surround sound. We found a superb audiophile system with tube amps, preamps, massive speakers, and a turntable that cost more than my car. We found a red leather sofa, loveseat, and recliner. We found that expensive camera on a tripod, its lens pointed at the sofa. We found a Heckler & Koch 9mm on the dark gray carpeting at the foot of the sofa. We found Michael Dillman's lifeless body slumped on the sofa with a chunk of the back of his head missing. We found that on the wall and sofa cushion behind him.

Vincent fainted, falling against the loveseat before hitting the floor. I left him there while I talked to Bursaw.

"Suicide. He bought the camera to record his goodbyes," I said.

"Looks that way. We'll know after the cops look at what's on the memory."

"He was so perfect. I thought he had to be the guy. Now I'm back to square one."

"Maybe he was too perfect, Moe."

"I guess. I'll call it in."

"Don't bother. I hear the sirens."

"I know you're the detective, Mike, but let me do the talking. If anyone's gonna take a hit here, it's gonna be me, but I think I can explain it so that we'll be all right."

He didn't argue with me and went over to revive Vincent. We had to get upstairs, outside, and put our weapons on the deck before the cops got there. Vincent came to and Bursaw shouted for us to go. I turned behind me to take one last look at Dillman. The dead often seem enviably peaceful, but not always. This was one of those times. Dillman didn't look at peace. He just looked brutally, horribly dead.

CHAPTER FORTY-ONE

It was nearly 4:00 A.M. when I got to Maggie's house in Crocus Valley. Nancy had been up, waiting, pacing when she saw my headlights flash through the living room window as I turned into the driveway. She opened the door and came out to me as I was getting out of my car. Even worried and stressed out of her mind at four in the morning, she made sure to be put together. God, I thought, the terrible weight of that, the pressure she put on herself. On the other hand, I must have looked like shit. I could see it in her eyes. I was falling down exhausted. My mouth was dry and I could smell my own sour breath. She put my arm over her shoulders and walked me into the house. I liked the feel of her against me.

The Southhold cops had bought my narrative without much skepticism. I was a licensed private investigator and I was doing a favor for a family friend. In the course of my investigation into another unrelated matter, I was alerted to the fact that Michael Dillman might be suicidal. I knew he was already in bad shape because of his recent divorce, the loss of his children, his job, and his pride. I was afraid that calling in the police might push him over the edge. Having met the man earlier in my investigation and having established a rapport with him, I felt it was safer for me to approach him on my own. After all, I had been twice divorced myself. I'd enlisted the aid of two close friends, both of whom I trusted and both of whom were licensed to carry firearms, to come along as backup in case things went awry or if we felt we needed to restrain Mr. Dillman for his own safety and the safety of others. When he didn't answer our urgent pleas to open the front door, we went around to the side of the house and looked through the basement window. Seeing Mr. Dillman slumped on the sofa and unresponsive to our pleas, I broke through the back door window, let myself and the others in. Unfortunately, we found Mr. Dillman had already committed suicide. We were about to call it in, but heard the sirens approaching.

It was all reasonable enough and, for the most part, the truth. If the Suffolk County Homicide detectives hadn't gotten involved in a pissing match with the local detective, we probably could have left it at that. But they had gotten involved in a pissing contest, and we had spent the better part of four hours telling and retelling and retelling our stories over and over again. It really seemed to chafe the Suffolk homicide detectives that two PIs and a Nassau County detective were operating on their patch. The Southhold detective got a real kick out of reminding his Suffolk PD counterparts that it was his patch, not theirs. At least Bursaw and Brock had reasonable deniability. "Hey, Moe's my friend. A friend asks me to help, I help. Wouldn't you do the same thing?" Chafed asses or not, once it was determined that Dillman had been dead for more than forty-eight hours, they let us go.

"I was sick with worry about you," Nancy said, ferrying me into Maggie's kitchen and getting me a bottle of water. "Your friend Devo's call didn't do much to comfort me. He's not a talkative fellow."

I laughed, remembering that I'd told him to tell Nancy as little as possible. That was cake for Devo. Nancy didn't appreciate my laughter. I didn't blame her.

"Do you remember Michael Dillman?"

A sick, mournful expression washed over Nancy's face. "Of course I remember Mike. I hated what happened to him and his family. That was the worst part of what Sloane did, how she hurt the friends closest to her. I don't think she meant to do it." She paused to think. I didn't argue with her about her daughter's intent all those years ago. "Wait a second. Wait a second . . . was Mike Dillman your lead? Did he have—"

"He's dead, Nancy. Suicide."

I told her the story of how my conversation with Valerie Biemann had got me thinking that if anyone had motive to hurt the Hollow Girl, it was Michael Dillman. Nancy sat in stunned silence as I built the case for her that I had built for myself against Dillman. He was perfect. Everything fit. Except it didn't. Now he was dead, and I was no closer to finding her daughter than I had been weeks ago.

"And tonight's post, did you watch it?" I asked after I finished and had given it a minute to sink in.

"More of the same, Moe, only a little worse." Tears ran down her cheeks. "The ropes seemed even tighter. There was more blood and she didn't even struggle. It looked like if you cut away the ropes, she would have just collapsed. Her eyes were closed most of the time."

"Was there anything else? Anything different? Was the photograph still at her feet?"

"The photo was still there. I'm not sure I noticed anything different about it. And I already told you what was different about the video." Her voice getting louder with stress.

"Okay, okay." I reached across the table and wiped her tears away with my thumb. "Is there a place I can get some rest? I need to think, and for that I need to sleep."

"Maggie gave us the guest room downstairs."

As we made our way to the basement, Giorgio Brahms's sour expression popped into my head once again. Exhaustion does funny things to a man's brain. I needed to get to sleep before I started fantasizing about Anna Carey and me drinking pitchers of margaritas on the veranda of our Cabo vacation villa.

CHAPTER FORTY-TWO

Bang! I woke up like I had a full body cramp. I had an idea. It wasn't much of one, I admit, but my good ideas didn't seem to be worth a damn either. I rolled over and saw Nancy was still asleep. I was long past the age where I found it thrilling or romantic to watch a woman sleeping, yet I found I couldn't stop watching her. She had been an object of fascination for me for so many years, and yet I hadn't paused to really think through what was going on between us. Maybe that was a good thing. Nothing beats the life out of something like overthinking it. I wanted to let her sleep, seeing as how she had gotten as little of it as I had. Neither what I wanted nor Nancy's sleep mattered. For my idea to work, I needed Nancy. It would turn on Nancy's performance. I just hoped we hadn't missed our window of opportunity. I kissed her on the neck and told her she needed to wake up.

"Sleep," she muttered, groggy. "Sleep."

"No sleep," I answered. "Sloane."

That did the trick.

* * *

Sloane's messages were the key, I explained to Nancy as we drove the short distance from Crocus Valley to her house in Old Brookville. Something about those messages—always so chipper, so full of vague promises—had bugged me from the start and now even Nancy had come to see them as a ploy. Still, she didn't understand how they were worth anything to us if they were phony or had been prerecorded. She wondered if I wasn't getting a bit desperate like her, clutching at straws.

"Do you think there's some code embedded in her messages? Are you going to have your friend Devo run them through a computer or something?"

"It's not the messages themselves, Nancy. It's not about what Siob—Sloane says in the messages or how she says it."

"Then what?"

"It's when they come. Have you noticed that they are always timed so that you're never at home to receive them? If they're prerecorded, like we're both fairly sure they are, what would happen if you were there to pick up the phone when one was coming in? If it's Sloane playing the hoax, it would make her look silly. She'd just hang up, or stop the recording and get on the phone with you. But if what we fear *is* true, that someone is holding Sloane against her will and has somehow gotten her to make these messages, he can't afford to have you pick up the phone when those messages come in. If you were home and picked up mid-message, the very means he was using to keep you from being alarmed would instead have the opposite effect."

"So what? I already know the messages are—"

"But he doesn't know that you know. And that's not the point, anyway."

She was exasperated. "Then what is the fucking point, Moe?"

"How does he know when to call? That's the point."

"Oh, my God."

"That's right, Nancy. He's watching your house, or he has someone watching your house. He waits for you to leave and then he calls."

"But wait. Hold on," she said. "I've checked caller ID and the messages come from Sloane's cell."

"Of course they do. He has her cell. When you leave the house, he uses her phone to call and he plays a digital recording into the phone."

She buried her head in her hands. The reality that her daughter might actually be someone's captive or worse was hitting home. "If her messages are prerecorded, then the video posts might be prerecorded, too. Sloane might be—"

"Don't even go there," I shouted at her. "Don't go there. If she was dead, he wouldn't be working so hard to delay you. He's buying time for something. He has a plan that requires the world seeing these posts. Otherwise he would be gone or covering his tracks, not risking capture by calling more attention to himself. She's alive, Nancy. She's alive. I'm sure of it. There's a reason he's doing this, presenting her to the world this way. It has to have something to do with the old Hollow Girl posts. It has to. I feel it in my belly."

"Remember what you told me, Moe, they cut half of that belly out."

"But not the half where I know things. Okay, we're almost at your place. Sit up tall in your seat. I need the press and anyone who might be watching to know for sure you're entering the house. Wave to them if you want to, blow them a kiss. Do anything to get their attention. I'm gonna drive in real slow. I need whoever is watching to get a good look at my car, too."

"Do you think this will work?"

"We won't know until we try it."

That wasn't the answer she was hoping for.

* * *

I realized this was a long shot at best. So far all of my gut feelings and machinations had added up to very little in the way of results. I'd been sure Mike Dillman was holding onto Siobhan Bracken, and it turned out the only thing he was holding onto was an overwhelming amount of pain. Even more than Giorgio Brahms's disgusted expression over his stupid walls, I could not get the vision of Dillman out of my head. He looked so unhappy even in death, it made me wonder if there ever really was rest for the weary. At my age, as sick as I had been, you think about shit like that. You think about it a lot.

That there was no message from Sloane on the house line's voicemail system seemed to bolster my theory. Rushing to the phone was the first thing Nancy had done after we'd finally waded through the phalanx of paparazzi and reporters. She had escaped from the media the previous day by hiding away in Maggie's trunk, so anyone watching the house would have assumed she had never left. If my theory was right, the watcher wouldn't have dared risk leaving a message had there been any chance Nancy was there to pick up. Of course there were hundreds of other more reasonable explanations for there being no phone message. The real test would come soon enough.

* * *

As I checked my watch there in the front seat of my rented Chevy Impala, I felt a fool. In the four and a half hours since driving away from Nancy's house—making sure everyone got a good look at me and my car—I'd done a lot of maneuvering, hoop jumping, and arm twisting. Now I was about to find out if it would amount to anything more than me looking like an idiot.

Only once before had I ever tried to pull off something as elaborate as this. And that one time, thirty years ago, it blew up in my face. I'd come this close from getting murdered in an abandoned hotel in Miami Beach. But it was too late now to worry about looking stupid. There. Nancy's gate opened—1:45 P.M., right on schedule. Time for her to head into Glen Cove for her regular two o'clock tennis game. Her red Porsche Cayman came rolling slowly out of her driveway. Nothing screams "Hey look at me" like a pretty woman in a red Porsche. She turned right and headed north up 107, passing me as she went. The countdown had begun. If I was right, Nancy's house phone would be ringing within the next hour, give or take.

Exactly thirty minutes later, at 2:15, my phone rang. It was Brian Doyle's cell.

"Her phone just started ringin'," he said. "I hope all this cloak and dagger bullshit is worth it to you. I nearly broke my freakin' ankle climbing over the back wall."

"Not now. How many rings?"

"Three. You're gonna look awful stupid if—"

"Forget that. How many—"

"Four."

"It'll pick up on the fifth," I said.

"Okay, here we—ah, fuck. False alarm. It's her pool guy. You might wanna tell the lady of the house that her pool guy is gonna be late on Thursday."

"I'll make a note of it."

"So, Boss, you really think this guy is gonna call?"

"He better. Now get the fuck off the phone and keep your head down."

Click.

Ten minutes later, Doyle was back on the phone. "Second ring," he whispered.

"What the fuck are you whispering for? Nevermind. Keep counting."

"Three . . . four . . . five. Her voicemail message is playing. This Nancy Lustig got a sexy voice."

"I'll let her know."

"Fuck me, you were right, Boss. There's a message comin' in. She's saying what you said she would, almost word for word."

"Good, now get upstairs and stay on the line."

I listened to him chugging up the steps and running into the guest bathroom on the second floor where he'd set up his camera. In a house with so much open space and so many glass walls, there weren't many places for Doyle to see out without being seen.

"I'm here. I'm here," he shouted breathlessly into the phone. "Fuck, I'm gettin' old."

"Tell me about it. Any cars pulling away on either side of the street?"

"No, nothin' yet."

A minute passed. A bead of sweat snaked its way down my side. "Anything?" I shouted into the phone.

"Jesus, Boss. I'm gettin' old, not deaf. Still nothin' . . . wait, yeah, yeah. Here we go. A black Chrysler 300C, about a hundred yards ahead of you. He's pulling out from between the two satellite vans. Do you see him?"

"No."

"He's facing the same direction as you."

"I see him. I see him. Tag number?"

"Fuck. It's a Utah tag. Probably a rental, Boss. I'll have somebody run it."

"Well, keep snapping until he gets out of range. I'm following."

I hung up and pulled into traffic behind, of all things, a white, orange, and blue-striped Nassau County police car. I almost didn't care about the cop because it felt so good to be right for a change.

CHAPTER FORTY-THREE

The good feelings didn't last as the three of us—the 300C, the cop's Crown Vic, and my Impala—wound our way south along Route 107 at a comfortable twenty-nine miles per hour. There were lots of majestic old trees to behold, many ridiculously enormous houses to laugh at or envy, and the occasional country club golf course abutting the road. The thing is, I needed to get a look at the guy at the wheel of the Chrysler. My view of him was limited to fleeting, distorted glimpses around the Crown Vic and through its windshield and rear window. As we approached the State University of New York at Old Westbury, I got a bit more hopeful. The road widened here and as we got closer to Hicksville, there'd be something like six lanes to choose from. But as long as the cop was between us, I really couldn't risk swinging out around him and speeding up. As much as I needed a better look at the guy driving the 300C, I didn't want to get pulled over for speeding and risk losing the Chrysler completely.

Although the road kept widening and exit ramps for Jericho Turnpike, the LIE, and the Northern State Parkway presented themselves, both the Chrysler and the cop seemed perfectly content to stay in single file and to maintain the same speed. My patience ran out. Coming to a red light, I changed lanes in an attempt to scope out the guy at the wheel of the 300C. It worked out well. With a tiny Fiat directly in front of me, I was afforded a clear view of the driver's left profile. The driver was a young man, maybe twenty-five, with a neatly trimmed brown beard and mustache. His hair was a little darker than his beard, longer, too, and not very carefully brushed. He wore heavy-framed black glasses à la Elvis Costello. His skin was pale and he didn't appear physically imposing. I guessed he was about five-eight and weighed about what I had weighed as a high school freshman. He wore a blue sport jacket over an open-collared light blue shirt. Doyle must've been right; the car had to be a rental. I couldn't see some skinny, twenty-five-year-old white boy choosing a 300C as his dream machine.

My cell buzzed in my pocket. I reached for it and was about to pull it up to my ear and answer when something told me not to do it. I looked to my right and saw the Nassau County cop eyeballing me. New York is a hands-free only state and if I had gotten the phone closer to my ear, I would have been screwed. As it was, the cop was sneering and shaking his head at me. I shrugged and waved sorry to him. He was unimpressed. When the light turned green, he was still shaking his head.

The three of us continued our little group dance as we passed the Broadway Mall. Finally, at the split between Routes 106 and 107, the cop veered off to the right for 106 and the black 300C stayed left with me on 107. Then, suddenly, the Chrysler jerked hard right to follow the cop. I yanked my rental's wheel harder right and cut off an oil truck that locked up his brakes and blasted his air horn at me. Then, just as I made it over to 106 where I could follow the Chrysler, he jerked his wheel hard left and got back on 107. This guy was either very, very good, or very, very bad. He was certainly unconventional. I wasn't sure if he had made me or if he had done the zigzag as a precaution.

I didn't bother trying to match him. Instead, I continued southwest, keeping an eye on him as I went. At the next opportunity, I made a left, then a right, and fell in a hundred yards or so behind the 300C. He stayed in the right lane and began adding speed. He didn't floor it, just accelerated at a steady rate until he hit fifty. I didn't know what he was up to or where he was headed, so I maintained the distance between us, trying to hide myself in traffic. We were deep in the heart of Little India now, an area of Hicksville that was packed with Indian restaurants and grocery stores. We kept this up for about another half minute. Suddenly, he accelerated around a car to his left, swung into the turning lane, and made a sharp U-turn in the opposite direction. Fuck, I thought, he'd made me.

I decided that I'd had enough of this cat-and-mouse shit, so I floored the Impala, weaving my way left as I went. A block past where the Chrysler had smoked his rear wheels making the U-turn, I made a similar turn. He must have thought he'd shaken me, because he had slowed to fifty again. Not me. Once I'd gotten the Impala oriented in the Chrysler's direction, I nailed the gas. I caught up to the 300C at Rave Street, swung left around him at Townsend Lane, and cut him off in front of an Indian restaurant, nail salon, and pizzeria. He pulled close to the curb, slammed on his brakes, and barely missed T-boning the Impala that I wedged in front of him. I jumped out of the car, .38 in my hand, but showing it only to the guy behind the wheel of the black Chrysler and not to passing traffic. I guess I sort of showed him my old badge, too. I put the badge away, not the .38.

"Out of the car, motherfucker. Out of the car, now!"

He did as he was told. Almost as soon as he got out of the car, I knew something was wrong.

First thing I noticed was that his arms were shaking and his lips were trembling. He was trying to speak but fear had robbed him of his voice. Second thing I noticed was the white press credential with his photo on it that hung around his neck on an orange lanyard. His name was Ian Kern. I holstered my .38 before I made an even bigger ass of myself.

"Relax, Ian. Relax. Nobody's getting in any trouble. Just take it easy. Deep breaths."

"Yes, sir."

"What was that zigging and zagging all about, and that U-turn? You could've gotten somebody killed," I said, as if I hadn't just done far worse.

"I was lost. I don't know my way around here. I'm from Michigan and I live in Williamsburg. My boss sent me to get Indian food for the crew from this place." He pointed at the big red and white sign on the restaurant. "My boss says it's the best Indian food on Long Island."

"Who's your boss?"

"Bob Mark. He's a producer at IENN, Independent Entertainment News Network. That's his car," Ian said, pointing at the Chrysler.

"What's with the Utah plates?"

"He has a ski—Hey, I recognize you. You're the guy who drove Nancy Lustig into her house this morning."

"My name's Moe Prager. I'm an old friend of Nancy's. I'm also an ex-cop and a private investigator. So let's keep each other's secrets, okay? I won't tell your boss you got lost and nearly caused a traffic accident trying to find a fucking restaurant, and you won't tell anyone I nearly shot you."

"Hardly seems fair," he said.

"How would you like an exclusive interview with the Hollow Girl's mom?"

His eyes got big and he smiled as if he'd just won the lottery. In a way, I guess he had. It seemed a long time ago that he was shaking and unable to speak.

"Are you kidding me? Fuck, yeah."

I handed him my card. "Listen, give me a few days. Things are still a little too crazy now and she won't do it. But you give me some time and I guarantee it." His brown eyes were understandably skeptical and I could see him weighing his options. I decided to help him make a choice. "Look, kid, it's worth the gamble. You think the cops are gonna give a shit about me pulling my gun on you? I'll just say you were driving erratically and dangerously and I felt compelled to stop you. Besides, I'm an ex-cop and I got friends. Trust me, and all you got is upside. C'mon, kid, think it—" I stopped myself. My phone was once again buzzing. When I saw it was Brian Doyle, I said, "Excuse me, Ian, I gotta take this." I picked up. "Yeah . . . ."

"It's not the black Chrysler," he shouted in my ear. "That car is registered to Robert Mark. He's a producer at Independent—"

"Entertainment Network News. I know. What else?"

"Just when I was finished snapping shots once you took off after the Chrysler, another car pulled out. A blue 2013 Toyota Camry with New York tags. I called you about it, but you didn't pick up."

"Long story. What about the Camry?"

"It's a rental."

"So?"

"You ain't gonna like this, Boss."

I lost it. "Just tell me what the fuck you gotta tell me."

"The name on the rental agreement is Siobhan Bracken."

That knot in my gut tightened again. I hung up the phone and slowly turned back to Ian Kern. As I did, I scanned for the blue Camry.

"Everything okay, Mr. Prager?" Kern asked, sensing something was up.

"Fine," I lied. "Go get your food. I got work to do, but I give you my word about the interview. You have a card, Ian?"

He dug one out of a black plastic case in his jacket pocket. "Here."

"Okay, thanks. Go on."

The kid must have had a good nose for trouble because he hesitated before starting for the restaurant. As he finally walked away, I pretended to stretch my muscles and scanned some more. It was only when I turned back to the Impala that I spotted the blue Camry. *Shit!* I'd been made. I'd gotten caught in my own trap. The Camry was parked a third of a block north of where I'd cut off the kid. There didn't seem to be anyone behind the wheel. No one was standing near the car. My eyes darted to the right. I saw a blur of a man and that's when the world jerked and tilted slightly to the left.

I saw the smoke, heard the wind-muted bang. It seemed that at the very instant I was hearing the bang, a crease appeared in the roof of the gray Honda Accord parked in front of the Impala. Another bang. Then a hole appeared in the Honda's windshield, its driver's side window shattered. Another bang. Something whistled by my right ear. I threw myself to the ground. I went down so hard, it knocked the wind out of me. I was gasping for air as I sidled under the Impala. Another bang. Another and another. To my left, the pavement spit out sparks where the bullets hit and skimmed like stones off the water. More sparks. Something exploded—a tire. Brakes screeched. Tires squealed past me. A car hit the low center divider and came to rest. My breath came back to me. The world jerked again, leveling to the right.

When I got out from under the Impala and stood up, I saw that a white Mercedes sedan had come to rest across both northbound lanes, blocking traffic. Its front right tire was shredded. The driver, a guy in his fifties, was cursing up a storm as he got out of the car. The blue Camry was disappearing around a corner when I turned to look. The time for me to be gone had come as well. I didn't need to spend another second more with the cops than I had the night before, and I wasn't in the mood to make any more deals with Ian. I'd already made too many promises that I wasn't sure I could keep.

CHAPTER FORTY-FOUR

One thing was finally for sure: Siobhan Bracken was in trouble. I got Bursaw on the phone, not that he was thrilled to hear from me after the previous night's misadventure. He was downright cynical about my certainty this time.

"Yeah, Moe, that's what you said last night."

"No one was shooting at me last night."

"Shooting at you? Where?"

"Broadway in Hicksville."

"Broadway in Hicksville in the middle of the day? Get the fuck outta here!"

"I don't have time to argue with you now," I said. "You keep your eyes and ears open. You'll be getting a report of shots fired soon enough. When you hear the report, call me and we'll talk then."

I raced back to Nancy's house and waited for her to return from her tennis game. Brian Doyle was there. I told him what had happened. He understood the implications immediately.

"He'll be nervous now that he missed killing you. Maybe he's gonna have to speed up his clock. That can't be so good for this Siobhan chick."

"I know, Brian. I know. But his shooting at me tells us something else."

"What's that, Boss?"

"He's an amateur. What I mean to say is that he has killed, but he's not who you would describe as a killer. If this is the same guy who killed the doorman, Rizzo—and I think it is the same guy—it says something. He tried to kill me for the same reason he killed Rizzo. It's the same reason he's been playing these stupid phone messages. He's trying to buy time."

Doyle asked, "For what? He's basically holding all the cards. He's got the girl, doesn't he? Why don't he just kill her, be done with it, and split?"

"Because it's not enough for him to just kill her. He wants to punish her and her parents first, and he wants us to know why. He wants us to watch it. There's a price to be paid. To just kill her without an audience would cheapen it, I think. This isn't something he thought of on the spur of the moment. No, Brian, he's been thinking about this, brooding over it for a long time. Believe me, I know the type. The guy who killed Katy, he was the same. He wanted her to suffer, and me to watch her suffer, and he wanted me to know why.

"This guy has a timetable, one he feels he has to stick to no matter what, even if it means killing people who get in the way. That's why I don't think he means to escape. Escaping isn't as important as following through. This took a lot of planning. The thing I have to figure out is why now? Why not last March or next February? What set him off? Once I figure out why he chose now to act, I'll be able to figure out who. The more I think about it, the more I'm sure this has to be connected to the Hollow Girl's old posts. Get back to your office and tell Devo to drop everything else except the fallout from the Hollow Girl's suicide post. It's got to be that. I'll pay you guys whatever it takes, but do it."

Brian Doyle didn't exactly hop to. "Boss, could you do me a favor?"

"What?"

"Help me over the back wall. I wasn't kiddin' about the fall I took before."

We found a ladder in the shed that made Doyle's return climb less traumatic. When I got back inside, my phone was at it again. It was Bursaw. The report had come in. At first the guy who owned the gray Accord couldn't figure out what had happened to the car's roof, his windshield and side window. But when a cop pulled up to see what the deal was with the Mercedes in the middle of the road, the owner of the Accord waved him over.

"Shit, Moe, this guy's serious. The initial report is he must've fired six or seven rounds at you."

"Then I'm lucky he can't shoot for shit."

Detective Bursaw could taste a promotion. "What do you want me to do?"

"For now, sit tight. I haven't told the mother yet."

"That time's pretty much come, don't you think?"

Just then I saw Nancy coming into the house. "Just sit tight for now, Mike. Gotta go."

Nancy walked in, looking as finely put together as always. And it was getting so that just the smell of her knocked me a bit off balance. The tennis seemed to have done her some good, but one look at me undid all that and then some. I was going to beg her for one more day without getting the cops involved and I wasn't sure she would give it to me. If I had been her, I wouldn't have. I told her all the things I'd told Doyle about the guy who had Siobhan having a timetable and needing to play this out at his own pace.

"You're contradicting yourself, Moe," she said, her face a map of worry. "First you say he has killed in order to keep on a certain schedule to hurt Sloane, and that he won't kill her until he's ready to. But in the next breath you say getting the cops involved might cause him to kill her. I don't understand."

"I know, Nancy. I know. And I know it's a lot to ask you to risk your daughter's life on a feeling I have about a stranger who just tried to kill me."

"You're asking me more than a lot. You're asking me for everything."

"He killed Rizzo and tried to kill me to buy time. That's what those stupid phone messages are about, too, and the disclaimers. All to buy time. It seems to me his only goal is to publicly punish and humiliate your daughter before finally killing her. He wants to tell us why, but he's not ready to. I think that's almost as important to him as the act of killing Sloane. That's what the framed photograph at the Hollow Girl's feet is all about. I'm sure of it. That girl or woman in that photo is the reason. But if we call in the cavalry now and there's some massive manhunt, he might feel forced to make a choice between killing Sloane according to his schedule, or killing Sloane before he gets caught. I'm afraid if it comes to that, he'll—"

"God, Moe, stop. I don't want to hear you say it again. Give me something more than all this conjecture."

"Okay. If I'm right, tonight's post will be more of the same or some variation of the same. The photograph will still be at her feet, but with one less strip of tape on the face. If I'm wrong, if it's much worse or really different, we'll call the cops immediately."

"But if you're wrong, Moe, we're giving this sick bastard six free hours to kill my daughter and get away."

"I have no right to ask, but I'm asking," I said, handing her the phone. "If you feel you have to call now, I will do everything I can to help the cops and no matter what happens, I won't ever second-guess your decision."

She took the phone. "What would you do if it was Sarah?"

"I guess I would call."

She handed the phone back to me.

CHAPTER FORTY-FIVE

I'd never been so relieved to be right, relieved but not happy. One look at the condition of the Hollow Girl removed happiness from the equation. She was terribly pale, and it seemed the ropes were so tight that she could barely breathe. Her eyes remained closed. I couldn't help but wonder if I had missed something about the ropes. Were they meant to be metaphorical? Was there a message in this about lack of mobility, or the inability to breathe? I could almost taste the answer, but being close was no good. The photograph was, as I suspected it would be, still at her feet, with one less strip of tape across the face. Now we could see the eyebrows, jawline, and nose of the girl in the picture. That much was clear from what had been revealed: She was a girl, not yet a woman. Surely, this had to be enough for Devo's software to get me an answer.

Then, about halfway through the post, my eyes drifted away from the center of the frame, away from the Hollow Girl and toward the blank white wall behind her. Staring at Siobhan, at her shallow, labored breaths, was gut-wrenching, hypnotic, and horrifying. Somehow, shifting focus to the wall behind her seemed like the most important thing in the world to me. Things came to me all at once: Anthony Rizzo's timeline, Nancy's timeline, the brief mentions of Millie McCumber in the press, Giorgio Brahms's sour expression. Giorgio Brahms and his fucking kitchen walls. I was sick of him living in my head, him and his petty bullshit. Then I remembered his parlor. Suddenly, I was on my feet, standing between Nancy and her TV, screaming.

"When did you say Millie McCumber came back into Siob—Sloane's life?"

"What does that have to—"

"When?" I shouted. "When?"

"Four, maybe five months ago."

"That's it! That's it, Nancy."

"That's what?"

"The key."

"To what?"

"Maybe everything. Stay here. I'll call you later. Just stay here."

* * *

The main floor of Brahms's brownstone was dark, but there was light coming from the second floor of his place, shadows, too. The problem was he didn't seem disposed to answer his front door, no matter how often I pounded on it. Nor did he answer his phone when I called from the stoop. So I did the next best thing: I threw a rock through his front window. When he didn't respond immediately to the sound of breaking glass, I got another rock, and another. That third rock was the charm.

"What the fuck!" he screamed, yanking his front door open. His feet were bare. He was shirtless, wet with sweat, and his gym shorts were untied. "I'm calling the cops."

"Please do," I said, pushing past him. "Get in here and shut the door."

"Who the fuck are you to order me around in my own house?" he ranted, shutting the front door and following me just the same.

I showed him my .38 and pointed it at him. "You wanna ask me that again?"

"Georgie, c'mon, Mama's waiting for you. I was so fucking close," a raspy-voiced woman called down from the top of the stairs. It was a voice with some mileage on it.

I whispered to Brahms, "Tell Mama you'll be up in five minutes."

"Me, too, honey. I was close, too. I'll be up in five minutes. Have another drink, honey," he called up.

I heard bare feet padding away. I nodded for Giorgio to follow me into the kitchen. He was good at following instructions, at least from a man with a gun.

"What's this about?" he whispered when we stopped.

"These walls," I said pointing the short barrel of my .38 at them. "When I was here, you couldn't take your eyes off them. You were muttering to yourself."

"You're holding a gun on me because my kitchen walls are unfinished? And they say theater people are crazy."

"The first time we met, you gave an earnest little speech about Millie McCumber and how you were so upset over her death because her family would take her money and exploit her, but that's not why you were upset, was it, Giorgio?"

He didn't answer, his face pinching up tight.

"Giorgio!" I growled, pointing the revolver at him once again. "I don't have time for this shit."

"Yes and no," he relented, and waved at me. "Will you put that damned thing away? You've made your point." He moved to the stove. "Tea?"

I put the .38 away. "No, thanks. What about Mama? Won't she get impatient?"

"Trust me, Mr. Prager, Mama will wait. But you're wrong about Millie. I did love her. I think I'm the only person who ever did. She didn't make it easy to love her, trust me."

"But she was paying you for something, Giorgio. She was paying you a lot of money."

"Some, not as much as you think, but some, in dribs and drabs."

"Then she died between a drib and a drab and left you and your walls high and dry. But why was she paying you? And please, don't make me pull it out of you, Giorgio. Just tell me, and tell me the truth because Siobhan's life depends on it. And if what you tell me isn't the truth and something happens to her because you lied to me, your life won't be worth shit."

He picked up the kettle and banged it on the stove. "Stop threatening me."

"Start talking."

"It had been a year since I'd seen Millie. She was staying with me here back then, because she had nowhere else to go and because she was as low as she'd ever been. That was saying something. There were no parts for her, and the drugs and booze had gotten completely out of hand. She was so desperate, she'd even tried to land work as an escort. A perfect job for her, one would have thought. That woman loved to fuck, and acting is acting, right? So you can imagine how crushing it was when they turned her down for that, too. One of the services told her that she was too old, and that only steak houses were interested in dry aged beef.

"She was ragged and one step away from living on the streets. One day, I left here to do some shopping, and she just split. But not before relieving me of all the cash I had in the house and most of my jewelry. I also had a collection of signed photographs and theater paraphernalia worth tens of thousands of dollars. She took all that as well. When she showed back up here in March, I nearly shit myself. I couldn't believe she had the *chutzpah*, but I remembered this was Millicent McCumber. She had no shame."

"Does this story have a point?"

The kettle whistled. He fussed with a mug, tea bag, and honey. "You're the one who threatened me not to leave things out."

"Okay."

"She strutted in here like she'd done nothing wrong. She acted as if robbing the most valuable possessions from her only friend, agent, and sometimes lover was perfectly normal. I couldn't speak, but I noticed that she looked fabulous: healthy, tanned, and dressed in several thousand dollars' worth of haute couture and fur. Before I could open my mouth, she handed me a check for thirty thousand dollars and promised there was more to come. She didn't apologize or ask after me. All she said was, 'Can you get me a bottle of water, George? Shopping is such thirsty work.' And when I came back with her water, she had spread herself out on my couch and commented on how dingy my place was. 'We have to do something about that immediately,' she said. When I asked about the clothes and the check and the water drinking, she said she'd sort of hit the lottery."

"Sort of?"

"A man, of course. A rich one," Giorgio said. "He'd come looking for her and had a proposition. He claimed to be a large shareholder in several media companies and had an idea for a project. The project was based on the whole Hollow Girl phenomenon of the late '90s and there would be a big part in it for her, but he needed access to Siobhan Bracken. He told Millie that his attempts to approach Siobhan directly or through that dried-up old bitch, Anna Carey, had been rebuffed. So he offered Millie a lot of money if she could insinuate herself back into Siobhan's life. He told her to spend all the money she needed and to get whatever help she needed to get close to Siobhan."

"Georgie!" Mama called from the top of the stairs, stomping her feet. "I need you, baby."

"He'll be up in a few minutes," I shouted to her. I turned back to Brahms. "Did you ever meet this money man?"

"Never had to."

"Did you believe there really was a project?"

"I believed his money."

"So what was your part in all this?"

"After Millie had worked her way back into Siobhan's good graces and her bed, I was invited in. After we'd all been together a few times, my job was to try and lure Siobhan away from Anna and to become my client. That way I'd be able to facilitate this guy getting together with Siobhan to discuss the Hollow Girl project. I told you the last time you were here that I'd tried to get her to be my client. When she refused to dump Anna, Millie told me it would be okay, that she would handle it and that I'd still get my money. But I knew it was too good to be true. Millie started using and drinking again. Then the payments slowed down. Then they stopped alto—" There was a knock at the door. "Holy shit! When did I become the most popular guy in town? Excuse me. I'll be right back."

Brahms got up from the kitchen table and walked to the front door. His hand was on the knob when I screamed for him to get down. He didn't get down, but turned sideways back towards the kitchen, his hand still on the knob. "What?"

That's when the holes appeared, one after the other, in the front door—splinters flying everywhere. Puffs of sawdust and plaster dust filled the air. Giorgio let out a sickening cry and thudded to the little oriental rug in the hallway. Mama was shrieking with panic at the top of the stairs. I headed for Giorgio at full speed, which, at my age, was only slightly faster than standing still. I raised my .38 to fire through the door, but stopped myself. I realized that if I missed I might hit a passerby or someone in a house across the street. Worse, if I hit and killed the shooter, we might never find Siobhan alive. I got to Brahms pretty quickly, just in time to hear feet scuttling down the steps and the screeching of car tires. There wasn't a lot of blood, but Brahms was holding his hands up over his face. I yelled up to Mama to call 911 while pulling Giorgio's hands away. I nearly passed out when I saw the needle-like sliver of wood sticking three inches out of the corner of his right eye.

"It's not in your eye itself," I told him. "You'll be fine. When the cops get here, leave me out of it or say I was someone else. Siobhan's life might depend on it."

I stood, opened the front door, and ran for my car.

CHAPTER FORTY-SIX

I had a rough timeline and the half-exposed face of a girl in a photograph. I hoped that was enough. It had to be. My guess was that the photograph girl's death was connected to the Hollow Girl's suicide post. I knew there was someone out there with a lot of money to throw around, but was the dead girl his girlfriend, his friend, his sister, his daughter, or his niece? Maybe the photo was an old picture of his wife or mother as a girl. Whoever she was, she had an angry angel out there willing to kill to get his revenge. That told me a lot about him. He was used to getting his way. I guess most people with a lot of money are used to that. Nancy and Julian Cantor certainly were. Maybe that's why he wanted revenge in the first place, because the universe had dared defy him; it had taken away something he treasured. And I couldn't forget that it was important that he do this thing himself and not hire proxies to do it for him. It wasn't enough to kill the Hollow Girl. It wasn't enough for him to do it. He had to be seen to do it.

What was the old saying? It isn't enough for justice to be done. It has to be seen to be done.

I counted backwards from Millie McCumber's reappearance at Giorgio Brahms's door in March.

He said she'd looked fit, tanned, and healthy. And given how Giorgio had described her when she'd left him the year before, I figured it would have taken at least three or four months to clean her up and get her healthy. That took me back to November or December of 2012. Regardless of how many resources and how much money he had at his disposal, it would take time to find a junkie on the run, even a semi-famous one. I counted back three months more. That put me in July or August. And I figured that in spite of all this guy's planning and apparent lust for revenge, it took him some time to make the decision to turn his dream into murder. It's one thing to plan to take a life. It's something very different to take one. So I counted back another month. That left me at May or June of 2012.

What I had was a girl—at least, she was a girl when the photo was taken—or a woman dying in the spring of 2012, somehow connected to the Hollow Girl's late-'90s posts. She was probably, but not definitely, from a wealthy family. Suddenly, it felt like all my figuring didn't add up to much. Before I started my computer search, I checked out the background material Devo had sent that had sat unread in my inbox. There was nothing there I hadn't expected. Both Millie McCumber and Anthony Rizzo had too much money in their bank accounts; Michael Dillman and Giorgio Brahms, not enough. That was all moot except for old Giorgio. At least he was still alive, though a bit worse for wear.

* * *

The phone was ringing in my head, and then in my condo. I'd been in that disoriented, groggy middle world between sleeping and wakefulness when I startled. *What day is it? What time is it? Where am I supposed to be? What am I supposed to be doing?* For the first few seconds, the only thing I was certain of was the ringing phone. Shaking the sleep out of my head, I looked at the clock and saw that it was nearly 4:00 A.M. I grabbed the phone.

"Yeah."

"What happened? Why didn't you call?" There was an air of sleepy desperation in Nancy's voice.

"I'm sorry. I fell asleep at my computer."

"I guess I fell asleep, too, and when I woke up and saw the time it was—"

"I'm sorry," I repeated. "But I'm close, I think. Someone tried to kill Giorgio Brahms tonight. Last night."

"What?"

"Nancy, let me make myself some coffee and call you back. I need to wake up for real, okay?"

"Don't fall asleep on me again, please."

"Give me an hour."

"Half an hour."

"Sold."

I scooped some coffee into the bottom of the French press, put up some water on the stove, and ran into the bathroom. When I came back, I stood at the stove remembering back to the night of Bobby Friedman's funeral and to Sarah listening to the tale of how I went from college student to cop. I had hardly ever looked back at that decision and, on those rare occasions I had, it was never with regret. Now, as I waited for the water to boil, I couldn't help but wonder how different my life would have been had I managed to reinterest myself in school. Then I thought of Katy and Sarah, of Mr. Roth and Marina Conseco, and stopped looking back or second-guessing.

The water seemed to be taking forever, so I sat back down at the computer and tapped a key. And there she was, from a search I'd started when I was nodding off: Emma Wentworth Johns, hiding beneath my screensaver. She had been a very pretty girl with short, dark brown hair, sad gray eyes, and a mournful smile. There was something about her calm pose that hinted at a darkness beneath it. Or was it that the words beneath her photo informed my judgment of her appearance?

Hartford Register
April 25, 2012
Insurance Heiress Succumbs
By Anita Thompson
After spending nearly thirteen years in a vegetative state, Emma Wentworth Johns died last evening at the age of thirty. A spokesperson at the Connecticut Institute for Long-Term Care gave the cause of death as pulmonary failure due to pneumonia. Miss Johns, who was to have inherited one half of the vast Johns family insurance fortune, had been the subject of much controversy during her long illness. Miss Johns was declared brain dead shortly after her arrival at the Glaxton-Sultana Medical Center outside of Hartford on the evening of February 14, 1999. In the intervening years, several attempts had been made by friends and family members to remove Miss Johns from the ventilator and feeding tube that kept her alive. All such attempts had been successfully rebuffed by her twin brother, Burton Wentworth Johns.

Controversy was a part of this sad Valentine's Day saga from the very beginning. It has been rumored that Miss Johns, who had battled clinical depression, had attempted suicide on several occasions. Although the family has consistently denied it, reports have since surfaced that Miss Johns's coma was the result of another failed suicide attempt. Reliable sources claim that there were ligature marks and severe bruising around her neck when she was brought into the hospital by her brother Burton on the evening in question.

Within months of the incident, the Johns family brought suit against the hospital and local emergency rescue squads for failure to respond to the family's repeated calls for an ambulance to be dispatched to their residence in Farmington Falls. Court filings reveal that there were seven 911 calls placed from the Johns's home telephone number between 10:32 P.M. and 10:59 P.M. on the evening of February 14, 1999, following the discovery of Miss Johns unconscious in the basement of the family home. Those suits never progressed very far, the courts ruling that the defendants could not be held liable for the extraordinary number of emergency calls on that particular evening.

When reached for comment on his sister's passing, Burton Johns stated, "I will miss my beautiful sister every day for the rest of my life." And "I will never forget who is truly responsible for Emma's death." When asked to clarify his last remark, Mr. Johns refused to do so. A private family service will be held for Miss Johns at the family estate. No further details were released.

It was a minute before I realized the kettle was whistling.

CHAPTER FORTY-SEVEN

Nancy's house was crawling with law enforcement types and none of them any too pleased with me. Frankly, I didn't give a fuck. I'd handed them their suspect on a plate and now it was up to them, but all I got was shit for not reporting this or that. It was that territorial thing again. It might not have been so bad had only the NYPD, Nassau PD, Suffolk PD, and the Connecticut State Police been involved. The presence of the FBI put all the other cops in foul moods. No one likes the FBI except the FBI. No one. I would have advised Julian Cantor not to ask them in, but Julian Cantor didn't ask my advice, and he was the type of man who had to flex his muscles in public.

For the first few hours I felt like the popular girl at a speed-dating session. Every agency on hand wanted to talk to me. And they all got their turns, except there was nothing speedy about it. The Nassau cops wanted to know why I hadn't reported yesterday's shooting. The NYPD wanted to know why I hadn't reported the shooting at Brahms's brownstone. The Suffolk PD wanted to know why I had given a false statement to their detectives after the discovery of Michael Dillman's body. The FBI didn't know what they wanted from me, so they made me give them the whole story from start to finish, and they made me do it four times. They all delighted in threatening me with arrest before telling me to get lost. It almost made me misty-eyed for Frovarp and Shulze.

I'd kept Brian Doyle and Devo out of it. I'd called them the minute after Nancy had called the cops and warned them to burn the bridges. That had always been our code for cleaning up after our messes and for scrubbing away the trails. I doubted the FBI would be looking at my computer until after they found Siobhan, if at all. Mike Bursaw and Vincent Brock seemed to be the only people on my side, which was like having Abbott and Costello as your backup. The only person whose backing mattered was Nancy, not because we were involved, but because it was her daughter's life at stake. That counted for something. It counted for even more when Nancy demanded that I stay and be kept in the loop. That made all the guys and gals with badges as happy as I'd been on the day I was diagnosed with stomach cancer. They deigned to show me a recent photo of Burton Wentworth Johns and asked if I recognized him from yesterday.

"No," I said, "he was a blur with a gun."

I'd kept the photo. He looked a bit like his sister—same color hair, same eyes, same sort of regal bearing—but not all that much for a twin. His face was rather more plain looking than Emma. Though he was only thirty-one years old, he had the ancient, mournful face of a Sioux Indian chief. I knew grief when I saw it, and I was seeing it. It was carved into him. I saw guilt there, too, but didn't understand it. What had he done to be guilty about? Emma had hung herself, presumably after watching the Hollow Girl overdose. Then there was a commotion, and I stopped wondering.

"Prager, get over here," FBI Special Agent Griggs, barked at me. "The rest of you, too, if you please." The "please" was an afterthought. Was it any wonder why people hated the FBI?

Nancy asked me if I knew what was going on. I shrugged my shoulders. "Maybe they want to use me as a human sacrifice. Who knows?"

He waited until we'd all gathered at the dining room table. "Okay, I just got word from the Bureau." He said *Bureau* with the same sort of reverence my old rabbi used when talking about God and Israel. "We're officially chasing our tails. Burton Wentworth Johns has been out of the country for the last three months." He held up some official-looking pieces of paper. "He put his family home up for sale and left for Qatar from JFK on Tuesday, August 13. Roughly fourteen hours later, his passport was stamped by customs. While there, he played golf with our ambassador and visited with the royal family. He has been traveling throughout the region since. Let's give ourselves fifteen minutes and reconvene for a discussion about a new approach."

"Fuck!" the Nassau detective who was working the Rizzo homicide shouted out.

"Couldn't'a said it better myself," Suffolk PD agreed. "Fuck."

The Connecticut State Police seemed more relieved than anything. Even in the twenty-first century, no one likes screwing with rich, powerful families. Rich people make campaign contributions, host fundraisers, and have access. Cops' lives are never worse than when politicians get all over their asses.

I waited for the tumult to die down a little before talking to the FBI special agent.

"What do you want?" Griggs asked, a superior smirk on his face. "You realize if you had come to law enforcement earlier—"

"Stick the lecture, Griggs. What I wanna know is if you're sure. This guy is apparently as wealthy as the Catholic Church. The rules don't apply for money."

"We have a record of him leaving. No record of his return. He's gone, and you've wasted everybody's time."

"Have you checked with Mexico and Canada?"

"Go back to the wine shop, gramps. You're in way over your head. This is serious business, not handing out littering tickets on the boardwalk."

"Did you major in Asshole at the academy?"

"That was almost funny, Prager. Now do me a favor and let the professionals do their work. You've done quite enough damage."

I did as he asked. Although I was totally unconvinced by his answers, I didn't have much choice. Once the law was called in, even if I'd been right, I would have been shoved aside and been told to sit at the end of the bench. I didn't want to think that's why I had been so reluctant to get the law involved, but now that the bitter taste of resentment was thick on my tongue, I guess I had to admit it was a possibility. I found Nancy and pulled her aside.

"Listen, I'm sorry about—"

"Don't be silly, Moe. It was my decision. I could have called anytime. I thought you were right. I believed what you told me," she said, a false smile plastered on her face. Things had changed between us, probably forever. I was okay with that. I wasn't sure that we would have survived this ordeal regardless of the outcome.

"You're not a very good liar, Nancy, but I appreciate you trying. If the law lets me, I'm going to get out of here. I'm only in the way now, and I'm only a reminder to you of what you think is a bad decision. Believe me, I understand about bad decisions."

If I'd thought or hoped she would stop me, I'd've been wrong. At least she was polite about it. "Are you sure?"

"Yeah." I stepped to leave. Stopped. Grabbed Nancy by the arm. "Just remember that there is someone out there, someone who shot at me and Giorgio Brahms, someone who killed the doorman. No matter what these guys tell you, someone has Sloane. Don't let these guys bully you, and don't let your ex bully you." I kissed her on the cheek. "You helped save me, Nancy. I won't forget that."

I left the house. When I turned to look behind me, no one was chasing after me with cuffs.

CHAPTER FORTY-EIGHT

As I drove home from Nancy's for what I was sure would be the last time, I was mesmerized by the forsythia atop the concrete center divider on the LIE. How, I wondered, could something so vividly yellow and beautiful in spring, so green and mundane in summer, turn into a chaos of ugly twigs in fall? What was forsythia, really—the yellow for a few weeks, the green for a few months, or the twigs? The twigs, I thought. It's what we all were beneath the façade of skin and civility: the ugly twigs.

At least I wasn't tempted to drink again. The thirst was gone. What I'd said to Nancy before I left was true. She had saved me. She had saved me even if she hadn't meant to. I wasn't sure what she had meant to do. I didn't know that I would ever understand her motives, or if they mattered. I wasn't sure she had actually believed her daughter was missing when she met me at the diner. Julian Cantor's words rang loud in my head: "Nancy fuck you yet?" He hadn't asked if I'd fucked her. To Cantor, I was an item thrown in the shopping cart and crossed off Nancy's grocery list. Maybe he was right. Maybe all I'd been to her was an itch for a bored, wealthy woman to scratch. She'd scratched it now, and I'd disappointed her by not being the white knight she had thought me to be.

I called Devo and Doyle and filled them in. I told them I didn't think they had anything to worry about, but that they should be diligent in cleaning up just the same. They knew that their job was to move on. Much easier said than done for me. I told Doyle to send their bill to me.

"Nah," he said. "Fuck it. I'll just pad your brother's bills until we make it up."

I didn't know whether he was kidding or not. I didn't argue with him. The bill would come due and get paid. Bills always did. The problem with bills coming due is that the wrong party often paid the price. I guess that's why I had never been able to buy into God. I didn't believe much in karma anymore either. Whatever goes around comes around. Nope. The longer I lived, the colder and more random the universe seemed to get.

I did receive one phone call from an FBI profiler named Lawrence Kerr. He was interested in discussing how I'd come to the conclusion that Burton Wentworth Johns had abducted Siobhan Bracken. He sounded like a nice enough guy. He even confided to me that I'd done well for an amateur. I told him to go fuck himself just the same. I had enough of the FBI and the cops to last me for several years to come.

* * *

That night, I watched the latest post on my computer. Things had changed and not for the good. Though the Hollow Girl was still bound tightly by the straw-colored ropes, she was no longer tethered to the lally column. She was now laid horizontally on a makeshift table of plywood and concrete blocks, a noose of the same sort of rope around her neck. The short rope was knotted to a wooden joist above her head. The rope near her crotch was dark with wetness. Her eyes were shut and her breaths were shallow.

The ball gag had been removed and a plastic oxygen mask had been placed over her nose and mouth. The framed photo of the girl was almost gone from the shot. Only the very top few inches of it was visible, and it appeared that all the black tape had been removed. There was something else, too: a soundtrack. For the entire fifteen minutes, the loud ticking of an analog clock could be heard in the background.

The knot in my *kishkas* was as tight as the rope that bound the Hollow Girl. Nothing I'd seen or heard dissuaded me. The noose, the oxygen mask, the photo nearly out of the shot, the ticking clock all convinced me I had been right about Burton Johns. It was hard to win an argument with a hunch and a knotted belly against stamped passports, airline tickets, and tap-in putts with an ambassador. Don't for a second think my dismissal didn't eat at me. It did. I was afraid for Nancy and for Siobhan. I knew death was in the air no matter what the FBI said, but I had been shown the door. I had a life to get on with and so I was determined, for once, to look straight ahead and carry on.

CHAPTER FORTY-NINE

Winter in October had come to Sheepshead Bay. The wind was blowing hard so that the trees across Emmons Avenue bent over like old men straining to touch their toes. I'd always thought of them that way, as old men. Fishing boats rocked and bobbed in the usually calm bay waters. There were reports of a possible nor'easter coming through in the next twenty-four to thirty-six hours, so it made perfect Moe Prager sense that I had decided to go up to Vermont to be with Sarah, Ruben, and Paul. The fantasy of playing with my grandson in the snow was a powerful motivator, and I wanted to be close to Pam.

I had dreamed of her, not as the woman beneath the wheels of a jeep, but as the woman who'd purposely rammed her car into mine. In the dream we were in Coney Island again, sharing hot dogs and french fries at Nathan's. We were naked, sharing wine in my bed. It was stupid and sentimental of me, I was aware, to want to smell her in her clothes before the bundles Sarah had made were shipped off to the Goodwill shop in town. I wanted to say goodbye without the grief and the Dewar's. I needed to say goodbye the right way: in love, not in sorrow.

Sarah was as crazy as me because she thought it was a great idea for me to come up and be with them if the storm came. She was a lot like Katy, but she also had the Prager streak of love before logic in her genes. Neither one of us had displayed it much since Katy's murder, especially not to one another, but it felt good that she was so enthusiastic about my coming up. Her fervor erased any doubts I had about making the trip. That said, neither one of us was totally *meshugge*. She demanded that I swap my car for Aaron's all-wheel drive Audi. It was an easy promise to keep, as opposed to the other ones I'd made recently that would go unfulfilled. I left the house, bag in hand, without booting up my computer or turning on the TV. I had had enough.

I met Aaron at Bordeaux in Brooklyn, on Montague Street in Brooklyn Heights. Of all our stores, Bordeaux in Brooklyn would be the only one I'd miss. It had been the only one in which I'd ever felt at home. It's where I'd kept my office, and it was close to 40 Court Street where Carmella and I had run Prager & Melendez Investigations, Inc. I didn't have any sentimental attachments to any of the other stores, not even our first store, City on the Vine, on Columbus Avenue by the Museum of Natural History. I had good and bad memories from all the stores, but it was the years I spent at Bordeaux in Brooklyn with Klaus, the punk rocker turned wine buyer and manager, that I would recall most fondly.

Aaron was waiting for me in my office, sitting behind my old desk. He threw his car keys to me as I came through the door.

"The last time you threw keys at me, you nearly took my head off," I said, flipping my keys to him.

"I missed, didn't I?"

"Not by much."

"You look good, little brother. A little tired, maybe, but good. So what's this trip?"

"I'm going up to be with Sarah and to work on Pam's house. I need to move on with my life."

He shook his head. "You couldn't wait until after the storm, yutz?"

"Mommy would be so happy that you still worry about me. But no, I've just gotta get up there."

"You're still sure you want to get out of the business? This office won't be the same without you in it."

"I'm sure, Aaron. It's time."

He stood, came around the desk, and gave me a hug. "I love you, you shithead. Even with all the *tsuris* through the years, I wouldn't have wanted to do this without you."

"I love you, too, big brother. I'll be back in a couple of days."

"Don't sweat it. Wine and cars, we got plenty. You go have fun and kiss them all from Uncle Aaron. The car's in the usual spot in the garage."

"Mine is in my spot."

I drove the big black Audi out of the garage, worked over to Court Street, and made my way to the Brooklyn-Queens Expressway. Almost unconsciously, I turned on the radio. I wished I hadn't, because Aaron had it tuned to a news station and the first thing that blared out of the speakers after the sports update was that annoying electronic theme music they play when there's breaking news. Part of me hoped it would be a weather update on the coming storm. For most of my lifetime, New Yorkers hadn't been too terribly weather conscious. Whatever the weather was, it was, and we managed. In recent years, after a flurry of superstorms, hurricanes, and historic snowfalls, the city had become nearly as weather crazed as Corn Belt farmers. But it wasn't a weather update. Somehow, I knew it wouldn't be.

The reporter spoke in hushed tones with the noise of people mumbling, chairs and feet shuffling in the background.

"This is Quinn Peters at One Police Plaza. We're here for an emergency press conference called by a joint task force comprised of the NYPD, several other local law enforcement agencies, and the FBI. We have not been briefed on what the conference is to be about, but rumors are it has to do with the current Internet phenomenon of the Hollow—hold it, the commissioner is stepping to the microphone. Here is Commissioner Riley."

"Good afternoon, ladies and gentlemen. In a moment, FBI Special Agent Stewart Griggs will be stepping to the microphones. After his statement, we will take questions, but I ask that you please hold those questions until we indicate we are ready to take them. This is a serious matter of life and death and we ask for your patience. Special Agent Griggs . . . ."

"Good afternoon. Thank you, Commissioner Riley. We have strong reason to believe the woman known to millions of Internet viewers as the Hollow Girl has been abducted and is in serious danger of losing her life. Here is a recent photo of her, alongside a still shot taken from a recent video post. Her legal name is Siobhan Bracken, and she is also known as Sloane Cantor. She is a thirty-one-year-old Caucasian. She has blue eyes, is five foot seven inches in height, weighing approximately one hundred and forty to fifty pounds. I will not spend the precious time we have here recounting her story, but please be aware that in spite of the disclaimers that have appeared before and after her recent posts, we believe she is in serious danger.

"The photo behind me is of Robert Allen Kaufman, the man we believe is holding Miss Bracken against her will. Kaufman, formerly of San Antonio, Texas, relocated to the New York metropolitan area six months ago. Kaufman, a photographer and videographer, has been in and out of psychiatric facilities over the past ten years. He has made threats against Miss Bracken, and apparently holds her responsible for the death of his mother in a traffic accident involving an ambulance some fourteen years ago in Texas. Kaufman is a forty-seven-year-old Caucasian and he, too, has blue eyes. He weighs approximately two hundred and twenty pounds and stands six feet two inches tall. He is considered armed and extremely dangerous. He is implicated in at least one homicide and a suspect in two attempted homicides. Under no circumstances should a member of the public approach Mr. Kaufman or anyone who might resemble him. Please call 911. All reports will be taken seriously and kept confidential. Again, do not approach him. To do so would put not only your life at risk, but Miss Bracken's as well.

"Kaufman's last known address was in Bayside, Queens, New York, but we have searched those premises and it appears he has not occupied that residence for a month or more. Mr. Kaufman, we believe, is most likely holding Miss Bracken somewhere on Long Island, within the confines of Nassau County or Western Suffolk County. He has been spotted driving a rented blue 2013 Toyota Camry sedan, New York tag number WH2001. With the storm approaching and time running out, we felt it important to enlist the public's cooperation. Again, I must stress, do not approach the suspect Kaufman under any circumstances. Call 911 immediately. After the Q&A, data sheets on both Miss Bracken and Mr. Kaufman will be handed out to those in attendance. That information is also available now on our website and the websites of the following law enforcement agencies: the NYPD, the Nassau County and Suffolk County PDs, and the Connecticut State Police. Questions?"

I switched off the news station and put on the '60s station on satellite radio. I didn't want to think about Robert Allen Kaufman, an admittedly perfect suspect, or the Hollow Girl. I wanted to get up to see my kid and hug her tight, and while I drove I wanted to listen to songs without irony or cynicism. It always amazed me that the music of the decade that gave us the Cuban Missile Crisis, the Kennedy and King assassinations, Vietnam, Selma, the Manson family murders, and so much more contained so much optimism and earnestness. When people sang about love in the '60s, it wasn't freighted with knowing ennui and impending doom. Then "Turn Down Day" by The Cyrcle ended, and Barry McGuire's "Eve of Destruction" came on. Figured.

CHAPTER FIFTY

I'd made it about as far as Hartford, Connecticut, before I decided to find a place to ride out the storm. The roads were still okay, but the storm was blowing freezing rain and snow all over the place. I was in no mood for a fender bender or to get stuck in the middle of I-91, so I found a hotel near the interstate and settled in. I called Sarah to let her know that I'd be delayed and where I was staying. She sounded relieved to hear it. I could also tell she was desperate for my opinion on the Hollow Girl situation.

"Go ahead, kiddo, ask," I said, resting my head against the hotel pillow and flipping on the TV.

"What happened, Dad? Why aren't you on the case anymore?"

"I came up with a different suspect. Doesn't matter. Even if they thought I was right, once the feds are called in, they're in charge. There would have been no place for me."

"You don't think it's Kaufman who has her?"

"No, he probably does. My guy is apparently in the Middle East somewhere. Kaufman fits."

"Do you really think he's going to kill her?"

"I do, and soon."

"Oh, my God, Dad. And here we all were watching him torture her."

"You couldn't know that. None of us could."

"Do you think it's just revenge, like they're saying? It was fourteen years ago."

"Revenge was motive enough for the men who killed your mother."

A painful silence echoed across both ends of the phone. Sarah hadn't been thinking in those terms. I guess I could have answered her without putting it that way, but I was through pretending with my daughter. The facts were the facts: Revenge has a long shelf life. I had ruined someone's career and marriage, and he took his revenge on my ex-wife in front of me nearly two decades later. It's why Sarah had barely spoken to me from 2000 to 2007. She blamed me for her mother's murder. Me, too.

"You're right, Dad. That was a dumb question. I'm sorry."

"No, kiddo, it wasn't. I'm sorry it still hurts so much."

"I forgave you a long time ago. Just be safe tonight, and get up here when you can. We're all excited to see you, and I've really got Pam's place pretty organized."

"Love ya."

"You, too, Dad. Very much. We all do."

I turned up the sound on the TV and clicked through the channels. Hotel television sucks at best—ten sports news channels, ten news channels, five business news channels, local over the air channels, and one movie channel—but when there's a storm closing in on the biggest media market in the country and a psycho killer is on the prowl, hotel TV is worse still. There seemed to be no other images available except those of swirling weather maps, hooded weather people standing in the sleet, bug-eyed Robert Allen Kaufman, and the Hollow Girl. There was the occasional image of Siobhan and of the young Sloane Cantor. But the news media, their standards of good taste ranging between that of a hormonal thirteen-year-old boy and of a British politician circa 1962, seemed to be fetishizing the bound and ball-gagged Hollow Girl. When I was a kid, we had posters of Raquel Welch and Brigitte Bardot on our walls. It wasn't hard to imagine that posters of the rope-bound Hollow Girl were already in production somewhere in a factory in China. The world had really come to shit, hadn't it?

I turned the sound down, and felt myself drifting off into a place where the world mattered less and where some sense of peace was still possible. When I woke up, the room was dark except for the strobing of the light from the TV. I found the bathroom, let some water out of me, and then splashed a few handfuls of cold water onto my face. I flipped on the light, trying to shake the sleep out of my head. I don't usually wake up from a nap hungry, but I hadn't eaten much all day. Amazing how when part of your stomach gets cut out it keeps your weight and appetite down. I found I was hungry and I wanted an excuse to escape from the TV. But when I picked up the clicker to shut the TV off, there was breaking news. I turned up the sound.

"That is correct, Mary," the gray-bearded anchorman said, "We can confirm that Robert Allen Kaufman has been found dead in a building in an industrial park near the towns of Westbury and Garden City in Nassau County on Long Island. Our sources tell us, though we cannot confirm it as yet, that there was no sign of Siobhan Bracken, better known to the world as the Hollow Girl. Wait, we have some video from our remote crew who was out on Long Island reporting on the fierce nor'easter bearing down on the area."

As he spoke, video came across the screen of a tan brick building, snowflakes falling furiously before the camera lens. In between the camera and the building were ambulances and squad cars, lights whirling, flashing, strobing.

"That is the building in which Kaufman's body was found," the anchorman continued. "We are expecting a statement from the FBI within several minutes. Garden City, as some of you will remember, was a locale hit very hard during the 9/11 attacks . . . ."

I stopped paying attention as I slipped into my coat. I looked at my watch: 8:43 P.M.

CHAPTER FIFTY-ONE

As I drove, I thought I might just have to give God another chance. Without the storm, I would have been in Vermont. I would already have had dinner with Sarah and Paul and the baby. I would have helped give Ruben a bath. By now, Paul and I would be sitting around, sharing a glass of good red wine as Sarah put Ruben to bed. As we sat, I would be telling Paul stories of how his biological father, Rico Tripoli, and I used to get up to all sorts of mischief when we were in uniform together at the Six-O Precinct in Coney Island. He would be happy and sad at tales of the father he never knew, as I would be happy and sad for having known his father too well. Being human was about functioning in the face of wild contradictions. In spite of Rico having betrayed me several times in ways that might have gotten me killed, I missed him terribly—more and more as I got older. I had once been closer to him than to Aaron. Rico and I had shared things as cops and men that could not be taken back or away by all the betrayal in the world.

But there had been a storm. There *was* a storm. I wasn't in Vermont, sitting around the fire with my son-in-law, drinking wine and bullshitting about how Rico and I had done this and that. Though I *was* missing Rico as I drove. It was easy for me to picture Rico—not the desiccated Rico who fairly drank himself to death after prison, but the Rico with the wavy black hair and twinkle in his eye—sitting in the front passenger seat next to me, laughing at me for being such a stubborn bastard. Then again, Rico always settled for the easy way, the path of least resistance, the crumbs instead of the cookie.

According to the GPS, my estimated travel time between the hotel and Farmington Falls—the town where the Johns family estate was located, according to the newspaper—was about twenty minutes. But given the road conditions and the rate at which the snow was coming down, it had taken me almost an hour. Then it took an additional few minutes to get the address out of the guy at the local gas station.

"Sure I know the Johns House," he said. "Everybody in town knows the Johns House."

The Johns House was the biggest Victorian in a town full of big old Victorians. There was a fancy wooden For Sale sign with engraved gold lettering posted by the stone and wrought-iron gate. The grand and fussy old lady was surrounded by a classic New England stone wall. Seeing the house they had lived in made it easy for me to picture the Johns as something out of Henry James or Poe. In spite of their fatal connection to the Hollow Girl, their lives and tragedies certainly seemed cut from the cloth of a long-ago era.

Just before I got out of Aaron's car, my phone buzzed in my pocket. It was Nancy Lustig. I wasn't mad at her for how she'd treated me. On the other hand, whatever magic there had been between us for all those years, a magic that had been enhanced in the dark of her bedroom, was gone, irretrievably gone. That was all right, I thought. Mayflies live for a few hours. Tortoises and lobsters live for hundreds of years, but in the grand scheme of things it's not about how long, but how well. At least, that's what I used to tell myself during chemo.

"Yeah," I whispered.

"Did you hear?"

"I heard. Listen to me, Nancy. Tell Griggs I'm at the Johns's old house in Farmington Falls. He'll know what to do. Thanks again."

I clicked off and shut off the phone. Didn't want it buzzing at the wrong moment.

Outside the car, there was that eerie quiet of falling snow. The wind whipped up and then fell back into a harmony of silence with the snow and the dark. I expected that it never got too loud in Farmington Falls to begin with. A diffuse pinkish light, the source of which I could not divine, fell across the blanket of snow that already covered the ground. I eased the car door closed behind me, checked my watch, and took in what I could from where I had parked. I'd made sure to drive past the house and not stop directly in front of it. The Johns's house was on a low hill with old trees placed strategically about the property to provide shade and privacy. Not quite buried in the silence, I could just about make out the snow-muffled trickle of running water from the wide stream that ran through the area. I had crossed over a quaint wooden bridge that spanned the stream a block east of the Johns's house. And there were suddenly other noises emerging from the pinkish dark: the putter and hum of a generator.

I did not look for lights in the upper floors of the house, as I was confident where this last act of the drama was meant to be played out. I needed to find the basement door, and quickly. As I hurried through the snow, I heard the ticking in my head that had played during last evening's Hollow Girl post. I was lucky that the snow that had fallen over the early sleet was powdery and did not crunch under my weight. On the other hand, it got pretty treacherous when my shoes hit the slick layer of ice beneath the fluff and I fell on my face.

"Fuck!" I whispered as I reached the padlocked steel bulkhead doors leading directly into the basement. At one time, these doors would have been made from wood. Now there was no hope of me gaining access this way. I had been pretty stealthy in my approach, fearing that Burton Johns would rather hang Siobhan than be stopped, even if it meant adjusting his timetable. When I heard the wail of sirens in the distance, it seemed to me that continued stealth was moot. I found the back door, put my elbow through the glass à la Mike Bursaw, and broke into the house. I switched my cell phone back on and used it as a flashlight.

I heard feet—no, paws—scratching on the wooden floor. I pulled my gun down, but something knocked my cell away. A sharp, searing pain shot up my left arm. I was down, a thick-bodied dog, a Rottweiler, trying to tear my wrist off my arm and my arm off my body. Drool dripped down onto my face from the dog's mouth as he shook his head side to side, my wrist in his jaws. I fought hard not to panic, no mean feat in the midst of the most primal of experiences. I suppose I could have just shot him in the side and been done with it, but I had seen too much innocent blood spilled in my life. So instead I put my gun to the dog's left hind quarter and fired. It yelped in pain and let go of my wrist. I scrambled to my feet, banged around in the dark as I lumbered away. Behind me, the dog struggled to get to its feet and chase after me, but couldn't manage it.

I found what I thought must be the basement door. Locked. I checked my watch. It was 10:13. If Johns hadn't already hanged the Hollow Girl and left her dangling at the end of the rope for the audience to see, he would soon enough. I didn't bother shouldering the door. I shot holes in the lock and the hinges, using all my remaining ammo to do so. Then I shouldered the door. It gave way more easily than I'd anticipated, and I toppled headfirst down a long flight of wooden stairs. It was a miracle I didn't snap my neck along the way. I lay breathless and stunned in a twisted heap of myself at the basement landing.

Siobhan's bound body was now propped up on the plywood and concrete block platform. She was on her knees, the noose around her neck, straining against her windpipe. She seemed to be unconscious. There was a camera on a tripod placed about ten feet in front of her, and Burton Wentworth Johns was standing just behind the camera. When I could breathe again, I gagged at the ammonia stink of urine and nauseating sewer pipe odor of old feces. As I forced myself to my feet, Johns calmly stepped away from the camera, walked over to the platform and kicked the concrete blocks out from beneath it. Siobhan's body unfolded like an Olympic diver's falling into the pool below, but she never quite made it to the water.

Johns had miscalculated. He hadn't anticipated that the makeshift gallows he'd built would create a pile of debris beneath Siobhan, preventing her falling with enough momentum to snap her neck. Her feet caught on the pile. I ran to her, wrapping my arms around her bound body, lifting her up, holding her as best I could. A fresh kind of pain rudely introduced itself to me, a pain so burning hot and powerful that it knocked me sideways and filled my body with fire. It happened so fast that I only heard the shot in retrospect. But I knew I could not let the Hollow Girl go. I had let too many people down in my life, their names and faces scrolling by in an instant. Then there was more pain. More noise. There was lots of noise, a world full of thunder and flame. Then darkness as quiet and profound as snowfall.

CHAPTER FIFTY-TWO

When I opened my eyes, the pain had me wishing for that profound darkness. I was getting jolted pretty good. There was a mask over my face. I was cold and wet and on fire. I saw tubes and plastic bags. My head fell to my left. There was a woman next to me. There was a mask on her face, too. There were plastic tubes sticking out of her arm. There were blurry men between us talking real loud and too fast, saying things I couldn't understand. Numbers. I remember they were speaking numbers.

* * *

Sarah was sitting next to me, asleep in a chair. The lighting in the room was dim, but I knew my daughter. I had watched her being born, her red curls preceding her into the world. It was still a feeling unmatched in my life, the moment of my daughter's birth. I knew I was in a hospital, knew it before I had even opened my eyes. Hospitals have that smell. I wanted to stop smelling it as soon as I could. Then I never wanted to smell it again.

* * *

The room was full of people, most of whom I was thrilled to see. Sarah, Paul, and Ruben were there. Aaron and Cindy, too. My little sister Miriam was there. Klaus. Fuqua. Bursaw. Marina Conseco and Carmella. *What?* Ferguson May, Rico and Katy. Bobby Friedman and Mr. Roth. *No, no. Wait.* Ferguson May, the Plato of the Six-O, had been stabbed through the eye during a domestic dispute thirty years ago. *And wait, these others* . . . I squeezed my eyes shut and made the dream go away. When I opened my eyes, I was alone. I stared up at the ceiling for the rest of the night and was happy to hear the whirring and beeping of machines.

* * *

The next time I opened my eyes, a doctor was standing over me. Dr. Whitaker, he said his name was.

"You're a lucky man, Mr. Prager."

Why do doctors always say that? If I was a lucky man, I wouldn't have gotten shot or had stomach cancer in the first place.

"You were shot through your left shoulder. The wound was a through and through that missed your heart by about this much." He held his index finger and thumb two inches apart. "The other shot is the one that did more damage, I'm afraid. It hit your right kidney and that slowed the bullet up so that it decided to plow around inside you. We've sewn you up pretty well, and we think we'll be able to save your kidney, but you have to take it easy. We've kept you pretty drugged up to this point, but now you have to begin your recovery in earnest. I'll be in to see you tomorrow." He shook my hand. "I've never saved a hero's life before."

"I'm nobody's hero, Doc. No such thing as a hero."

"There's someone here to see you who might disagree."

When he left the room, a woman walked in past him. I hardly recognized her without her ropes and with her eyes open. We didn't really talk. What was there to say? She just wanted to hold my hand, and I let her.

EPILOGUE
Vermont, April 2014

Brooklyn would live only in my memory now that Sarah had sold my condo in Sheepshead Bay and I had settled into my life as grandpa in semi-residence in Vermont. I would go back—had gone back—but it was different. Although it had taken almost two-thirds of a century to do it, I'd finally cut the umbilical cord that had kept me tied to Coney Island.

A wise man once said that a place, anyplace, stops existing once you've left it. He was wise, but wrong. Brooklyn would live inside me. I would be able to breathe in the salt smell of the ocean breezes that blew along the boardwalk until I shut my eyes for the last time. And carried on those breezes would be the coconut scent of summer girls covered in suntan lotion, and the raw perfume of boiling oil from Nathan's. I would hear the *thud, thud, thud, thud* of bicycle tires and *clickety-clack* of women's sandals on the weathered planks of the old boardwalk. The shrieks and screams of kids on the Cyclone would always ring in my ears. Some of those shrieks were mine. On quiet days in my new house I could call up the sound of balls bouncing off the concrete walls at the West 5th Street handball courts. I would be able to taste the oniony potato knishes from Hirsch's. And the fireworks . . . there would always be fireworks on Tuesday nights on the boardwalk in my mind.

It had taken months for me to recover from the gunshots, but it was cake compared to the cancer. The dog I'd shot recovered in less time. I was glad of that, and that I'd chosen not to just kill him. Burton Wentworth Johns had not recovered from his wounds, which was just as well. According to papers they found after the shootout, Johns hadn't intended to live much longer anyway. I'd been right about him, just not right enough. He was guilt-stricken over his sister's suicide because he had been a driving force behind it. It came out that he had sexually abused Emma one way or another since they were eight years old. Love, I thought, had as many ugly permutations as beautiful ones. No wonder Emma could relate to the Hollow Girl.

As I suspected, Johns had slipped back into the United States from Mexico through Arizona. Johns had been willing to go further than I'd imagined in order to avenge Emma. Not only had he enlisted Millicent McCumber and Anthony Rizzo's help, but he'd also been wise enough to use Robert Allen Kaufman as a kind of insurance policy, a hedge in case the wheels started to come off the original plan. Kaufman, so blinded by his own hate and thirst for revenge, had no idea what Johns ultimately had in mind. It had been Burton Johns himself who'd called in the anonymous tip to the FBI about Kaufman. And when they checked Kaufman out, the FBI found everything Johns had left for them to find. But the real genius of the plan was how he had lured Siobhan Bracken so willingly into it.

He had set up a TV production company, but meant to focus on the emerging Internet TV market and not the traditional ones. He'd even had some mediocre reality shows produced and aired. Old world, new world, it didn't matter: money talked. He'd tried to approach Siobhan through Anna Carey. No dice. And, as

Brahms had told me, also through him. That hadn't worked either. But Millie McCumber had worked her considerable charms: She convinced Siobhan to meet with Johns in the Hamptons after returning from Ireland. Johns then persuaded Siobhan that the Hollow Girl could be used as a means to the career she so craved.

"He was very persuasive, Mr. Prager," Siobhan told me when we met for lunch at her mother's house last month. "He knew what I so desperately wanted. I could write the shows, act in them, make it a showcase for my talents. I would have free rein, but the Hollow Girl had to be the starting point. I hesitated. I didn't want to do it at first, but he wore me down. And Millie was always in my ear. I had a real weakness for Millie.

"During that week in the Hamptons, we would drive to the building he'd set up as a studio in Westbury and record some things I thought we were just trying out. He said he didn't drive, so he had me rent the car and promised to reimburse me. He had me write some monologues and record them. It was really kinda fun and liberating. I guess he knew it would be, revisiting the Hollow Girl. That had all ended so badly."

Once he had her committed to the project, the rest fell into place. He drugged her drink one night after they had shot her monologue, and held her captive. The remainder of his fourteen-years-in-the-making revenge fantasy was out there for the world to see. He had planned it all so carefully. And I had to admit that if Millie McCumber hadn't died of a heart attack, it all might've worked just as Johns had hoped. But me finding Millie dead in Siobhan's apartment set in motion a series of missteps that eventually ruined Johns's dream. He panicked and paid Anthony Rizzo to ransack the apartment as a diversion. Of course it backfired, and when Rizzo saw it as an opportunity to blackmail Johns . . . *au revoir* Anthony. It's still unclear if it was Johns himself or Kaufman who killed the doorman. And we'll never know which one of them shot at me and Giorgio Brahms. We do know it was Johns who blew Kaufman's brains out and left him to be found by the FBI.

I did extract one thing from Nancy and Siobhan that day I went for lunch. They had done no interviews since the rescue. That, I told them, was about to change. I handed Siobhan Ian Kern's card.

"I kept my promise to your mother," I said. "Now you're going to keep my promise to him."

Aaron and I have dissolved Irving Prager and Sons, Inc. We had named the partnership after our dad. It was the only way to do it. I needed to cut that tie, too, like I had with Brooklyn. I needed to be completely out of it, and not at the fringes. I was okay with just letting go, but my big brother insisted I be bought out, some in cash and some on a note. I knew better than to argue with him. I didn't need the money. I had all the money I was ever going to need. The one demand I made was that Aaron keep Brian and Devo on as security. That, of all things, my brother grumbled about.

"I don't know about those guys," he said. "The bills for the last few months have been a little high."

I managed not to laugh.

Bursaw had come up to Connecticut to see me, as had Vincent Brock. Julian Cantor couldn't be bothered. Bursaw didn't get a bump, but had managed to hold onto his shield for the time being. He told me that the Suffolk cops, as a courtesy, had shared what was on Dillman's suicide tape. The return of the Hollow Girl had been the last straw. He didn't think he could deal with the bad publicity again, not after the divorce. When I saw Siobhan at Nancy's house, I'd been tempted to tell her about the Hollow Girl's part in Dillman's suicide, but I realized the pain and guilt had to stop somewhere. Dillman's was over with, and I decided not to be a conduit for more. Vincent thanked me for saving Siobhan. I think I appreciated his coming to see me more than anyone else beside my family, because I knew he didn't much like me. He had no other agenda. He just wanted to say thanks and shake my hand. When he had done those two things, he got back in his sparkly maroon BMW with the stupid vanity plates and drove two hours back home to Long Island.

When we were clearing out my drawers to make the move up to Vermont, Sarah came across a piece of my past that I had assumed had just vanished with time. She found the replica detective's shield Katy had had made for me decades ago, in lieu of the one I'd never gotten from the NYPD. Over the years I had come to realize that not getting my real shield was probably the single best thing that had ever happened—or, to be precise, *not* happened—to me. Not getting it had made me a husband, father, and ultimately a grandfather. Not getting it had introduced me to Mr. Roth and Klaus, and made me a success in business, if a reluctant one. Not getting the shield had helped me help get a measure of justice for people from whom it had been stolen or delayed, and it helped me help save people's lives. What else could a man do better with his own life than those two things? We never did find my PI license, but that was okay. I was never going to need it again.

Nancy came up to visit me last week. I'd tried to get her not to come, but she insisted. I don't know, maybe it was that I felt uncomfortable having her in Pam's old house. Maybe it was that I was afraid she would try to rekindle that brief flame we had shared over the course of a few weeks last September and October. Maybe I was just afraid. I needn't have been.

We shared lunch at a local diner, neither of us ordering a drink and both of us managing to be civil to the waitress. She had simply come up to say thank you and to wish me well. She said that her brief time with me had woken her up, and that maybe she would try and do some good in the world instead of trying to improve her tennis game. It was good of her to say, though she was as impeccably put together as ever and still smelled fantastic.

"There is one more thing," she said as she stood to go.

Uh oh. "Yeah."

"I know you won't take more money from me, but I want to give you something. Nothing extravagant. Let's call it a gesture between old friends and lovers."

"A gesture like what?"

"A trip anywhere you want to go. I know you can afford to do it yourself and you can go anywhere you'd like for as long as you'd like, but I think I know you a little bit now. You won't do it yourself. So let me do it for you."

"Israel," I blurted, though I could scarcely believe it.

There were a thousand reasons that it made no sense. For one thing, I wasn't so much a lapsed Jew as a collapsed Jew. That and I didn't believe in God, second chances notwithstanding. I also didn't care much for the hawkish nature of current Israeli politics. I had sent my daughter there and the rest of my family had gone, Aaron several times.

Nancy looked nearly as surprised as I felt. "Why Israel?"

All I said was, "It's about time."

We hugged long and hard, and I watched Nancy Lustig walk away. The tickets arrived yesterday.